AN ELUSIVE PURSUIT

THE PARABLES
BOOK 1

KENNETH A. WINTER

WildernessLessons

JOIN MY READERS' GROUP FOR UPDATES AND FUTURE RELEASES

Please join my Readers' Group so i can send you a free book, as well as updates and information about future releases, etc.

See the back of the book for details on how to sign up.

An Elusive Pursuit

A young man's journey to discover his dream

Book 1 in the series, **The Parables**

Published by:

Kenneth A. Winter

WildernessLessons, LLC

Richmond, Virginia

United States of America

kenwinter.org

wildernesslessons.com

This story has been inspired by true events.

However, the story, characters, and incidents portrayed in this production are fictitious.

Edited by Sheryl Martin Hash

Cover design by Scott Campbell Design

ISBN 978-1-9568662-3-0 (hard cover)

ISBN 978-1-9568662-4-7 (paperback)

ISBN 978-1-9568662-5-4 (e-book)

ISBN 978-1-9568662-6-1 (large print)

Library of Congress Control Number: 2023916182

DEDICATION

In memory of
my grandfather,

R. Eugene Foresman

whose personal journey
as a twenty-three-year-old young man
inspired this story.

∽

A man's heart plans his way,
But the Lord directs his steps.

(Proverbs 16:9)

∽

CONTENTS

1

MONDAY, APRIL 1, 1912

~

*T*oday is All Fools' Day! It's probably not the wisest day for me to set out on this journey, but then again, I'm not superstitious.

I boarded this railcar at half past six this morning, and my heart is so full of excitement it might burst wide open—just like my suitcase, which may come apart at the seams at any moment! I've been looking forward to this day for a long time. I am keeping a diary of my journey so I can one day look back on how it all began. I feel certain this will prove to be my greatest adventure—or at the very least, one of many great adventures.

Allow me to introduce myself. My name is R. Eugene Fearsithe. The "R" stands for Robert, but that's my father's name. I go by Eugene, but my friends call me Gene. I have traveled very little during my twenty-three years, so some of the things I find uncommon you may consider quite ordinary.

For example, I am completely captivated by the sights scampering past my window. It's not that the landscape is so beautiful, rather it's just moving at a speed I've never seen. The almanac may say spring is supposed to be blooming here in Central Pennsylvania, but someone apparently forgot to tell winter that its time is over. It has turned out to be a cold, rainy day.

The first leg of my trip was from my hometown of Williamsport to Lock Haven. The journey took about forty-five minutes by train, which was a lot faster than when I traveled there by horse and buggy with my father.

As I boarded my next local train to Bellefonte, I realized I was about to travel the farthest west I had ever been. But I quickly realized I would be doing so going backward! The engine was on the east end of this train. I spent the entire thirty-minute trip seeing where I'd been instead of where I was going!

I changed trains once more in Bellefonte and traveled to Tyrone, where I would catch the main line to Pittsburgh. I was grateful to again be facing forward even though it was the bumpiest ride I had experienced all morning. A short, bespectacled fellow about my age was seated next to me on this leg. As it turned out, Ed McKee was the son of a Pennsylvania Railroad executive.

He asked me where I was headed. "Out West," I answered.

"What business takes you to Pittsburgh?" he inquired.

I laughed when I realized he thought I meant western Pennsylvania.

"No," I said, "I'm not going to Pittsburgh. I'm on my way to the real West! I'm going to the western United States!

"The western part of our country is the land of opportunity. Arizona just became the forty-eighth U.S. state less than two months ago, and New

Mexico the forty-seventh state just a month before that. I've frequently heard that the best opportunities for young men with gumption are out West. So, I've decided this is my chance—and I'm taking it!"

"Well, good for you!" Ed said with a smile. "I've thought about doing the same thing, but my father keeps reminding me I have responsibilities right here. He says I don't need to head off to the West to find opportunities, a man will find them right where he is, if he just looks for them."

"That may be," I replied, "but I want to make my mark out from under the shadow of my father. I want to become known for who I am, and not who my father is."

We fell silent for a few minutes, before he asked, "So, who do you favor as our next president—William Howard Taft or Teddy Roosevelt?"

Like most people, he considered the two Republican candidates to be the only options. There had been only one Democrat elected president since the Civil War, so no one considered the presumptive Democratic nominee, Woodrow Wilson, to be much of a possibility. The Republican candidate would be chosen at the convention in Chicago in a couple of months. The November election would simply be a formality.

I had never been bashful about talking politics.

"Given all that President Roosevelt did to foster expansion in the West," I said, "while at the same time preserving its natural beauty, I definitely want to see him come back for a third term. Taft is too concerned about preserving the way things have always been done. We need change, and Teddy will bring it!"

I could tell by Ed's reaction that he was a Taft man. Oh well, so much for common ground! We traveled the remainder of the ride to Tyrone in silence. As soon as we pulled into the station, I ran to catch my 10:55 a.m. train to Pittsburgh. But first, I hurried across the street to a bakery to buy a sandwich for the next leg of my journey. As I boarded my next train, I noticed the two large engines up front were already building up steam. They certainly looked up to the task of pulling the long line of cars behind them.

I found a seat by a window and looked around at my fellow passengers. Most of the men were dressed in business attire—and all had their noses glued to their newspapers. I noticed a picture of a large ship on the front page of the paper. The headline announced the maiden voyage of the largest and safest passenger ship ever built, scheduled to depart from Southampton, England, in a little over a week. Its destination is New York City.

From what I could read, the ship is considered to be the best of the best, and the crown jewel of the White Star Line. It must be since they are making such a fuss over it! Even its name indicates its grandeur: the RMS Titanic. I imagined one day sailing the seas on the Titanic and hobnobbing with all of the swells on board. I could easily picture myself smoking a Cuban cigar and drinking a fine sherry in the company of people such as the Astors and the Guggenheims—once I've made my fortune, of course!

I have no doubt I'll be there one day. That's why I am making this trek. I have set off to make a name for myself. I plan to invest all my money in a sure-fire opportunity and become a millionaire before I'm age thirty. I have big dreams and big plans. My father tells me to get my head out of the clouds. But that's exactly where I want my head—up in the clouds, rubbing shoulders with people who think like I do!

Suddenly, a bump on the rail brought me back to reality. I glanced around to see if anyone had noticed me smiling through my daydream. But no one appeared to be looking, and no one seemed to have any interest in conversation. So I gazed out the window at the passing countryside. It was all still fairly stark, but it had a rustic beauty. Those bare trees are like my plans; soon they will take shape and bloom!

Our second stop was the town of South Fork. It was midafternoon and a parade was forming on the street running alongside the tracks. Members of a local school band, dressed in their shiny uniforms, were getting into position and warming up their instruments. Someone shouted at them to play a few songs for those of us on the train.

Their first number was a Tin Pan Alley song, *Alexander's Ragtime Band*. It had quickly become a hit for Irving Berlin, who wrote it over a year ago, and the kids obviously enjoyed playing it. A lot of my fellow travelers were tapping their feet despite a few sour notes here and there. But we gave the band an ovation like they were the Pennsylvania Philharmonic Orchestra! They didn't even wait for us to ask for an encore. They immediately struck up with a more conventional marching song, *Stars and Stripes Forever* by John Philip Sousa. Our train pulled out of the station just as they were completing the final grandioso strain.

The music seemed to boost everyone's spirits, and the atmosphere was less subdued. The wall of newspapers disappeared, and people began to chat with one another. I introduced myself to the young man sitting across from me. I was somewhat surprised when he replied with the most pronounced British accent I had ever heard: "Pleased to meet you, mate. Alfred Hudson is my name."

Alfred told me he was from Manchester, England. A tall and lanky fellow like me, he said his father owns one of the largest commercial construction firms in the city. He had dispatched Alfred to Pittsburgh to intern at a major construction company. I found out Alfred is about my age, and his father has pretty much mapped out his life. We had that in common—or at least we did! All that changed this morning when I set out on this journey.

As we neared Pittsburgh, I asked Alfred where he would be spending the night. He told me arrangements had been made for him to stay at the Carrick Hotel near the station. I decided to see what they had available since my next train wouldn't leave until tomorrow.

As we pulled into Union Station, I could see it was much newer than the others I had visited thus far. It was certainly a dandy, but as we passed through it, I found it lacking. It took me a moment to realize what it was missing. But then it came to me. Where was the fragrant aroma of the Amish bakeries that one finds in the Reading Terminal and Union Station in Philadelphia? I quickly realized I was hungry. The sandwich I picked up in Tyrone had been good—but that was a long time ago!

The Carrick Hotel was quite grand, though it was a little pricier than I had planned. I decided I would make up the additional cost on my next stay and enjoy the night in a comfortable bed. The hotel also boasted a fine dining establishment. Alfred and I made a reservation and arranged to meet for dinner at 7:00 p.m.

Alfred introduced me to a number of dishes I had never tried. We ate like kings. In fact, the food was of such quality and the atmosphere so formal, I felt like one of the Astors or Guggenheims. When I received the substantial bill, I wished I *was* an Astor or a Guggenheim!

After dinner, we parted company and I decided to explore the city. I walked down to the riverfront of the Allegheny River. I was amazed at the long bridges that spanned its width. Without question, they were some of the most remarkable engineering feats I had ever seen.

Though Pittsburgh isn't the largest city in Pennsylvania—that designation belongs to Philadelphia—I was still impressed by the multitude of electric lights illuminating this city. I watched as coal barges unloaded onto horse-drawn wagons; a task heretofore limited to daylight hours. The horses pulled the filled wagons to an inclined plane elevator at the base of a hill, which then carried the load—wagon and all—to the top of the high ridge. I was mesmerized by this amazing sight of industrial innovation!

Pittsburgh is truly a city built in the hills in the same way I envision medieval castles of old dotted impregnable cliffs. But these castles are modern bastions of industry, and others are the palatial homes of the leaders of industry that bear witness to their great achievements. Unquestionably, this is a day of opportunity—a day when almost anything is possible. And I plan to take full advantage of it!

I made my way back to the hotel to get a few hours of sleep before my early morning train.

∾

2

TUESDAY, APRIL 2 – WEDNESDAY MORNING, APRIL 3

~

Though this is only the second day of my journey, Williamsport feels as if it is a long ways away. My heart tells me the city in which I was raised is no longer my home. The past twenty-four hours have already shown me the world is a much bigger place than I envisioned. I am now a man in search of my home. My family is not those I left behind, rather it is made up of the men and women I am meeting on this journey

Early this morning, I boarded my Northwest Railway train for my departure to Columbus, Ohio. Not only am I going farther west than I have ever been before, but for the first time in my life I am leaving the Commonwealth of Pennsylvania.

Someone had left a copy of the previous day's *Pittsburgh Gazette Times* on my seat. My eye was drawn to a picture of First Lady Helen Taft and the Japanese ambassador's wife planting a Yoshino cherry tree on the northern bank of the Potomac River. Apparently, the mayor of Tokyo had given 3,000 cherry trees to be planted in our nation's capital as a sign of goodwill from their nation to ours.

The story recounted how an earlier shipment of 2,000 trees sent in 1910 had been infested with insects and nematodes. Those trees had been burned when they arrived in Washington, D.C. in order to prevent an infestation of the local vegetation. As you can imagine, the destruction of the trees had created quite a delicate diplomatic stir, resulting in this most recent gift. "Hopefully this shipment of trees is bug free," I said out loud to no one in particular.

My seat companion, however, thought I was speaking to him, so we struck up a conversation about cherry trees. William E. Bird was a middle-aged man and wore a distinguished bowler hat. He told me he was the secretary of the Columbus Typographical Union and had been in Pittsburgh for an appointment with his counterpart in that city.

Columbus, Mr. Bird explained, was the fifth of fifteen chartered locals that originally comprised the International Typographical Union, formed to improve working conditions for those in the printing trade. These men and women produce newspapers and magazines, which makes them the gatekeepers to our information. As Mr. Bird reminded me, "If you didn't read it in the newspaper, it didn't happen!"

He studied me for a moment, then said, "Gene, if you're looking for an opportunity to get in on the ground floor and make your mark, you don't need to travel any farther. You need to invest your life in the newspaper business in Columbus. I'll introduce you to two friends of mine, Harry and Robert Wolfe. Those two brothers started out selling shoes, and now they own the two main newspapers in town: the *Columbus Dispatch* and the *Ohio State Journal*.

"The *Dispatch* offices burned to the ground a few years ago, which would have put most men out of business. But not Harry and Robert! They had the paper back up and running out of temporary offices in three days. These are men who have never met a challenge they couldn't overcome. They are going places, and they are always looking for sharp young men like yourself to partner with them."

Mr. Bird convinced me to get off the train and stay overnight in Columbus. He seemed to have nothing else on his schedule other than selling me on settling there! First, he took me to the nearby Chittenden Hotel. He said this was the third building the hotel had occupied—the first two had burned to the ground.

Once I learned my room for the night was on the fifth floor, I was trusting they wouldn't experience their third fire while I was there! It was a fine hotel, and its room rates proved it. So much for saving any money that night, but if I was going to meet the swells, I knew I would need to look the part!

Mr. Bird treated me to lunch in the hotel, then we headed over to the newspaper offices. Unbeknownst to me, he had made an appointment for me to meet the owners at two o'clock that afternoon. The Wolfe brothers were extremely cordial and gave me a grand tour of the paper, introducing me to their staff along the way. I was amazed they were taking so much time out of their busy schedules for me. Almost an hour passed before I realized there had been a mistake.

Somehow Mr. Bird was under the false impression I was the son of a wealthy Philadelphia financier. He had read about such a person being in Pittsburgh the day before. When he had seen me leaving the Carrick Hotel that morning, and then as I told him on the train I was traveling west to explore business opportunities, he had mistakenly believed me to be the financier's son. Though I was carrying a significant bankroll on my person for someone of my station, it was by no means to the degree that he had thought. Once the confusion was settled, everyone looked for a polite—but expedient—way to conclude my visit.

Ten minutes later, Mr. Bird and I were back out on the street. He apologized for his confusion and assured me if I ever had any interest in finding employment in the newspaper business, I should look him up. With that, he shook my hand and left me to navigate my own way back to the hotel.

Since I was already rebooked on a train to Chicago the following morning, I set out to see what else Columbus had to offer. As I walked along High Street, I immediately noticed the dozens of arches that spanned the street. I discovered they were the reason Columbus had earned the nickname, "The Arch City." And though they were impressive by day, the arches became magical at night when their electric lights illuminated the city.

I also learned the first water filtration plant in the world had been constructed here due to the high incidence of typhoid and cholera deaths. Since the city boasts of having one of the most efficient streetcar systems, I hopped on one and rode out to see the plant. On my return, the conductor informed me about a streetcar workers' strike two years earlier. The strike had turned into a violent riot that cast a pall over the city from which it had yet to recover. After hearing about fires, riots, and disease, I was more than ready to board my train the next morning.

I was pleased to find I had a seat to myself. My sightseeing had kept me out quite late, so I didn't get much sleep. I decided to take advantage of my solitude and get a little shut eye. The trip between Columbus and Indianapolis was scheduled to take four hours, so I settled in for a good nap. The only problem was my body didn't want to cooperate. Try as I might, I couldn't fall asleep. So I decided to stretch my legs and walk through the coaches.

In the next car, I came upon two unlikely travel companions having an animated conversation. Both fellows appeared to be about my age, but that's where any similarity ended. One was well-groomed and dressed like a gentleman. His distinct accent told me he was a Brit. The second fellow was dressed in an outfit that apparently had been pieced together. His pants were two sizes too big, and his coat was at least two sizes too small. His ruddy appearance suggested he lived in the country; his pronounced drawl quickly confirmed it.

The British fellow called out to me, "Excuse me, sir. Perhaps you could help settle a dispute. My name is Reginald Dandefore, and this chap's name is . . ."

"My name is Ernest Cluck and I'm from Fayetteville, Pennsylvania," the other fellow added.

"Well, I'm pleased to meet you both. My name is Eugene Fearsithe," I replied as I shook their hands. "But I can't make any guarantee that I can settle your dispute. What's it about?"

"It's quite simple," Reginald responded. "Ernest and I were discussing the game of football. I recently had the pleasure of watching a match between two of the finest teams in the sport before I came here to the States. Sheffield United from South Yorkshire decidedly defeated Bradford City of West Yorkshire by a score of seven to three.

"Ernest insists the Canton Athletic Club is the best football team in this country, and they would resoundingly defeat either Yorkshire team. I assured him that couldn't be the case since, to the best of my knowledge, football isn't even played here in the States—."

"Of course it's played here," Ernest interrupted. "Canton defeated the Massillon Tigers for the championship this past December!"

After I quieted Ernest down, I told them, "Yes, I believe I can help you settle this."

I explained that the football played in England and the football played in the States are actually two different sports. It took a while to clarify the differences to them, but by the time I was done, they both had a good laugh over their misunderstanding. In fact, they seemed keen on learning the finer points about the other's version of football.

I left them to continue their conversation while I returned to my seat. This time I was able to settle into a nap that lasted until the conductor announced our arrival in Indianapolis. As I looked around to get my bearings, I saw that Ernest was sitting in the seat beside me.

"I wondered if you were ever going to wake up, Eugene," he laughed. "I was finally able to straighten out that British fellow about the real football. Once I had, it appeared we didn't have anything more to talk about. So I decided to come talk to you!"

"Where are you headed, kid?" I asked. I later found out Ernest was only a year younger than I am, but he seemed so much younger.

"Logansport, Indiana, to visit my kin. I have to change trains here in Indianapolis and catch the #19 train."

The poor guy looked as lost as a star in the daylight, so I decided to help him find his way.

"Well, I'm catching the #19 for Chicago myself," I told him. "So it looks like we're headed in the same direction. Our train leaves at 12:25 p.m., so we have an hour and a half to explore Indianapolis. Grab your suitcase and let's go."

He gave me a big grin and nodded excitedly. "I need to get a postcard to send to my family. Do you think we could find one as we explore?"

"I definitely think we can find a postcard. Maybe two or three! We'll look for a drugstore."

So off we went and soon came upon the Imperial Hotel. It was quite a sight. We walked into the hotel and surveyed the lobby. Ernest gawked at all of the swells and the ladies as we passed by them. He obviously felt—and looked—very out of place. We probably could have gotten a postcard there, but by now he was so excited about going to a drugstore, I didn't want to disappoint him.

Back outside, Ernest looked up and saw some of the guests on the third- and fourth-floor balconies enjoying the morning air. He waved at them enthusiastically as if they were long-lost friends. Most looked at him not knowing quite how to respond. I was glad to see a few returned his wave. It occurred to me he may never have seen a balcony before. This guy truly had never been to a big city before!

We walked to the corner and saw a storefront with a window full of bottles. "This must be the drugstore!" he called out as he dashed inside. He walked around for the longest time looking at the variety of liquor bottles lining the shelves. When he eventually told the clerk he was looking for postcards, the man gave Ernest a quizzical look.

I decided to rescue them both and said, "My friend here is looking for a drugstore where he can buy postcards. Can you kindly point us in the right direction?"

The liquor store clerk told us where to find the nearest drugstore, and on the way I explained to Ernest what kind of store we had been in. He couldn't believe alcohol came in so many different kinds of bottles.

"City folk sure are funny!" he commented more to himself than to me. "Where I come from, it all comes out of the still and goes into plain glass bottles."

When we arrived at the drugstore, he glanced at me to be certain this was the right place. Ernest's head swiveled from side to side as he looked at all the merchandise on display. The proprietor saw his bewildered look and asked what he needed. "I just need a postcard to send to my family."

"Would you like a stamp to go with it?" Ernest nodded, and the proprietor announced, "Then that will be two cents, please."

Ernest carefully counted out two copper pennies and placed them on the counter. Then he asked if he could borrow a pencil to write his message. He labored over what to write, but twenty minutes later he finally completed his two sentences and handed the card back over to be mailed. I told him we needed to hurry back to the station or we would miss our train. Halfway down the block, I realized he had left his suitcase in the store.

I was exasperated as I watched him run back to get his case. This wasn't the way I had planned to spend my time in Indianapolis, but I would be in Chicago by nightfall—without Ernest—and I'd be able to explore that city to my heart's content!

We made it back to the station and boarded the train just as the conductor shouted, "Last call! All aboard!"

~

3

WEDNESDAY AFTERNOON, APRIL 3 – FRIDAY MORNING, APRIL 5

~

*A*s we made our way north, Ernest told me he was traveling to Logansport to join his cousin at the Western Motor Company manufacturing plant. The company makes engines for the rapidly growing automobile industry, and Ernest's cousin had started working there six months earlier. The money was good, and the work was steady, so Ernest decided to come get in on the ground floor of a growing business.

As it turns out, he and I are really not all that different. Both of us have set out on our respective journeys to pursue our dreams and make our marks in this world. It doesn't matter whether we were raised in the country or in the city, deep down we're both young men with big dreams. He was leaving farm work behind to become successful in the emerging automobile business. His father was not happy about his choice. I could relate to that! At two forty-five that afternoon, I bade him farewell as he departed to pursue his dream in Logansport.

Mr. J.T. Shaw from Chicago boarded the train and immediately took the seat next to me. He was a balding fellow who appeared to be about the same age as my father. He looked tired, as most older men do, and wore a fine tweed suit that had experienced a lot of wear. Soon after the train pulled away, he introduced himself and struck up a conversation.

"Where are you headed?" he asked.

"Out West."

"What's out West?" he countered.

"My future," I replied.

He looked me over for a moment. "Yes, young men are always gazing longingly toward the future—until the day comes they look regretfully back to their past. What do you see in your future?"

"Fame and fortune," I responded without hesitation. "Opportunity is calling out to me, and I intend to take the Roman poet's advice of 'carpe diem' and seize the day!"

"Just like many young men before you," Mr. Shaw chuckled, "including me! When I was your age, I set out from Scranton, Pennsylvania, to discover my fame and fortune working for a man named Thomas Chalmers. Mr. Chalmers was a fellow Scotsman who immigrated here, found work as a blacksmith, and soon made himself and his employer, a Mr. Gates, very wealthy men.

"I was certain if I attached my wagon to his, I, too, would prosper. He gave me an opportunity as a salesman with his new division selling boilers and pumps throughout Illinois, Indiana, and Michigan. It hasn't made me a wealthy man, but I've been able to make a good living."

"Where do you live now?" I asked.

"I live in an area on the south side of Chicago called Washington Heights," he responded. "Our neighborhoods are becoming quite the international community—made up of Scots, Germans, and Swedes. It's been a good place for my sons to grow up, and they both are planning to stay in the area and work for the Allis-Chalmers Company as well. But they both have a better education than I do, so I expect they will end up in management positions that don't require the constant travel that my job does."

"So you travel a lot?" I asked innocently.

"Laddie," he said with a laugh, "I travel all the time! Gratefully, I'm headed home now and will be able to stay there for a few days. But if I'm not traveling, I'm not selling. And if I'm not selling, I'm not making any money. 'Seizing the day' comes at a cost. Be sure you're willing to pay the price!"

That made sense. But I didn't plan to be a salesman. I wanted to seize my opportunity on the ground floor and work my way up, just like Thomas Chalmers had done. I had no intention of settling for a well-worn suit and a home in the suburbs. That's what I was leaving behind!

I steered the conversation in a different direction.

"What do you recommend I see in Chicago while I'm there tonight? My next train doesn't leave until ten o'clock tomorrow morning, so I want to take advantage of the time and see some of the city."

Mr. Shaw took a moment to consider before he answered.

"You'll be arriving at Union Station, one of the busiest stations in the country. It's located on the banks of the Chicago River right in the heart of the city. You'll be needing a place to stay. You can find a reasonable room for a dollar fifty at the Adams House right near the station. I stayed there on a few occasions during my earlier days. The food is good, and the rooms are clean.

"Of course, if you want to stay where the rich and famous go, that would be the Blackstone over on Michigan Avenue. It was built about two years ago. So, if you have money to burn, I hear they are asking about nine dollars a night.

"The city is booming. You'll find a theater on Michigan Avenue. If you were staying over tomorrow, you could see if the Cubs were playing over at West Side Park. It will cost you a buck if they have any seats left. Since it's a Thursday, you might just be able to get in. There's talk they are going to build a new stadium over at Weeghman Park and double the seating capacity. But that will probably also double the price!" he added with a laugh. "But since you're only staying the night, you'll miss seeing them play.

"Instead, you can walk along Lake Michigan and see all the construction taking place. Wherever you go, you'll see a lot going on!"

By the time he was done, I knew exactly what I was going to do. I was going to delay my departure for Friday morning, stay at the Blackstone two nights, and go see a Cubs game tomorrow. My schedule was somewhat flexible, and I had no idea if I'd ever make it back to Chicago. I might as well enjoy the time while I can!

Mr. Shaw and I continued talking most of the way to Chicago, mainly about his work and his family. Twice he asked about my family, and I redirected the conversation back to his. There was no need for him to know about my family. We arrived at Union Station right on time at 5:45 p.m. Mr. Shaw and I shook hands, and I made my way to Michigan Avenue.

The Blackstone was even more impressive than the Chittenden Hotel. As it turned out, the hotel was the tallest building on Michigan Avenue. I decided to request a room on one of its lower floors. As I walked through the lobby, I began to feel completely out of place. and would have remained as such if the hotel clerk had not been so friendly and helpful.

"What brings you to Chicago, Mr. Fearsithe?" he asked.

"I'm just passing through and decided to spend an additional day in your fair city."

"Well, it's too bad you're not staying a little longer," the clerk continued. "This Saturday, the hotel and its adjacent theater will celebrate the second anniversary of our grand opening. The owners of the hotel and theater, the Drake brothers, have made big plans. The famous actor, William Crane, is in town to perform the Chicago debut of his new play, *The Senator Keeps House*. I hear that all 1,200 seats for opening night have been sold out, and there will be a lot of celebrities attending the performance and staying here in the hotel.

"I even heard that former President Teddy Roosevelt will be here. In fact, he was present for the grand opening. He and Timothy Blackstone, the namesake of this hotel, are good friends, so he agreed to make this an official stop on his campaign tour for the Republican presidential nomination. It's too bad you won't be staying to see it all. It should be quite a spectacle!"

"It sounds like a grand event," I told him. "But I can't delay my travels that long. I'll just have to come back for a future celebration once I've made it big out West."

"Then I'll hob-nob with all the swells," I added with a smile. "But in the meantime, where can a guy find a ticket for the Cubs game tomorrow? And what team are they playing?"

The bellboy standing near me spoke up.

"Their regular season doesn't start until next week, but tomorrow they are playing a warm-up game against the St. Louis Cardinals. I can get you a ticket for a seat in the upper section behind home plate."

"How much will it cost?" I asked, checking to see if he would tell me the same price Mr. Shaw had mentioned.

"They went up this year. It now costs a whole dollar—even for a warm-up game—plus whatever you want to give me for my efforts," the bellboy replied rather sheepishly. "Would you like me to get you a ticket?"

"Why not?" I replied. He offered to take my suitcase up to my room, but I told him I could manage.

The room was grand! I was on the fifth floor and had a great view of the city. Since I had splurged again on my accommodations, I decided to take my meals in the hotel's café instead of the swanky restaurant.

After I'd eaten, I walked the streets well into the evening. The front desk clerk advised me to avoid an area called "The Levee," home to the city's gambling saloons and brothels. Although I was a little curious, I heeded the clerk's warning about the city's "Moral Division" making nightly mass arrests. With my interest dampened, I confined my wanderings to Michigan Avenue before returning to the hotel.

The next morning, the bellman arrived at my room with my ticket for the ballgame. As it turned out, it was an excellent seat in the upper section behind home plate. It was well worth the price, including the generous two-bit tip I gave the bellman. I even splurged for a hot dog, a bag of peanuts, and a soda pop during the game.

I almost got hit by a foul ball, but fortunately I moved in time and the guy seated behind me caught it. I later regretted not having tried to catch it myself; it would have been a great memento from the day. The Cubs beat the Cardinals with a score of nine to two. The entire city seemed to erupt in celebration.

After the game, I set out to explore the Chicago River. I had read about this engineering wonder! Twelve years ago, they completed the work to reverse the flow of the river. Instead of the river emptying into Lake Michigan, it is now being fed by the lake. Since the river is used as a means of processing the city's sewage, they were at risk of polluting the lake, which is the primary source of drinking water for the city. With the flow reversed, the engineers were now able to construct a series of canal locks that safely enables the sewage to be processed and carried away from the lake.

I doubt most visitors to Chicago rank exploring the river as a highlight, but for this engineer it may have even overshadowed my time at West Side Park. And I didn't have to spend a buck twenty-five to see it! Nonetheless, they were both highlights I wouldn't soon forget. I returned to the hotel in time for a late dinner and settled in for the night.

As I headed out the next morning, I remembered the shops and businesses would be closing up that afternoon for Good Friday. If I were still at home, I would have been attending church services with my father, listening to the minister preach for three hours about the seven last words of Christ on the cross. I must confess, I was pleased to be avoiding that sermon this year.

I arrived at the train station well ahead of my 10:00 a.m. departure time. The #5 train on the Union Pacific line would ultimately take me to my destination of Portland, Oregon. "That will be sixty-five dollars," the man at the ticket window told me. "And if you want a sleeping berth, that will cost you an additional ten dollars."

I hadn't planned for the additional ten dollars. It was another one of those expenses I had not counted on when planning my trip, but since I was going to be sleeping on the train several nights, I decided it was worth it. I would just have to save money somewhere else along the way.

As I made my way to my seat, I passed a young woman who reminded me of my girl back in Williamsport. Leaving her behind had been the hardest part of this venture. She and I both liked to dance, which had been another source of contention between me and my father. He didn't approve of dancing—but then again, he didn't approve of a lot of things.

My thoughts were suddenly interrupted by the arrival of my seatmate, whom I stood to greet.

"My name is Eugene Fearsithe," I said somewhat nervously as I extended my hand.

"It is a pleasure to meet you, Mr. Fearsithe. My name is Ethel Martin, and it appears we are to be travel companions," the beautiful young woman smiled as she gently returned my handshake. My prospects for this journey had just vastly improved!

"All aboard!" the conductor called out. And in a few minutes the train began to pull away from the station.

~

4

FRIDAY AFTERNOON AND EVENING, APRIL 5

~

*D*ark clouds gathering overhead quickly extinguished the morning sun as we departed Chicago's Union Station. The conductor announced we would soon be traveling through heavy rain. Forty-five minutes later, his forecast became reality as sheets of rain pelted the windows. The accumulating rainwater in the fields on both sides of the tracks made it appear we were gliding across a large lake with no sign of dry land.

The train's engineer soon slowed our speed by more than half. When the conductor came by to punch our tickets, I asked him why we were now traveling so much slower.

"In a heavy rain like this, there is always a good chance of washouts," he explained. "The crew is keeping a close watch on the track ahead, and the engineer has slowed down in case he needs to make an abrupt stop. It's normal procedure in a storm like this. There's nothing to be worried about."

"Oh, I'm not worried," I lied. Then looking at my seatmate, I added, "We're just curious."

As the conductor continued down the aisle, Miss Martin turned to me and quietly said, "Well, you may not be worried, Mr. Fearsithe, but I can assure you I am. I was once on a train that almost descended into a ravine because the bridge had washed out. And I have no desire to relive that experience.

"Are you a religious man, Mr. Fearsithe?" she suddenly asked.

"Not as much as some, but maybe more than others," I replied. "Why do you ask?"

"Well, seeing it's Good Friday and all, I thought maybe a little prayer would do us some good about now. But I think it only works if you're religious, and that leaves me out."

"I'm not sure it even works for those who are religious," I responded. "My father is one of the most religious men I know, and he used to say he was praying for me to make the right decisions about my life. But then he told me I was making all the wrong decisions. So I don't think prayer was working much for him.

"And I tried praying, and I didn't get what I wanted either. So I stopped praying because I don't think anyone is listening—even on Good Friday."

My last statement seemed to hang in the air when Miss Martin didn't respond. She acted like she was pondering what I had said. After a few minutes of awkward silence, I asked, "Do you travel by train often?"

"As of late, I seem to be spending quite a bit of time on trains," she laughed.

"Why is that?"

"My work takes me from place to place," she answered. "I am a stage actress."

"How delightful! Are you currently in a show?"

"Yes, I am playing the role of Puck in William Shakespeare's *A Midsummer Night's Dream*. We just closed our production at the Blackstone in Chicago, and next week we open at the Paris Theater in Denver."

"Puck? I thought that character was a 'he', not a 'she,'" I replied in surprise. "It is hard for me to imagine an elegant lady such as yourself playing the role of a male fairy."

"Well, that is why we call it 'acting,' Mr. Fearsithe. On the stage, we can make anything and anyone become whatever we want. And if we do it well enough, our audience will believe us," she added with a demure smile.

"I never imagined I would be sharing a seat on this train with an actress, Miss Martin."

"I'm not sure if you mean that as a compliment or a statement of concern," she replied with mock shock.

I assured her I was completely sincere.

"Mr. Fearsithe, I believe I made you blush. I was only kidding with you," she said playfully.

That exchange broke the ice, and we began a real conversation. Miss Martin told me she was originally from Indianapolis and had begun acting at age eighteen with the full support of her parents. She had recently played the role of Gretel in the stage production of *Hansel and Gretel* before taking her current role of Puck. Though I found out she was ten years my senior, Miss Martin's petite frame and youthful attractiveness belied that fact. She was well-suited to play those younger roles.

Not surprisingly, the more we spoke, the more smitten I became. And I was quite content when the engineer further reduced our speed. He could stop the train altogether as far as I was concerned! I was in no hurry to arrive in Denver.

"Mr. Fearsithe, you now know a lot about me, and I know absolutely nothing about you. What brings you on this train?"

"Miss Martin, if we are going to continue sharing our innermost secrets, then you should by all means call me Gene."

"Well, Gene, I didn't know we were divulging our deepest confidences, but if that's the case, you must call me Ethel!"

 "Well, I am traveling to Portland, Oregon, to embark on a new career. One of my good friends from my hometown in Central Pennsylvania is there, and he has encouraged me to come join him. The city is exploding with opportunities for smart young men who are willing to apply themselves and work hard."

"And are you a smart young man who is willing to apply himself and work hard?" she quipped.

"Yes, I am. There is no limit to what a man can do if he puts his mind to it. And I am headed to Portland to make my mark."

"What is your profession or trade?" she inquired.

"I have been trained as a mechanical engineer," I replied, "but my training also equips me to turn big dreams into reality. Oregon is a place of ambition, and a place where I can discover my own big dream. I plan to find mine and bring it to fruition, so I will not limit my exploration to an engineering position.

"Over the past few days, I have seen a river flow in reverse and bridges that span the widest rivers. All of those feats can seem impossible to some, but not to me! I plan to face the impossible and overcome it."

"That is quite a dream, Gene," Ethel replied, "and I believe you are the man who can do it. But be careful! Don't ever let your dream take control of you; make sure you are always in control of your dream. I have seen too many men become consumed by their dreams. They were so obsessed with achieving success, they began to ignore everything and everyone else around them."

"Oh, I would never do that!" I declared.

"I know you would never set out to do that," she agreed. "No one ever does," she added with a hint of sadness. Ethel abruptly changed the subject. "Do you have a girl back home in Pennsylvania?"

"I do. Her name is Sara. Or I guess I should say, 'I *had* a girl,'" I answered clumsily.

"Well, which is it, Gene? You either do or you don't," she replied curiously.

"Well, I would have to say I did, but I don't anymore," I responded. "I told Sara I would send for her once I made my fortune in Oregon, but she told me she did not want to leave her family in Williamsport. She said if that was my plan, there wasn't much hope of a future for us.

"I anguished over her answer for a while, but finally I decided I needed to pursue my dream. If I don't do it now, I never will. I'm twenty-three years old, and I have my whole life in front of me. I can't give that up—not for Sara, not for my father, not for anybody."

Suddenly the brakes hissed and screeched as the train slowed. A couple of passengers standing in the aisle almost lost their footing. Everyone tried to see what was happening outside the windows, but we couldn't see anything but water. The train fell silent as we all braced, fearing the worst. It was probably less than a minute before we came to a standstill, but it seemed like an eternity.

We all breathed a sigh of relief. The conductor made his way to our car and announced, "There's a washout up ahead, folks. Nothing to worry about. Our crew is already working to shore up the track. It's to be expected in weather like this. They'll have the track repaired in short order, and we'll be on our way. In the meantime, please remain in your seats and out of the aisles."

He didn't stop for questions, instead he hurriedly made his way to the next car to make the same announcement.

"My husband will be absolutely beside himself," Ethel declared. "He has a business appointment in Denver once we arrive, and he will not like this delay one bit."

"So you're married?" I asked, somewhat startled. "And he is here on this train, but the two of you are not seated together?"

"Oh, yes," she replied. "Horace and I never sit together on trains. He prefers to travel in the smoking car, and I detest being surrounded by all that smoke. So, early on, we decided it was best for us to ride separately."

"Won't he be coming to check on you since the train has stopped?"

"No, he will be much too preoccupied discussing how delays like this could be avoided with anyone who will listen to him," she answered matter-of-factly. "He will be content in his belief that if I am troubled in any way, I will come and seek *him* out."

"What does Mr. Martin do for a living?" I inquired.

"No, not Mr. Martin," Ethel corrected me with a chuckle. "Martin is my stage name. His name is Horace Browning, which makes me Mrs. Ethel Browning. Forty years ago, Horace's father founded the Pittsburgh Sheet and Tube Company, a steel manufacturer. It's quite possible the rails we are riding on were made by his company. Horace's father took advantage of low wages, a shrewd investment in infrastructure, and an efficient oper-ation to make cheap steel he could sell for a large profit in a time of growing industry.

"Ten years ago, soon after Horace and I married, my father-in-law sold his company to J.P. Morgan's U.S. Steel for an outrageous sum. That allowed him to retire without any financial concerns whatsoever. Sadly, he died of a heart attack two years later. All of his fortune then passed to his only son —my husband.

"Horace generously uses a portion of his inheritance to invest in theatrical productions—those that star his wife. So, he has enabled me to pursue my dream, while he pursues his dream of being an industrialist. Truth be told, though, he's never really worked a day in his life. I don't say that as a criticism; it is merely the way things are. So he gives the appearance of pursuing a dream that eludes him, and I pursue my love of the stage. We both have what we want—but we do not *share* a dream . . . and individual dreams rarely keep you warm at night," she remarked with a hint of regret.

We both fell silent while I considered what Ethel had just told me. And I found myself thinking of Sara, more than I had since my trip began. I was jolted from my thoughts by the eerie blast of the train whistle as we lurched forward.

At ten past eleven that night we pulled into the station at Council Bluffs, Iowa, for a brief stop. Then we made a short, ten-minute journey across the state line to Omaha, Nebraska. A few fellow travelers exited the train at both stops, only to be replaced by new passengers quietly boarding the car.

We pulled out of Omaha station a few minutes past midnight. I knew I had a sleeping berth awaiting me, but Ethel gave no indication she would be leaving her seat. I did not want to leave her by herself, so I decided to wait to see what she did. In a few minutes, her head rolled gently onto my shoulder as she fell fast asleep. Maybe prayer does work—even though it isn't Good Friday any longer!

≈

5

SATURDAY MORNING, APRIL 6

~

"*N*ow stopping at Columbus, Nebraska!" the conductor announced.

The train car was still dark, but his announcement, combined with the slowing of the train, stirred me from a deep sleep. Ethel abruptly raised her head off my shoulder. She turned with a start and looked at me.

"Oh, Mr. Fearsithe, I am so sorry," she whispered. Even in the dark, I could tell she was blushing.

"You have nothing for which to apologize, Mrs. Browning. We both appear to have fallen into a very sound sleep—and it was the best sleep I've had in several days, I might add," I continued, grinning. "Please don't think anything about it, and let's not revert back to calling one another by our surnames."

"You are most kind, Gene," Ethel replied with a smile. "I think my busy schedule for the past few weeks has caught up with me. That was the best sleep I've had in quite a while as well—even if it was only for a couple hours. By the time Horace purchased our tickets there were no sleeping berths available, so I feared I wouldn't be able to get any rest. But I was obviously mistaken."

She had now answered my earlier question—but had placed me in a dilemma. I decided chivalry is always the best option.

"I have a sleeping berth that I am not using tonight. Why don't you go ahead and take it? There is no sense in leaving it unoccupied."

"Gene, that is most kind of you, but I couldn't," she said. "Besides, why are you not using it?"

"I decided I sleep better sitting up on the train," I lied. "But I'm not able to get a refund for the reservation, so I would feel so much better if it was being put to good use. You can tell me if it did the trick in the morning."

She hesitated, then took me up on my offer and set off to find the berth. The train had arrived in Columbus at quarter past two in the morning. By two thirty we were on our way. I spent the rest of the night trying, unsuccessfully, to find a comfortable position in which to sleep.

At half past six, the sun started to make its way into the rail car as we passed through miles and miles of prairie land. I knew from my geography lessons that two-thirds of Nebraska lies in the Great Plains. Now I was seeing it unfold before my eyes. The scenery was much different from what I was accustomed to in Central Pennsylvania. But, then again, Williamsport felt like it was a world away.

The car was still very quiet, other than the melodic clickety clack as we headed down the tracks. My fellow passengers also seemed to be easing themselves into the day. Even the conductor was quietly making his rounds through the car.

He stopped to inform me Ethel had made a reservation for the two of us to have breakfast in the dining car at eight o'clock. I had avoided taking meals in the dining car in order to save money, but I had eaten all of the sandwiches I brought on board—and my stomach was starting to protest. I wasn't about to turn down her invitation!

Ethel and I arrived at the dining car at the exact same time. The steward showed us to our seats where, as it turned out, we were joining another couple. The man reached to shake my hand and introduce himself: "My name is John Clapp, and this is my wife, Beatrice."

"I'm Gene Fearsithe and this—" But he didn't give me time to finish. He took Ethel's hand and began to nervously shake it, saying, "Miss Martin, we know who you are. We saw you perform at the Blackstone Theater three nights ago in Chicago. We were spellbound by your performance and never imagined we might be dining with you on our train ride home."

"It is a pleasure to meet you, Mr. and Mrs. Clapp," Ethel politely replied. After we were settled into our seats, she continued. "I am so glad to hear you enjoyed the performance. As I recall, the audience that evening was particularly responsive to each scene. You all were a delight to perform for, and I am so grateful for this opportunity to meet the two of you personally."

I already knew Ethel was masterful at putting everyone she met at ease— after all, I had experienced it firsthand. I watched as she adeptly made the Clapps quickly feel like her long-lost friends. Once she learned they were returning to their home in Denver, she invited them to attend another performance of *A Midsummer Night's Dream*, which they assured her they would.

John then turned to me and asked, "Mr. Fearsithe, do you perform on stage as well?"

"No, I'm afraid I do not have Miss Martin's talent," I replied.

"Actually," Ethel interjected, "Gene is an accomplished mechanical engineer soon to make his mark here in the West. His name may not yet be known in every household in the country, but one day it will be," she added, nodding at me with a twinkle in her eye.

"Well there is no question that you will succeed, Mr. Fearsithe, with Miss Martin by your side," Mr. Clapp remarked. "How long have the two of you been together?"

His question surprised me. Though I had spent the past several hours wishing it were true, I knew that it never would be. Our association would only continue for a few more hours. I feared the flush on my face gave away my true feelings. But I did my best to take control of myself and replied, "I fear we may have given you the wrong impression. Miss Martin and I only met yesterday morning. I have the privilege of being her seatmate on this journey."

"And he kindly allowed me to use his sleeping berth last night so I could get a good night's rest while he selflessly sat up in his seat," Ethel added. "He is a gallant gentleman whom I will now forever count as a dear friend."

"Well, hurrah, Mr. Fearsithe. Well done!" Mrs. Clapp declared.

Our conversation was interrupted when the waiter arrived with pastries and coffee, and to assist us in making our selections for breakfast. The menu choices and the service were no less than that of a five-star restaurant—at least from what I'd been told. I ordered the eggs benedict after hearing the waiter's glowing recommendation.

During breakfast, I learned that Mr. Clapp, who insisted I call him John, was a prominent banker in Denver. When I told him my plans for Portland, he suggested I might consider Denver instead. He told me about his friend, David Sturgis, who was preparing to open an electric company in the city.

"He has great dreams just like you," John added. "I think the two of you would hit it off! He's the kind of man you can depend on to get the job done. Why don't you get off the train in Denver and spend a few days in the city? I'll introduce you to him. At the very least, you'll be able to get some ideas from the plans he is developing!"

If John ever tires of being a banker, he can most certainly earn a grand living in sales. By the end of breakfast, he had sold me on the idea of staying over in Denver. We agreed I would meet him at his bank at nine o'clock sharp Monday morning. Though I was anxious to get to Portland, I was now even more intrigued with the prospect of meeting Mr. Sturgis. Besides, a delay of two or three days certainly wouldn't hurt anything. It's not like anyone was waiting for me in Oregon!

The Clapps excused themselves and returned to their car, while Ethel and I remained sipping our second cups of coffee. When the waiter arrived with our bill, she discreetly paid it despite my protests.

"That is the least I can do for the gentleman who gave up his sleeping berth for me," she said. I grudgingly capitulated. As we made our way back to our seats in the railcar, I asked her, "Ethel, don't you want to visit the smoking car and look in on your husband?"

"Oh no!" she laughed. "Horace will be preoccupied in conversation, and my arrival will only be seen as an interruption. We agreed to meet up when the train arrives at Denver's Union Station. In the meantime, we will continue our journey in the way that suits us both. We have found that works best. Besides, Gene, are you trying to get rid of me?"

"Of course not," I insisted. "I just know if you were my wife, I wouldn't want to be apart from you."

"Gene, that's the sweetest thing anyone has said to me for quite some time," she replied, "but I fear if you knew me for more than one day you might develop a different perspective."

"I am most certain I would not," I countered but decided to let the subject drop.

I asked Ethel if she had visited Denver before, and if so, if she had any recommendations on where I should stay.

"Horace and I will be staying in private lodgings this time around, but we previously visited the city about two years ago," she answered. "We stayed at the Windsor Hotel on Larimer Street. It is the grandest hotel in the city and boasts a palatial marble bath with Turkish, Russian, and Roman pools.

"During our stay, however, there was quite an uproar one night when a prominent socialite flushed her diamond and platinum necklace down the water closet following an argument with her husband. It was quite the talk at the time—and apparently quite an ordeal for the staff to retrieve it from the hotel's plumbing.

"But I must warn you that the hotel is quite pricey. You may want to put off staying there until after you have made your fortune. When you do, though, be sure your wife leaves her expensive necklaces at home," she added with a laugh.

"In the meantime, you may want to explore the St. Elmo Hotel. It's only two blocks from the train station and it's much more reasonably priced. You must promise me, however, regardless of where you stay, if you're in town for more than a week, you will come see me perform at the Paris Theatre. I will arrange for you to have a seat in the center of the front row."

"That would be dandy," I replied, "but I doubt I will be staying that long. However, if my schedule changes, I will certainly let you know. In the meantime, I think I will heed your suggestion and see if the St. Elmo Hotel has a room available."

We spent the rest of the morning and afternoon talking about a variety of topics. We discussed the growing tension brewing in Europe and the fears it would end in war. Though those concerns didn't have anything to do with the United States, we somehow knew a war would have global ramifications.

"I hope war does not occur for many reasons—but one of them selfishly is that Horace and I have tickets to cross the Atlantic this fall on the RMS Titanic," Ethel added excitedly. "You probably know it will be setting sail this coming week on its maiden voyage. I've never sailed across the ocean, but everything I have heard indicates the Titanic is the safest and grandest ship on which to do so. Horace says that by the time we board her, they will have worked out all the bugs on the new ship."

"Will you and Mr. Browning travel separately on the ship like you do on trains?" I asked.

"We have reservations for one stateroom, but I would expect our daytime hours will be spent in different pursuits," she replied with a look of chagrin.

Our conversation eventually turned to politics here at home, most notably the upcoming presidential election. Ethel and I agreed that Teddy Roosevelt was the wisest choice, and neither one of us could imagine President Taft being reelected. Other than Sara, I had never had such a comfortable conversation on such diverse topics with a woman. The time flew by.

It wasn't long before the conductor passed through the aisle announcing, "We will be arriving at Denver's Union Station in ten minutes. If you are exiting the train, please make sure you have all your belongings. You will be exiting through the rear door of the car."

I realized my time with this remarkable woman was drawing to a close.

"Mrs. Browning, it has been delightful spending this time with you," I told her. "I could never have imagined such a rare pleasure. I will hold this time we had in my memory for as long as I live."

"As will I, Mr. Fearsithe. I do hope you find what you are looking for. I have no doubt you will excel at whatever challenge you choose to pursue. And if you decide to stay in Denver until next week, it would be delightful to see you sitting in the front row."

Ethel extended her hand—but I was not inclined to shake it. Instead, I was preparing to kiss it when a rather portly gentleman about twenty years my senior stopped in front of our seat and said, "Ethel, are you ready to go?"

Ethel had been looking at me but now turned toward the man who had interrupted us in such an untimely manner. "Horace!" she exclaimed. "How kind of you to come seek me out."

"Well, you know me, my dear," Horace replied. "I am your ever attentive husband. And who is this fine gentleman sitting beside you?"

"Horace, this is Eugene Fearsithe," she answered. "He has most graciously put up with all of my rantings throughout our travels."

"Mr. Fearsithe, my name is Horace Browning," he said as he reached out to shake my hand. "I hope you were able to enjoy your journey and were not too distracted by my wife. Though she is a gracious and charming woman, she can sometimes be very talkative. But then again, most actresses are."

"I do not know about most actresses," I replied, "but Mrs. Browning has been a most delightful traveling companion. As I just told her, she has been the highlight of my trip. It has been a pleasure to meet you both."

"Well good! Glad to hear it," Horace declared. "Well, my dear, let's make our way to the door so we can exit the car as soon as we stop. There's no sense holding up this gentleman any longer."

"I quite agree, Horace," Ethel responded and reached out to shake my hand. "Mr. Fearsithe, it has been a rare pleasure. I wish you Godspeed."

"And to you, Mrs. Browning," I replied as I slowly shook her hand. It appeared Mr. Browning had no intention of graciously moving away so Ethel and I could exchange an affectionate farewell. I settled for a shake of her hand—and a day and a half filled with pleasant memories.

She looked back and gave me a warm smile as the two of them made their way down the aisle toward the exit door.

~

6

SATURDAY AFTERNOON, APRIL 6 – SUNDAY MORNING, APRIL 7

~

a s I exited Union Station, I passed through a large arch with the word "Welcome" inscribed on it. That seemed to be mighty friendly. I had not seen anything like it at the other train stations I visited. After passing under the arch, I looked back and saw the word "Mizpah" spelled out with light bulbs on the outward face of the arch.

All those years of listening to my father read the Bible was now paying off. I knew Mizpah was a Hebrew word used in the 31st chapter of Genesis that says, *"May the Lord keep watch between you and me when we are away from each other."*[1] I decided that was a nice way for the city of Denver to send off a parting visitor, but it also had another meaning for me at the moment. *Mizpah, Ethel,* I thought.

As I slowly walked in the direction of the St. Elmo Hotel, I spied a barber shop. I had been acutely aware during my time with Ethel that I needed a shave and head wash, so I decided to stop. The barber did a fair enough job, but he could have knocked me over when he said, "That will be eighty-five cents."

"Eighty-five cents?" I gulped. "It's only two bits where I come from in Pennsylvania!"

"Well, mister, you're not in Pennsylvania anymore," the barber replied, holding out his hand. I counted out the change and placed it in his palm, but his hand stayed outstretched. I realized he was waiting for a tip. I got stung to the tune of a whole dollar for a shave and a head wash! That will teach me to ask the price *before* I get the work done next time. Another lesson learned!

As I continued on to the hotel, I couldn't help but think it would be nice to see Ethel again now that I was cleaned up. Though I doubted that would happen, I decided I would at least look more presentable tomorrow for Easter Sunday.

The St. Elmo Hotel was a suitable enough place. Ethel had described it well. It was built to accommodate weary travelers, not the swells. The lobby was modest but functional. The clerk informed me the hotel had sixty rooms on three floors. My room was simple – a bed, a dresser, and a washbasin. I didn't need anything more. What the dining room lacked in ambiance was more than made up for in the quality of food. Though the fare was still slightly higher than my budget, it was far superior to the pricier meals I had eaten in Pittsburgh and Chicago.

And the entertainment in the hotel lounge that night was also more than satisfactory. A singer named Nellie Beauford, accompanied by a small band, sang a mix of ragtime and blues with a haunting voice that penetrated the soul. During her second break, I worked up the courage to invite her to join me at my table. I was both relieved and pleased when she accepted my invitation.

It turned out she was originally from Scranton, Pennsylvania—a town not far from Williamsport, and one I had visited on multiple occasions. She had left home a year ago and made her way westward by singing at hotels along the way. She had been in Denver for the past three months.

"What brought you out West, Miss Beauford?" I asked.

"The same thing that brings most people out here," she replied. "The West has become the land of opportunity. That's true for just about everything, and entertainment is no different. It seems like every month they are building a new hotel in this city, and every one of them is looking for an entertainer.

"I sing in some of the finer hotels in the city, as well as some that aren't quite as grand—like this one. But the St. Elmo is my favorite. The guests here tend to be more hospitable and don't put on airs like those at the more expensive hotels. But I'm grateful there is no shortage of opportunities here, and I can sing as much as I like and earn a decent living."

"There is no question you have a beautiful voice," I commented. "Yours is the type of voice that moves the soul. When you sang *My Melancholy Baby,* you had me thinking about love lost."

"Tell me about the love you've lost, Mr. Fearsithe," Miss Beauford coaxed.

"I will, but please call me Gene."

"Okay, Gene, and you can call me Nellie."

"Well, Nellie, there's not that much to tell. I decided I couldn't stay where I was in Pennsylvania any longer. Sometimes a man just has to set sail, leave the shore, and seek out new and better opportunities. That means leaving people behind. Some of those people are easier to leave than others; and some you invite to go with you, but they refuse. My lost love falls into that latter category."

"So your girl refused to come with you?"

"I told her when I made my mark I would send for her, but she said she had no interest in leaving her family. The way I saw it, we'd be starting a new family, and no longer tied down by the dictates of our existing families. However, she didn't see it that way, so we ended things. All I knew was I couldn't stay in Williamsport any longer. So here I am, and there she is."

"I'm sorry, Gene," Nellie said consolingly.

"Yeah, you and me both," I replied, "but I figure it's the way it has to be."

Just then the bandleader approached our table and told Nellie it was time for her to return to the stage.

"It was good meeting you, Gene," she smiled as she got up from her seat. "I hope you find the dream you are pursuing—and a love that will last. Be careful that you don't become so focused on the former that you miss out on the latter. Or you'll end up being that melancholy baby."

"Oh, I won't," I said somewhat unconvincingly. "And don't you either, Nellie!"

It was approaching midnight, so I decided to head up to my room. But I lay awake for quite some time thinking about Sara, wondering if she missed me or even thought of me. I didn't fall asleep until the sun was about to come up. As a result, it was 10 a.m. before I made my way downstairs to celebrate the day.

After a quick bite of toast with jam and a cup of coffee, I meandered outside. The sun was shining brightly, and the temperature was cool but comfortable. The cobblestone streets were beginning to fill up with people traveling hither and yon—some on foot, others on the parade of streetcars, and a smattering in horse-drawn carriages.

Everyone was sporting their Easter regalia. The men were similarly attired to me in their suits, vests, dress shirts, ties, and hats. The women wore colorful, full-length dresses fitted at the waist. And I had never seen such a variety of hats, from large and elaborate to small and simple! It seemed the entire town of Denver was headed to church.

Though I was not particularly religious, I thought it appropriate to attend a church service on Easter Sunday. The front desk clerk suggested I try the service at the First Baptist Church, which was only a ten-minute walk from the hotel.

First Baptist, like every other church in town, was obviously expecting its largest attendance of the year. The greeter at the front door welcomed me as if I were his long-lost cousin. "Howdy, mister! Welcome to the First Baptist Church. He is risen!"

I failed to remember the traditional response, so I shook his hand and said, "Why yes, He sure is, isn't He?" Neither of us appeared to know what else to say, so I continued on into the sanctuary. It looked a lot like the church my family attended back in Williamsport. Multiple stained-glass windows, displaying scenes from the Bible, stood watch over uncomfortable wooden pews, a choir loft, a pulpit, and a pipe organ in desperate need of tuning.

The pastor's name was Rev. Dr. James Ashenhurst. As preachers go, he kept my interest with his sermon on Jesus being raised from the dead. It was a message I'd heard at least twenty-two times before, so I was pretty familiar with what he was going to say. But he interspersed his message with enough interesting stories to hold my attention.

All in all, it was a pleasant experience, and I enjoyed being surrounded by nice people attempting to do the right thing on Easter. The preacher stood at the door greeting everyone as we left.

"I hope you'll come back and see us, young man," he told me as he shook my hand. As I was walking down the front steps, I heard a familiar voice call out my name. I knew for sure it wasn't the pastor!

"Gene, is that you?"

I turned around to find John Clapp reaching to shake my hand. "I thought that was you!" he exclaimed with a pleasant smile. "I never thought I would see you here in church this morning. But I should have known. And what's more, I should have invited you to join us. Please excuse my lack of courtesy."

"John, it is a delight to see you, and you have no need to apologize. I just decided this morning to attend a church service, and the hotel clerk suggested this one."

By this time, John's wife had caught up with him and extended her greeting as well.

"Gene, will you do us the honor of joining us for Easter dinner?" she asked.

"I would hate to impose, Mrs. Clapp."

"It would be no imposition! We would consider it our good fortune to have you dine with us. John frequently says, 'There is always room for one more around our table.' And that is particularly true on such a special day as Easter. Please, you would be doing us a great honor."

"Mrs. Clapp, how could I possibly refuse such a cordial invitation? It will be my pleasure to join you and your husband."

"Wonderful! And please call me Beatrice like all the rest of my friends."

"Now I am doubly honored," I told her as I tipped my hat, "that you should count me as one of your friends."

"Well that settles it!" John exclaimed. "Join us at two o'clock at the Windsor. It will be the three of us along with a few other friends. Just tell the maitre'd that you are a member of our party."

The Clapps climbed into their red Model T Touring automobile and waved goodbye. I stood there watching as they drove away—with more than a little bit of envy. I would need to buy one of those automobiles one day!

I had two hours to kill before dinner, so I decided to take a walking tour of the city. I passed a number of impressive buildings, including the state capitol. It was striking with its white granite façade and its distinctive gold dome soaring as high as an eighteen-story building. A plaque said the dome was finished with real gold leaf commemorating the Colorado Gold Rush.

At the west entrance of the building were the words "One Mile Above Sea Level" etched into the fifteenth step. As I stood there looking out at the Rocky Mountains, I realized three things. One, I had never stood at this height before—I was standing a mile high! Two, the Rocky Mountains are magnificent. As pretty as the Allegheny Mountains are, they are but foothills compared to the Rockies. It occurred to me I was standing higher than the highest peak of the Alleghenies.

Three, I knew this was just the beginning. I would go even higher, see things of which I had only dreamed, and accomplish more than my father had ever imagined. I would show him . . . and everyone else for that matter. Even Sara would have to admit she made the wrong choice. I could see it all so clearly from where I was standing!

As I walked on, I came upon the Brown Palace Hotel. Back in the late 1800s, people from all over the country were flocking to the West, seeking their fortunes in gold and silver. Apparently, everyone stopped in Denver —either on their way to or from the mountains. Some settled, some moved on, but they all needed a place to stay.

A carpenter from Ohio named Henry Brown moved to Denver in 1860 and had the foresight to buy up all the land he could. As it turned out, that was where the real gold was to be found. Over the next twenty years, his land rose in value, and he became a very wealthy man. He eventually built the Brown Palace Hotel in 1892.

The Italian Renaissance-style hotel was constructed using Colorado red granite and Arizona sandstone. For a finishing touch, Brown commissioned the creation of twenty-six medallions—each carved in stone and depicting a different Colorado animal. Those "silent guests" of the hotel are located between the seventh-floor windows on the hotel's exterior.

I was surprised to learn that no wood was used for the floors and walls. Instead, they were built using hollow blocks of porous terracotta fireproofing, making the Brown Palace the second fireproof building in America. I was starting to wonder if I was staying in the wrong hotel!

Henry Brown spent close to two million dollars to build and furnish the hotel! I can't even imagine that much money. But since he's charging twelve to fifteen dollars a night per room, he'll soon make that back and then some. That's the kind of thing I'm going to do when I get to Portland.

As I continued my tour, I came to the Daniels & Fisher Stores Company—the tallest building between the Mississippi River and the state of California, standing at 325 feet. It was modeled after the bell tower at the Piazza San Marco in Venice, Italy. The clock tower rises twenty-four stories and has clock faces on all four sides. You never have to guess what time it is when you're in downtown Denver!

In fact, I suddenly realized it was rapidly approaching two o'clock, so I picked up my pace and made my way to the northeast corner of Eighteenth and Larimer streets. The grand entrance led into what was described as the most luxurious hotel in Denver. Though I had been impressed by the Brown Palace, I must say the Windsor took my breath away. Ethel had certainly not overstated its opulence. Walking through the lobby, I now truly understood how "out of place" Ernest had felt in the Imperial Hotel in Indianapolis

I surveyed the dining room filled with swells and spotted the maitre'd. He was looking out across the room with an air that clearly communicated he was in charge. I doubt anything took place in that restaurant that he didn't know about. I walked over and asked, "Can you tell me where I can find Mr. John Clapp? I'm a member of his dinner party."

The maitre'd looked at me in disbelief. It was obvious he felt I was unworthy of the Clapps' company. And the longer he looked down his nose at me, so did I. Finally he said, "Yes, Mr. Clapp told me to expect you—and he described you to a 'T.' Follow me."

As he led me to my seat, I couldn't help but feel like everyone was staring at me, wondering who had let me in. Eventually we arrived at a private room. Gratefully, I saw John and Beatrice Clapp speaking with two guests whose backs were to me. Without question, they had the ability to make everyone feel welcome. It appeared their small number of friends had grown to a party of no less than twenty people.

Now I felt even more underdressed and provincial. But John caught sight of me and began walking toward me with his hand outstretched. It was then I realized with whom he had been speaking. All my apprehension melted away as the woman turned . . . and I locked eyes with Ethel.

---

1. Genesis 31:49

7

SUNDAY AFTERNOON, APRIL 7 – MONDAY, APRIL 8

~

I could not take my eyes off Ethel as I shook John's hand. "Well, it appears I have surprised you with one of my other guests, Gene," he chuckled.

"Yes, I am surprised—not only by your kind invitation, but also with the unexpected pleasure of seeing Mrs. Browning again. This is becoming a day full of wonders. First, coming upon you and your lovely wife at church, and now dining with Mr. and Mrs. Browning. This will without question be an Easter to remember."

"Well Gene, we are so glad you are here. Aren't we, Ethel?" John asked, as he and I both turned to the rose standing between us.

"Gene, it is delightful to see you again," Ethel confirmed. "I had no idea you would be here when John and Beatrice extended their kind invitation to Horace and me."

At that moment, Horace Browning appeared beside his wife, looking none too happy to see me.

"You're Ethel's seatmate from the train, aren't you? It's Eugene, isn't it?" Then he added to no one in particular, "What a surprise to see you here."

I thrust out my hand to shake his as I said, "Yes, it's a bit of a jolt for all of us. It is a pleasure to see you both again." But Horace didn't shake my hand; rather, he just stared at me until it became awkward.

John spoke up and enthusiastically announced, "Gene, please allow me to introduce you to the rest of our guests." Everyone else in his dinner party was most cordial. Several men worked at the bank with John, and a few others had moved to Denver from back East during the past year.

I soon realized John and Beatrice were probably two of the Denver Chamber of Commerce's most effective ambassadors. Throughout the afternoon, I repeatedly heard stories from their friends of how the couple had convinced them to settle in Denver. I am certain they have singlehandedly been responsible for much of Denver's growth. I had a hunch they were going to try to convince me to stay here as well!

As we were seated for dinner, I was honored to be between Beatrice on my left and Ethel on my right. However, I don't believe Horace was as pleased. Soon, though, he was engaged in an animated political conversation with the banker seated to his right—and appeared to forget anyone else was present.

"Are your accommodations at the St. Elmo satisfactory, Gene?" Ethel asked.

"Very much so. I'm sure they are not as swell as a place like this, but they suit me just fine. Thank you for the recommendation."

"And were you able to get a good night's rest in a comfortable bed after having sacrificed your sleeping berth on the train for me?" she asked, her eyes twinkling.

"It was no sacrifice, and yes, I had an excellent night's sleep!"

"And what do you think of Denver?" she continued.

"Quite worthy of its reputation," I replied. "I am enjoying its many differences from the East Coast. There's a freshness in the air, and a greater spirit of adventure. You can sense it among everyone you meet. It's as if everyone is excited about what is going to happen next. My expectations of the West are already being confirmed. If Portland is anything like Denver, I am certain I will do very well there."

"Oh, so you haven't yet considered the possibility of making Denver your home?" she asked lightheartedly.

Having overheard our conversation, Beatrice turned and said, "That's because you haven't yet spent enough time with John. I am certain he will have you convinced to stay here before he is done. After all, we need more industrious young men like you here in Denver, and you will find our city to be a very welcoming host."

Right then, the waiters arrived with the first course of our dinner. Before the meal was completed, we had dined on the finest roast lamb I had ever tasted, accompanied by a variety of vegetables and other sides, all seasoned to perfection. The meal was topped off with a delicious Simnel cake, blending a variety of fruits with a layer of marzipan.

As we all savored every morsel of our food, Beatrice became absorbed in conversation with the woman to her left; Horace remained fully focused on his political discussion. So Ethel and I were able to carry on a conversation without interruption, just as we had on the train.

She captivated me with more details about their production of *A Midsummer Night's Dream*. The week of rehearsals would start in the morning and run each day from early morning until late, right up to opening night.

"We have a number of actors who were not with us in Chicago, so in many respects it is a new cast," she explained. "Do you know yet if you will be staying long enough to see the show?"

"I don't believe so," I replied with a touch of regret. "Though I don't have a fixed schedule, I do need to be diligent about finding work. My travels thus far have been an enjoyable holiday of sorts, but I have already taken more time than I planned. So I am going to head out for Portland Tuesday morning."

"I am sorry to hear it, Gene," she said, "but I know you are a man whose mind is set. Your friend has obviously convinced you to come to Portland, but I don't understand why you won't consider other opportunities, such as those in Denver. And you've never actually told me why you had to leave Pennsylvania to pursue your dream?"

"Because I wasn't allowed to pursue my dream there. I was expected to pursue my father's dream—just like he had pursued *his* father's dream. All my life, my father told me everything he owned would one day belong to me. All I had to do was follow in his footsteps, whether I wanted to or not. That applied to my educational pursuits, my vocational pursuits, and even my religious pursuits. I wasn't allowed to have my own original thoughts," I confided to her. "I was simply to do what he told me.

"One day, I'd had enough. I decided to take what little I had saved up and get as far away from Williamsport as possible. When my friend wrote me about his terrific opportunity in Oregon, I told my father I was going to Portland. Anything short of that destination will feel like failure."

Ethel said she understood. She had also left her hometown to pursue her dream.

"Be careful, Gene, not to be so set on your plan that you miss a golden opportunity when it presents itself," she advised. "But also be careful to count the cost before you make any compromises."

I knew she was speaking from personal experience, and I also knew we couldn't pursue that conversation any further. So I shifted our conversation back to more superficial subjects. I wasn't in any hurry for the dinner, or our time together, to end. But end it did, and much too soon we were again saying goodbye.

Horace announced he and Ethel needed to leave for another engagement. Ethel and I were forced to bid one another an abrupt farewell once again. As I watched them walk out of the restaurant, I knew this would truly be my last time to enjoy the pleasure of her company. But there was nothing to be done—she was another man's wife.

I thanked my host and hostess for their kind hospitality and assured John I would see him at his bank at nine o'clock the next morning as we had arranged. I replayed the conversation with Ethel in my mind as I walked back to the St. Elmo. By the time I arrived back in my room I realized I was tuckered out and needed to catch up on my sleep. I decided to call it an early night.

I arose early the next morning, fully rested and looking forward to the day's events. I leisurely enjoyed toast and coffee in the café while reading the newspaper. A front-page article discussed the primaries taking place in Illinois the next day. Republican candidate Teddy Roosevelt was favored to beat incumbent President Taft. The Democrats were deciding between

Speaker of the House Champ Clark from Missouri and New Jersey Governor Woodrow Wilson. It didn't much matter which Democrat won; come November, I was pretty certain Teddy would be the winner.

I arrived at the First National Bank of Denver at five minutes before nine. John had told me the bank was one of the oldest in Denver. William G. Evans was bank president and John served as vice president and cashier. Both men were widely respected, and it was no surprise that John was well acquainted with most, if not all, the leading businessmen in the city. I was still amazed he was taking time out of his busy schedule to introduce a nobody like me to his friend, David Sturgis.

John walked briskly toward me from his private office, his hat in hand and a smile spread across his face.

"Good morning, Gene. You're punctual, I see. My father always said, 'If you're not five minutes early, you're late!' And I have always abided by that principle. I'm glad to see you do as well. Let's be on our way. It's a ten-minute walk to David's office and we have an appointment to meet him at quarter past nine."

On the way, John explained that David was originally from Ohio and came to Denver seeking opportunity and fortune at the age of thirty. He went to work for Denver Gas and Electric Company, just as they were beginning to generate electric power, and worked his way up through the company. He left there about a year ago to start up the Sturgis Electric Company.

"You remind me a lot of him when I first met him," John continued, "and I pride myself on helping like-minded people connect with one another. I have no motive other than to put two young men together who might be an encouragement to one another."

We arrived at Mr. Sturgis's garden-level shop on Fourteenth Street and were immediately shown into his office. After introductions, his first question was, "What is the first thing you think about when you wake up in the morning, Gene, and the last thing you think about when you lie down to sleep?"

When I hesitated, he spoke up again. "For me, it is about what I need to do to provide affordable, reliable electricity to the people of Denver. I have been driven by that question for almost twelve years now. It shapes my every thought, conversation, and action throughout my day. It guides me even in this conversation with the thought, 'What can this fellow Gene Fearsithe do for me or say to me that will ultimately help me provide dependable electricity?'

"Gene, if you're going to achieve your dream, whatever that is, you must be that singularly focused. And if you don't yet know what your dream is, you must be singularly focused on finding it. It must be something bigger than you can accomplish by yourself, and something that you will never fully achieve no matter how hard you try. It must be something that will always require more to be done and something in which you can invest your life passionately.

"Are you seeking that kind of dream, Gene?"

"I am," I replied, "but I don't yet know what it is."

"I was you once," David smiled. "I knew I didn't want to spend the rest of my life in Ohio. I decided I needed to go somewhere else to find my dream. The West seemed like the place to go looking for it—and when I arrived in Denver, I knew I didn't need to search any further. I needed to stop running and let the dream find me.

"It sounds like your *place* may be Portland, Gene. But only you will know for sure once you get there. If it turns out to be *your* place, let your dream find you, then pursue it with all the strength and ability you have."

"David, I didn't know what to expect from our time together," I told him earnestly. "but I was grateful for John's willingness to introduce us and your agreement to meet me. I thought maybe I would learn about the business of electricity, but you have inspired me with so much more. You've helped give me clarity on what I am seeking—or more importantly, how I can find the clarity I need.

"Up until this point, I think I've been traveling *from* something. Portland had merely been the destination on that ticket. And I do believe I need to go there. But you've helped me see that I need to be headed *to* something. And I think you have helped me know what that is when the time comes. I can't thank you enough!"

"Gene, it is always a pleasure to help a fellow dreamer, and I look forward to one day hearing that you've discovered your dream," David replied. "In the meantime, Godspeed in your pursuit."

"And to you the same, David. By the way, I was walking around Denver last night admiring all the lights. I couldn't help but wonder what they would look like if they were different colors instead of just white light. Have you ever thought about painting your light bulbs and giving them some color?"

David looked at me thoughtfully. "No, I haven't, Gene," he said, "but that idea is not half bad. You may have just given me something I can take away from our conversation as well." We shook hands and parted ways.

As John and I walked back to the bank, he said, "Well, that didn't go quite the way I had planned. I had hoped the two of you would strike up a conversation that would convince you to stay here—but he appears to have convinced you to travel on to Portland.

"Nevertheless, I hope you will consider staying over until next week in order to see a certain actress perform in her play. Perhaps the city will grow on you in that time and you will decide to stay."

"John, you have been most kind," I replied. "You and your wife have almost persuaded me to change my plans. But David is right; if I don't go to Portland, I will always wonder what might have been."

"Their gain will be our loss, Gene. But please know you are always welcome here."

We parted ways when we arrived back at the bank. Since my train was not departing until Tuesday morning, I decided there was one more place I wanted to see. I inquired as to the address of the Paris Theatre and set off to find it.

One of the front doors was ajar so I was able to slip into the theater unde-tected. The only light was coming from the stage. I made my way up to the balcony and settled into a seat in the shadows. Cast members were running through their lines, while the director was blocking their move-ments. I sat there for several hours watching the rehearsal. Ethel was correct—they needed a lot of practice before next week's opening night.

I was mesmerized by Ethel every time she moved or spoke a line. In all fairness, she probably wasn't a great actress. But I decided it really didn't matter because she would forevermore be my favorite actress. There were a couple of times she said something that almost made me laugh out loud. But I resisted the urge because I did not want to be discovered, nor did I want her to know I was there. I just wanted to drink it all in.

I will admit I spent some of those hours wondering "what if." I had only felt this way about two women—the one I left behind in Pennsylvania, and this one who could never be mine. But I was grateful for the time I had spent with them both. Just like with Sara, these few days with Ethel had made me a better person. She had made a mark on my life I would wear forever.

Eventually I worked up the resolve to quietly get up and exit the theater without being seen. I knew this was now my final farewell.

8

TUESDAY, APRIL 9

∾

*I*t was a few minutes before 8:00 a.m. when the Denver & Rio Grande Railroad conductor called out, "Final call for Train #1. Now departing for Salt Lake City and Ogden, Utah! All aboard!" I was already settled in my seat as the train began to pull out of Denver's Union Station. I stared out the window to catch my last glimpses of the city as the train began to gain speed.

Although Denver offered impressive buildings and beautiful terrain, my memories would always center on a charming woman who had stolen my heart. Denver would simply be remembered as the backdrop for that encounter.

My seatmate for this leg of my journey was quite a change! I would venture that Mr. Thomas Smeltzer was well into his sixties and had that well-worn appearance of a man who had worked hard all his life. He was lanky like I am, but shorter in stature. The one thing I noticed right off was that he sported a mustache that twitched whenever he spoke. After we exchanged introductions, he told me he was headed back home to Salt Lake City.

"What do you do there?" I inquired.

"I work for the Ontario Mining Company, just like my father did before me," he responded. "The company sent me to Salt Lake City in 1874 to work as one of the foremen overseeing the mining operations of a silver mine they had just acquired. Located in the Oquirrh Mountains outside the city, the mine remains one of the largest producers of silver in the region."

"Are you still one of the foremen there?"

"No, over the years I've received a number of promotions. Now I am the mine superintendent, overseeing the work of a dozen foremen and 200 miners. They represent half of our company's overall workforce of approximately 400 employees."

"I had no idea a mining operation could be that large," I replied.

"Oh, yes," Thomas assured me. "In addition to the miners, the total workforce includes those who extract the silver from the ore, those who transport it, our engineers, electricians, maintenance workers, and office clerks. It takes a lot of people to make it all work—and we're not even one of the largest mines in the area. Some of the largest mines employ several thousand workers."

"How about you, Gene?" he asked. "What do you do for a living?"

I explained I was traveling to Portland to find out the answer to that question. When I told him my training was as a mechanical engineer, his eyes lit up.

"Do tell! I am currently looking to employ a good mechanical engineer," Thomas said. "You should get off the train at Salt Lake City and apply for the job. You seem like you are an industrious fellow. Maybe you don't have to go all the way to Portland to find your opportunity. As a matter of fact, why don't you come be my guest for a day or two, apply for the job, and explore the city? I am confident you won't be disappointed."

We wouldn't be arriving in Salt Lake City until the next afternoon, so I promised Thomas I would consider his offer. In the meantime, he proved to be an excellent guide along our journey. He told me he was a widower whose wife had died eight years earlier of consumption. They had one child—a daughter who was now married and living in Denver. He tried to make the journey between the two cities as often as possible. As a result, he was practically an expert about the points of interest between the two cities.

Along the way we passed by a prominent, tower-shaped butte appropriately called Castle Rock. Thomas said the original settlers of this entire region were various Indian tribes, most notably the Ute and Arapaho tribes.

"The first white settlers were drawn to the area by the prospects of gold," he elaborated. "But instead, they discovered rhyolite stone. Though that discovery did not attract the hordes who were searching for gold, it was enough to prompt the settlement of a town that quickly was named after the castle rock towering above it."

A few hours later, we passed through the picturesque Royal Gorge. My personal guide explained the gorge is about 1,000 feet deep and ten miles long. It was formed by the Arkansas River cutting through the granite rocks over thousands of years.

"Now there's an engineering challenge for you," Thomas told me. "There's talk they want to build a suspension bridge across the gorge 956 feet above the river. Whoever successfully engineers that bridge will most definitely leave their mark!"

His comment reminded me that opportunities like that existed everywhere you went in the West. I was certain the same would be true for Portland.

Not long after, he directed my attention to a peak off in the distance. "Have you ever heard of the Mount of the Holy Cross?" he asked.

"Of course, I've heard of it," I replied, "but I never thought it was real. I've seen pictures, but I just figured it was a picture card fake."

"Well, if it's fake, what's that you're looking at?"

I strained my eyes to see where he was pointing. Lo and behold, I saw the cross-shaped snowfield up on the face of the peak.

"The pictures you're referring to were taken by a photographer named William Jackson almost forty years ago," Thomas continued. "There are some folks who say that cross was God's way of affirming the westward expansion of our nation. I, on the other hand, think it was pure greed that drove the expansion. People got a thirst for gold, and they would do anything to try and satisfy that thirst. But the cross story seems to fit well with the church folks.

"What about you, Gene? Are you a religious man?"

"I spent a fair part of my youth sitting on those uncomfortable seats in the church building," I answered, "but I wouldn't consider myself to be a church-going man. Don't misunderstand me; I believe in God! I don't know how anyone could look at all of His handiwork around us and not believe He exists. I just don't believe He cares one way or the other whether I live in Pennsylvania or Oregon."

"Well said, Gene!" Thomas exclaimed. "My sentiments exactly."

As our conversation hit a lull, I found myself nodding off. The next thing I knew, a sudden change in the train's movement awoke me from my nap. The view outside had changed dramatically. Everything was covered in snow—and a lot of it! And the snow was still falling by the bucket. The train had obviously slowed down.

"When did we encounter snow?" I asked Thomas, once I had my bearings.

"It started about two hours ago after we pulled out of Canon City," he replied, "but we didn't enter into this heavy stuff until about ten minutes ago after we pulled out of Salida. It appears there may be some delays ahead as a result."

Those words had barely left Thomas's mouth when the train slowed to a stop. After a few minutes, the conductor came through our train car announcing, "Nothing to worry about, folks! The engineer has stopped so the crew can clear the track. It's not unusual here this time of the year. Just sit back and relax, and I'm certain we'll be out of here in no time."

Thomas apparently sensed my anxiety and told me, "The conductor's right. This has happened prit'near every time I've passed through on my way to or from Denver. Could be a holdup of an hour or so, but not much beyond that. Did you bring some food with you for dinner, or do you plan to eat in the dining car?"

"I've already finished the food I brought from Denver, so I guess I'm going to have to eat in the dining car," I stated, not having considered the matter before this. "How about you?"

"It's likely to be two to three hours before we arrive in Buena Vista, and even with that, I doubt there will be enough time to get off the train to purchase food in the station. So I reckon I'll take supper in the dining car as well."

"In that case, let me see if I can go make a reservation for the two of us," I volunteered. "It will give me time to stretch my legs."

Dinner reservations were delayed until the train started back up and we were on our way. When our time arrived, it was none too soon for me. I was ready to eat one of everything on the menu. We were the first to be seated at our table. A few moments later, two men who looked to be in their forties, and who were traveling separately, joined us.

The first introduced himself as Frederick Felt from Boise, Idaho, and the second was Emmett Hall from, of all places, Portland, Oregon. I was beyond excited to finally meet someone who could give me more insight into the city.

After Thomas and I introduced ourselves, it was actually Thomas who said, "I expect that Mr. Fearsithe here will have a lot of questions for you Mr. Hall, given that he is headed to your fine city."

Mr. Hall raised his eyebrows and asked, "What takes you to Portland, Mr. Fearsithe?"

"A quest," I replied. "I am in search of a dream, and I believe I will find what I am looking for in Portland."

"Why is that?"

"I know our entire nation is a land of opportunity," I began. "But I also know the western states are facing unique challenges—taming a land without the shackles of established traditions. I perceive it as an area looking for innovation as well as industrialization, and a place where a man is only limited by the size of his dream and his determination to see it fulfilled."

"But I am sure Mr. Felt would tell you the same is true in Boise, and Mr. Smeltzer would say the same for Salt Lake City," Mr. Hall commented. "And as a current resident of Portland, I would not contradict them. Portland is actually more established than those cities. So why Portland specifically?"

"Portland has earned the reputation of being environmentally responsible," I replied. "Instead of polluting and ravaging its resources like so much of the country, Portland has sought ways to protect its natural resources. Your leaders have shown great innovation in addressing the concerns of a growing city. And they have demonstrated a social responsibility that can be an example for cities across our nation. Portland may have sixty years of history, but it is still an adolescent compared to the East."

"Spoken like a true easterner who is looking to break free from the problems of the East," Mr. Hall said with a smile.

"And I cannot ignore the other important factor Portland has going for it," I said.

"What is that?" he asked.

"Portland is also nearly 3,000 miles away from my home," I replied as I returned his smile.

"Now that is spoken like a young man looking to make his own mark!" Thomas interjected with a gentle slap on my back. "Hear! Hear!" the other two men chimed in.

Frederick Felt told us he was the chief engineer of Boise Street Railway Company. He had been raised in Chicago and made his way to Boise when he was my age. Emmett Hall was the secretary of the Oregon-Washington Railroad and Navigation Company based in Portland and headed up their steamship division. As it turned out, he had made his way to Portland from Baltimore when he was in his early twenties.

"So all three of us have that in common," Frederick declared. "The only difference is you still have your whole life in front of you, and ours is half over. Oh, to be twenty-three again!

"But, Gene," he continued, "though I have heard your impressive reasons for wanting to go to Portland, I would be remiss if I did not encourage you to visit Boise before you make a final decision. Ours is also a growing and prosperous city, ripe with opportunities for young men such as yourself. And I will tell you that my company is always seeking talented engineers."

I sat back in my seat and smiled while all three men began to "sell" me on their respective cities. Emmett knew he didn't have to try as hard since my mind was already made up in favor of Portland. But the other two clearly were not to be put off!

As we finished our meal, I told them I would consider their kind invitations overnight and looked forward to seeing them again in the morning. I then set off to find my sleeping berth. I was determined not to spend the evening sitting up in my seat. Besides, I had no prospect of a beautiful young woman's head falling gently on my shoulder this time!

I really had no idea what to expect in a sleeping berth as the attendant showed me to Number 14. It was made of wood with a hinged door I could lock from the inside. It was a narrow bed, made up with a pillow, sheets, and a woolen blanket, and folded down from the wall.

I quickly discovered there was no room to move around once the bed was down. Twice I hit my head because the lighting was so dim. There was no washbowl or any other amenities. Before I settled in, I walked to the shared facilities at the end of the train car to wash up.

I sighed as I realized my legs extended three inches beyond the end of the bed. Whoever designed these berths never expected men to grow beyond six feet tall. I pulled up the blanket and shivered. It was cold outside—and it wasn't much warmer inside.

These berths were obviously designed for function rather than comfort or luxury. I had wondered if the noise and vibration of the car might make it difficult to sleep. But that concern soon melted away. I lay there briefly pondering the invitations from my dining companions—but fell asleep in no time at all.

≈

9

WEDNESDAY, APRIL 10 – THURSDAY, APRIL 11

~

*I*t was still early morning as we pulled into Grand Junction Depot, but I had already been awake for a while. Though I much preferred sleeping in the berth over spending the night sitting up in a seat, neither one of them was ideal. So I got up, dressed, and walked the aisles of the train.

I spotted the conductor and asked, "How long will we be stopped here?"

"Thirty minutes and no more," he replied, looking at his pocket watch.

"Is there a bakery near the depot or somewhere I can get a bite to eat?"

"Yes, there's a good bakery just beside the depot," the conductor told me. "It's run by an Amish family from back East, and their sticky buns are the best in the West," he added with a smile. "You won't have enough time to eat there, but you should be able to buy something to bring back on the train. If you decide to go there, be sure to be quick about it!"

The conductor abruptly turned and continued on his way through the car. I followed him to the back of the car so I would be ready to hop off as soon as we came to a complete stop.

The depot was quite impressive and apparently fairly new. It was a simple two-story structure that was more pleasing than imposing. It was constructed of white brick with terra cotta ornamentation under a red tile roof.

The only people inside were those waiting to board our train. I quickly made my way through the main hall and exited onto the street. I didn't need to look around to find the bakery—all I needed to do was follow my nose. The pleasing aroma of freshly baked bread and pastries made my mouth water and my stomach rumble.

A pleasant, middle-aged woman wearing an apron and a prayer kapp was placing trays of freshly baked treats on the shelves of a display case. Though it all looked—and smelled—delicious, my eye was drawn to the pan of sticky buns that had just come out of the oven.

"Good morning, young man," the woman greeted me with a smile. "What can I interest you in?"

After surveying the trays, I replied, "Those sticky buns look amazing. I'll take two, packaged, so I can take them on the train."

As the woman readied my order, I asked, "Where are you originally from?"

"My family moved out here a few years ago from Lancaster, Pennsylvania," she replied. "Have you ever heard of it?"

"I sure have," I grinned. "I passed through it once with my father on my way to Philadelphia from Williamsport."

"Are you from those parts?" she asked, obviously pleased I knew of her hometown.

"Yes, I lived there all my life until a little over a week ago," I told her. "And I grew up eating sticky buns that looked and smelled just like these. My mother used to make them!"

"I'm glad to hear that," she said, her eyes sparkling. "Hopefully they'll provide you with a taste of your mother's home cooking. Where are you headed?"

"To Portland, Oregon, ma'am."

"What's taking you out there?"

"I'm chasing a dream, and I hope to find it in Portland."

"Well, I hope you find what you're looking for, young man. But I'm sure your mother misses you."

"Not really, ma'am. My mother passed away a few years ago, so it's just me and my father."

"I am so sorry to hear it. I'm sure that was hard for you both. Your mother was obviously taken much too soon."

"Yes, ma'am it was—it is. I don't reckon it's something he and I will ever truly get over."

"I believe there is a special bond between a mother and her son, young man. My only son died in an accident on our farm a few years ago. It is an ache that never truly goes away. That's actually why my husband and I moved out here. Everything in Lancaster reminded us of our son. It was hard to move on; I wasn't even sure if I wanted to go forward.

"A loss like that causes families to grow apart or grow closer together. Gratefully, my husband and I grew together. We knew we needed to start fresh, for the sake of our Eli, to honor his memory and not run from our loss.

"I hope that's what you're doing, young man. I hope you're headed to Portland to honor your mother's memory—and not run from her loss."

I didn't quite know how to respond to her statement. Because no matter how hard I tried to convince myself I was running toward my dream, there was a part of me that knew I was running *away* from something. And I knew I was running away from those to whom I needed to be drawing closer.

Just then, I heard the train whistle, and I knew I needed to hurry back.

"How much do I owe you for these, ma'am?" I asked.

"Not a thing, young man," she replied tenderly as she handed me the bag and patted my hand. "They're in honor of your mother. Think of them as a gift from her."

Suddenly there was a lump in my throat I couldn't swallow. Just then, I did something I had never done with a stranger. I gave her a big hug—and she hugged me back. And for a moment, I felt like I was in my mother's embrace.

As I walked out of the store, I heard her say, "Run toward your dream, Gene; don't run away from it."

Halfway to the train, I was struck with a thought: *How did she know my name?* But I knew I didn't have time to go back and ask her.

I arrived back at my seat with only a few moments to spare. Most passengers were still asleep as the train left the station. Thomas was nowhere in sight, so I had the seat to myself. I was glad for no interruptions as I mulled over my conversation with the Amish woman. The conductor was counting heads as he passed my seat, but this time he turned and stopped.

"I see you made it back in time," he said, noticing the bag in my hand.

"I sure did. And this one's for you," I added as I handed him the bag. "Thanks for the recommendation. You're right! They are most definitely the best sticky buns in the West . . . and so much more!"

～

While we were stopped at the depot, a batch of today's newspapers were brought aboard the train. I picked one up as my eye caught a huge headline:

White Star Liner Titanic Sets Sail on Her Maiden Voyage

. . .

The front page had a lengthy article about the massiveness of the vessel, its luxurious appointments, and its grand send-off in Southampton. It also boasted of the ship's seaworthiness and claimed it was unsinkable. But my attention was drawn to an editorial on an inside page:

The White Star Liner Titanic, which left Southampton for New York today on her first Atlantic voyage, surpasses in size and luxury, but especially in luxury, anything else afloat, if not also the Waldorf-Astoria and the Royal Automobile Club. The information that she is 883 feet long, 104 feet deep (or high) from keel to bridge, and displaces about 60,000 tons of water probably means no more to most of us than the astronomer's assurance that the sun is 90,000,000 miles away, and much less probably than the statement that her rudder is as tall as a six or seven story building, weighs more than a hundred tons, and swings on pintles nearly a foot thick.

But the appointments of the ship make one realize how remote the sea and its associations are from the up-to-date Atlantic passenger. Squash racquet courts, Turkish baths, gymnasium, swimming bath, electric passenger lifts, reception rooms, Ritz-Carlton restaurants, concert halls, Parisian cafes "in French trelliswork with ivy creepers," parlor suites with private promenade decks—could anything be much more foreign to old-fashioned people's ideas of a sea voyage?

Still, to do them justice, the designers of the Titanic, preoccupied though they were with the tastes of cosmopolitan millionaires, have made at least one small concession to those of us

who regard the sea as something better than a
dreary slum surrounding a Grand Babylon Hotel.
We learn from one enthusiastic description that
on the upper promenade deck one can look
through the windows, and, safely sheltered from
contact with the outer air, obtain "a full view
of the sea, so much appreciated by passengers."
Let us be grateful for that kindly provision.[1]

I was lost in thought as I pondered what it must be like to be a passenger on the main decks—not steerage. Horace and Ethel would know firsthand this fall. Hopefully, I, too, would one day be able to join those ranks. But in the meantime, I was simply amazed by the overall proportions of the ship and the engineering detail that went into its manufacture.

As I considered those things, Thomas arrived. He told me we had been invited to join Frederick and Emmett in the dining car for breakfast. "But I didn't make a reservation," I told him.

"Neither did I," Thomas replied. "They made the reservation for both of us. They sent word to your sleeping berth, but apparently you had already set out for the day. They are already seated at the table. Let's not keep them waiting!"

As we headed to the dining car, I rehearsed in my mind the decision I had made regarding the three gentlemen's invitations. They were very kind to extend me such generous opportunities. I did not want to offend them in any way.

The easiest offer to accept was Emmett's—not only due to its location, but also the tremendous prospects of advancement the railway and shipping business would afford. I definitely planned to explore that opportunity as soon as I arrived in Portland.

Thomas's offer in Salt Lake City was the easiest to reject. Thomas had spent a lifetime working for his company and had only made it to middle management. There appeared to be some kind of invisible barrier designed to keep people from reaching the top of his company. Thomas was content with that, but I knew I would not be.

I especially wrestled with Frederick's offer. Boise would require a slight detour to visit, but I decided I would always regret it if I didn't investigate the city. It would be easy enough to get back on the train and proceed to my original destination if I weren't impressed.

Frederick was overjoyed when I told him I would join him in Boise. Confident that he would still prevail, Emmett handed me his business card and said he looked forward to seeing me in Portland in about a week. Thomas was gracious and told me if I ever changed my mind, I should look him up in Salt Lake City. "There will always be an opportunity there for a determined young man like yourself," he said.

Thomas disembarked at the Salt Lake station and gave me a final wave before disappearing into the crowd. As the train rolled on, I looked out my window to gaze at the impressive Great Salt Lake. After seeing the lake and all the birdlife, I began second-guessing myself about whether I should have made a brief visit. No, I decided, Boise was a necessary excursion; Salt Lake City was not!

An hour later we arrived in Ogden at four in the afternoon. Snowfall had slowed us down, so we were about ninety minutes late. As a result, Frederick and I had missed the train to Boise. The next train wasn't until 1:00 a.m.

"This isn't the first time I've had to spend a few extra hours in Ogden," Frederick told me. "Allow me to show you the town!"

Ogden was a bustling city with a population of about 35,000 people. It had become a significant railroad hub, and as such, a major center of commerce in this region. The downtown appeared to be thriving. We passed numerous shops and hotels, as well as a variety of cultural venues, such as museums, art galleries, and libraries.

But what stood out to me the most was the fact that I don't believe I saw one girl or woman who was not made up. It will forever be the city of painted ladies to me. And the reality was, none of them needed to wear makeup, because each one was pretty already. I suddenly thought about Ethel and Sara. Ethel, of course, paints her face because she's an actress. Sara, however, doesn't wear makeup or need to in order to look pretty.

When I made my observation to Frederick, he replied, "It's the new style. My wife tells me all the women in Paris, France, paint their faces. And since they are known for their glamour and beauty, every woman in America wants to be just like them—apparently, especially here in Ogden.

 "Speaking of France, do you like French food, Gene?"

"I don't know that I've ever tried it."

"Well, we need to remedy that this very evening," Frederick said. "Let's take the streetcar."

He explained that our train passes enabled us to ride on the streetcars free of charge. Utah boasts of having one of the most efficient streetcar systems. I don't know about the entire state, but my experience in Ogden supported that claim. Frederick, however, smugly pointed out that I would find Boise's streetcar system superior.

We got off the streetcar on Washington Avenue and Frederick led me to the Paris Café. He told me it was one of his favorites.

"It's owned by a couple who emigrated from France and came directly to Ogden," he explained. "No one knows why they chose this town of all places, but there is no question they serve the finest French food west of the Rocky Mountains."

At Frederick's suggestion, I chose coq au vin as my entrée, and it was an excellent choice!

We ate a leisurely meal, then slowly made our way back to the train station. As we passed a barbershop, we decided we could both use a shave. It turned out to be the best shave I ever had—unlike the rude barber who robbed me in Denver! I doubled my Japanese barber's charge and paid him a full fifty cents. He earned every penny!

Back at the station, we learned our train would be delayed another two hours. Since everything in the city was closed for the night, we waited in the station and talked.

We finally departed Ogden at 2:55 a.m. We made an unscheduled stop in Pocatello, Idaho, later that morning to make repairs to the train engine. When the conductor informed passengers we would be here for at least two hours, Frederick and I decided to get breakfast in town. Since Frederick had treated me to dinner, I felt compelled to reciprocate. It was another unplanned expense, but it tasted like a wonderful, home-cooked meal.

We pulled out of Pocatello with a new engine at 10:30 a.m. and eventually made it to Boise just before 8:00 p.m., after changing trains in Nampa. I didn't know what to expect when we arrived in Boise, but I was by no means disappointed!

---

1. Published in The Manchester Guardian on 11 April 1912

10

FRIDAY, APRIL 12

~

*F*rederick assured me his wife would be more than amenable for me to stay in their home, but I wanted the unfettered opportunity to explore the city of Boise on my own. Though we had enjoyed our time together, I also sensed we now needed some time apart.

When I pressed him for suggestions, Frederick recommended the Bristol Hotel.

"It's a ten-minute walk from the Union Pacific Train Depot," he said, "and an even shorter distance to my offices, so it is very convenient. It is not the most luxurious hotel in the city, but I think you will find the accommodations adequate."

As we parted at the train station, Frederick said, "I'll leave it to you to get settled into your hotel for the evening. Come to my office at eleven o'clock in the morning and I'll show you around."

When I approached the reception desk at the hotel, I had the distinct impression I had been here before. But the truth is, all these hotels were starting to look alike. I breathed a sigh of relief when I was able to get a room on the second floor. The story Mr. Bird had told me in Ohio about hotel fires was never far from my mind!

After dropping my suitcase in my room, I ventured down to the hotel dining room and enjoyed a supper of meatloaf, mashed potatoes with gravy, and garden peas. It was actually one of the simpler meals I had eaten since departing on this journey, and it was a welcome change.

Though I wanted to explore the city after I finished dinner, I was so exhausted I decided to retire early and catch up on my rest. Within moments of stretching out on the bed, I was fast asleep. The sunlight streaming in my window woke me a little before six o'clock the next morning.

It was a comfortable spring day. As I strolled down Main Street, the air carried the invigorating scent of blooming flowers, and the trees along the sidewalk were budding. Sunlight filtered through the intermittent gaps between buildings, casting a warm glow on the bustling street.

I was fascinated by the architectural diversity of the city. Victorian-era facades stood boldly alongside newer structures embracing a more neoclassical influence. The ornate storefronts beckoned me to enter with their colorful signage and carefully placed wares.

The rhythmic clatter of horse-drawn carriages and wagons resonated through the streets, blending with the hum of conversation and the occasional bursts of laughter. The sounds created a melody that was different from any of the other cities I had visited. The sidewalk teemed with pedestrians as street vendors endeavored to capture our attention with the goods on their carts. I soon felt as if I had been absorbed into a symphony that was unfolding around me, and I was but one of the solitary notes.

As I continued exploring, I found the clothing store the hotel desk clerk had recommended. I purchased some clean linen to replace my soiled shirt and collar. I wanted to look my best for my interview.

On my way back to the hotel, I passed a newspaper boy energetically shouting the day's headlines and waving his papers to catch people's attention.

"On this day fifty-one years ago, Confederate forces opened fire on Fort Sumter and started the Civil War! Read a never-before-heard account from one of the soldiers who was there!" I decided it must be a slow news day.

I arrived at the offices of Boise Street Railway Company at five minutes before eleven. Frederick's secretary greeted me and said her boss would be delayed. He had given instructions for me to meet with Fred Bechtel, head of the company's personnel department. Frederick and I would meet up later for lunch.

Mr. Bechtel was an affable fellow, about the same age as Frederick. He had worked his way up in the company from streetcar operations and scheduling.

"I am living proof," he told me, "that a man can climb the ladder of success here at Boise Street Railway from the bottom to the top if he has the gumption and determination to make the journey.

"Mr. Felt tells me he sees that kind of determination in you. He says you have traveled from the East to find an opportunity where you can grow and succeed. Tell me about yourself. What kind of education and training do you have?"

"I have an associate degree in engineering from the Williamsport Dickinson Seminary in Williamsport, Pennsylvania. While attending school and for the four years since then, I have apprenticed under my father, Mr. Robert D. Fearsithe, the chief engineer of Keller and Company. Keller is a successful regional manufacturer of a variety of steam boilers, tanks, and engine supplies. My work at the company has centered around product design and manufacture."

"Very interesting," Mr. Bechtel replied. "And what has prompted you to leave your position to seek another?"

"I no longer wish to work in the shadow of my father," I responded. "Neither do I want to pursue the career path he has set out for me. Though I am grateful for his tutelage and the experience Keller and Company has granted me, I want to explore opportunities that lead to future inventions beyond boilers. I want to be a part of designing and creating solutions for the future."

"How did your father respond when you told him you were headed out West?" Mr. Bechtel asked.

I probably should have anticipated someone asking that question. In retrospect, I should have already composed an answer that sounded professional. But the fact was, my decision to leave Williamsport caused great upheaval in the company—and with my father. No one understood why I wanted to leave.

They all felt I was abandoning my father. Truth be told, his two partners at Keller had accused me of doing just that.

"You are his only living family," they chastised. "The two of you are all each other has since the death of your mother. How can you possibly leave him and travel to the other side of the country? How can you be such an uncaring son?"

The situation was further complicated because Sara's father was one of the other partners. He was angry I was walking out on his daughter.

"If you cared about either of them, you would marry Sara and settle down, raise your family, and work here alongside your father," he insisted.

The silence following Mr. Bechtel's question began to feel awkward, so I finally spoke up.

"My father was not happy to see me go, but he did not try to talk me out of it." That part was true. My father never tried to convince me to stay. I knew I had wounded him, but he had just responded with a stern silence.

"There can always be challenges when you mix family and business," Mr. Bechtel replied. "Do you have any letters of reference?"

"Yes, I do," I answered as I reached into my coat pocket and withdrew an envelope. "Though my father did not want me to leave, he still provided me with this letter of reference."

Mr. Bechtel read over the letter slowly. "Your father has written an excellent reference letter for you. He obviously thinks very highly of your abilities, and he has written it in such a way that someone would be hard pressed to accuse him of being biased."

My conversation with Mr. Bechtel continued for another forty-five minutes, during which he asked me more questions about my abilities. I asked him questions regarding opportunities at Boise Street Railway. When the interview was completed, he told me Frederick made the final decision about hiring new employees in the engineering department. I left with the impression I had passed his part of the interview, and anything further would be entirely up to Frederick—and me.

Mr. Bechtel walked me back to Frederick's office to make sure I didn't get lost. I thanked him for his time, and he extended his good wishes that he hoped to see me again.

Frederick walked out of his office and shook my hand. "So, how did it go?"

"I think everything went fine," I replied, "but you'll need to ask Mr. Bechtel to get his opinion."

"Oh, I will, Gene," he said with a smile. "Let's go get a bite of lunch."

We walked two blocks to the restaurant inside the Idanha Hotel. Frederick told me it was the grandest hotel in Boise, but I had already surmised as much before we even entered through the intricately carved doors. I was impressed that everyone in the hotel seemed to know Frederick and cordially greeted him.

"Gene, I highly recommend the trout. I'm not quite sure what the chef here does to it, but it's the finest I have ever tasted," Frederick said once we were seated in the dining room. I followed my host's recommendation, confident I would not be disappointed. Once the waiter had taken our orders, Frederick began to speak in hushed tones.

"I apologize for not greeting you when you arrived this morning, Gene. Our president, Mr. Howe, called an unscheduled meeting of all our executives. We discussed important matters that will weigh heavily on our future plans as a company. One of the things you will soon learn, if you haven't already, is that you always need to be looking ahead in order to anticipate the next great revolution.

"For example, the Boise Street Railway Company is not really in the street railway business; we're in the people-moving business. Ten years from now the street railway business as we know it today will look very different. A chap in England, by the name of Frank Searle, has designed what they call a double-decker bus. They are gas-powered vehicles that can carry eighty passengers and do not require a track, an electric line, or a horse. Just like the automobile, it travels on the open road and can go anywhere.

"Can you imagine what that flexibility will do to the planning of future passenger routes within cities? The miles of tracks and the overhead electric cables will become obsolete. It will revolutionize the people-moving business. The London General Omnibus Company is already producing hundreds of these double-decker buses each year, and soon other manufacturers—including some right here in the U.S.—will join their ranks. The street railway companies that do not adapt to these changes will soon find themselves out of business.

"Accordingly, Mr. Howe has announced numerous changes our company will be making. Regrettably, those changes mean we no longer need to hire additional mechanical engineers. I'm so sorry, Gene, but the position I brought you to Boise for no longer exists."

Slowly, his last statement began to sink in. Though Boise had never been my intended destination, I considered the city an example of what lay ahead of me in the West. I had envisioned unlimited opportunities ripe for the picking by someone like me. I never imagined being told there wasn't a position available for me.

"How will these changes affect the engineering staff you already employ?" I asked.

"I'm not sure," Frederick replied. "But we can't have our employees fearing for their jobs. The big changes are really years away, and steps will need to be taken gradually.

"During our time together, I have come to think of you as a brother-in-arms seeking to slay the challenges of the future with finesse and success. So I think it only fair to tell you I no longer believe Boise Street Railway is a good fit for you. I owe you that much honesty and transparency since I convinced you to come to Boise. But I hope you understand the confidentiality with which I share this information."

"I do, Frederick, and I am honored that you would confide in me so freely. Be assured I will not betray your confidence. If you don't mind my asking, what will these changes mean for you?"

"I don't completely know yet, Gene," he admitted. "That will depend on how forward thinking our owners are, and whether they are willing to make the radical changes the future will require. If not, you may see me one day in Portland!"

For the remainder of our lunch, we discussed other examples of how things will change in the future. We are in the industrial age! Innovation and invention are the watch words of the day. Fifty years ago our nation was in a civil war, and now we are becoming a major power in the world. Nothing stays the same, and opportunity only comes to those who seize it. I soon realized it was that truth I had come to Boise to discover.

Frederick and I parted ways after lunch, and I stopped by the train station. I booked my travel to Portland and made a reservation on the Oregon Short Line Train No. 14 departing at half past seven the next morning.

Since I doubted I would ever return to Boise, I decided to explore more of its sites. The state capitol building had just been completed a few days earlier. A beautiful structure made of sandstone, it featured a 5'2" copper eagle atop the building's intricate dome, majestically overlooking the entire region.

From there I walked to the U.S. Cavalry Barracks and the reserve on the edge of the city. I learned that the U.S. Army is in the process of vacating the site and turning it over to the National Guard. Because it was in transition, the sergeant at the entry gate gave me permission to walk through the areas that previously housed the stables and barracks. I decided the men who had served there led a nice life!

By the time I got back to the hotel, I was bushed. I enjoyed a bowl of soup in the dining room before going to bed. Just before I lay down, I looked out my window and admired the blanket of stars twinkling across the cloudless sky. That is a picture of Idaho I will never forget!

~

11

SATURDAY MORNING AND AFTERNOON, APRIL 13

∼

*A*t quarter past eight on Saturday morning, my train rolled into the train depot in Nampa, Idaho, after a short, forty-five-minute ride. I now had slightly more than eight hours to kill before my next train departed for Portland. We had passed miles and miles of farmland as we approached the city.

My seatmate, who introduced himself as John Reynolds, informed me that Nampa and the surrounding areas were thriving farming communities.

"At harvest season," he said, "those fields will be filled with corn, wheat, potatoes, sugar beets, and the like, as far as the eye can see."

John had pointed out the sugar beet factory on the outskirts of the city—an impressive, multi-story brick structure with large smokestacks to accommodate the boilers and steam engines. Though the factory looked idle, John said by late summer and early fall it would be running at full capacity, employing a significant seasonal workforce.

"Where do the seasonal workers come from?" I inquired.

"In addition to the managers and supervisors who live here year-round, some workers are area farmers who depend upon the additional income during the harvest season. Most workers, however, are beet laborers who come here just for the season. They follow the sugar beet harvest as it progresses from one region to another. While they are in town, they stay in those barracks right over there," he added, pointing to a row of buildings on the eastern side of the factory. "The population of the city more than doubles during those months."

"How many people live here year-round?" I asked.

"About 3,000; it's one of those towns where everybody seems to know everybody else. Even the majority of the seasonal workers come back year after year. So it's easy for the townspeople to keep an eye on newcomers and keep any nonsense to a minimum."

Before we disembarked, I asked John to recommend a place where I could get a good meal while I waited for my next train.

"There's always the dining room at the Dewey Palace Hotel," he said. "But if I were you, I'd choose the Longbranch Saloon. The food is much better, and you'll find it to be more entertaining."

As I struck out to find the saloon, I was bowled over that the streets didn't run north to south and east to west like most places. Rather, they were perpendicular to the train tracks, which ran northwest to southeast. That shift seemed to play tricks on my mind as I struggled to get my bearings. Though it was a small town, I decided to limit my exploration so I didn't get lost.

I made my way along Front Street to Twelfth Avenue, which appeared to be among the few paved streets in town. I encountered an electric streetcar that connected Nampa to Boise and was operated by Boise Street Railway. I felt fairly certain this route would one day be replaced by one of those buses Frederick had mentioned.

When I walked through the swinging doors of the Longbranch Saloon, I suddenly felt like I had gone back in time to the old West. The cornerstone was engraved with the date of 1903, so I knew the building wasn't that old. But the décor and furnishings felt like they were right out of the 1880s.

I suddenly pictured myself wearing a tall cowboy hat and spurs on my boots, swaggering up to the ornately carved bar to order a shot of whiskey. The only problem? I don't own a cowboy hat or a set of spurs, and I don't drink whiskey. As I looked around, I discovered none of the other patrons looked like cowboys either.

A middle-aged waitress called out to welcome me as I entered and told me to take a seat at any one of the empty tables. I selected one by the wall so I could look out across the entire saloon. I didn't want to miss a moment of the experience.

 "So, are you travelin' through town on the train, mister?" the waitress asked as she approached my table.

"Yes, I am," I replied. "How did you know?"

"Because you've got that wide-eyed look of someone from back East who has never stepped foot inside a saloon," she said with a smile. "What's your name?"

"My name's Gene Fearsithe. What's yours?"

"Everybody calls me Sadie, Mr. Gene Fearsithe. Where you from?"

"I'm from Pennsylvania, heading to Portland."

"So you're going west to pursue your fortune. Am I right?" she asked.

"Well, yes you are!"

"Don't be too surprised, Gene Fearsithe. You're not the first young man I've met who is doing just that. As a matter of fact, you're not the first young man *today*," she added with a grin. "But you may be the best lookin'!"

Before I could respond, she laughed and said, "Well, Gene Fearsithe, I think I've gone and made you blush! Let me go ahead and take your order so I don't embarrass you anymore. What are you gonna have?"

"What's on the menu, Sadie?"

"Well, the special of the day is steak, eggs, and potatoes," she replied.

"Anything else?" I asked.

"No, just that. That's why it's our special of the day!" she responded with a wink.

"In that case, I'll have the special of the day," I answered, amused. "And I'll take some coffee to go with it."

"You must have been here before, Gene Fearsithe, because that's all we have to drink at this time of the day!"

I couldn't help but chuckle as she walked away. I surveyed the other customers scattered around the room; no one was paying any attention to me. Apparently, they had not paid any attention to Sadie's banter either, which told me she had probably had the same conversation with each of them.

It took only a few minutes for Sadie to return to my table with my plate of food and my coffee; I guess having just one special of the day has its advantages. My plate was heaping with generous portions, and my first bite confirmed that John's recommendation had been right on target. I decided this meal was going to last me all the way to Portland.

When Sadie returned to refill my coffee, I told her as much and asked her to give my compliments to the chef. She said, "Oh, there ain't no chef here —only Bob. But I'll tell him you like his cooking!"

Since I had plenty of time to kill, I ate slowly and savored every bite of my breakfast. The saloon soon emptied out, and I was the only remaining customer. Sadie came by again to refill my coffee, but this time she had a second cup in her hand.

"Would you like some company while you finish your meal?"

"I would consider it an honor," I replied. "Please take a seat."

She had been bustling from table to table during the entire breakfast rush, so I could imagine how tired she must be.

"Sadie, I hope the owners appreciate how hard you work," I told her.

"I think they do," she replied with a smile. "But thanks for mentioning it."

"How much longer is your shift today?"

"We serve food from seven in the morning until seven at night," she replied. "So my day will end about eight tonight after we clean everything up."

"That's a long workday! How many days a week do you work?"

"Seven," she answered.

"You work thirteen-hour days, seven days a week?" I asked in disbelief.

"I sure do."

"Well, I certainly hope the owner appreciates all you do," I said.

"They do," Sadie declared. After a pause she added, "Would it surprise you to learn I'm the owner—or at least a co-owner?"

I raised my eyebrows in wonder. I'm not sure why I hadn't considered that Sadie might be the proprietor. But now her playful banter with the customers and her non-stop work ethic all made sense.

"How long have you owned the saloon?"

"My brother, Bob, and I came to Nampa from Cleveland, Ohio, twelve years ago," she began. "We were just like you—pursuing our dream! We wanted to open a restaurant and decided an old Western saloon would be just the ticket. So we took the seed money we came out here with and built this place. It's been open for almost eight years now."

I noticed her "old West" drawl was now gone from her speech. Before I could mention it, she said, "Yes, the Western drawl is all part of the atmosphere. We try to make the experience as real as possible for East-erners like you who are making their way through town. The residents get a kick out of it, but they keep coming because they like our food. Those who are passing through just think we're the real thing!"

"Well, Sadie, you had me fooled," I replied. "My compliments for a deli-cious meal and a realistic atmosphere. I would venture you have found yourself a gold mine here."

"Not quite a gold mine," she said, "but it has been the fulfillment of our dream. Oh, and by the way, my name is actually Sarah—Sarah Long. Thus the 'Long'-branch Saloon. Sadie is my character's name. I put that persona on every day. Some days I forget to take it off."

"So why did you decide to let me in on your secret?"

"Well, it's really not a secret," she confided. "Everybody in town knows our real story. I meet a lot of people every day who are passing through Nampa pursuing their dream, but every now and again I encounter someone like you. I'm not sure what it is about you, Gene, but I felt you needed to hear my story. My brother and I could have started a restaurant anywhere. But this place at this time came together to work perfectly.

"That may be what happens when you get to Portland—or it may not be. Nampa is not what determined our dream. Rather, we had a dream, and Nampa became the best place to fulfill it. Remember that! Your dream will not come from the place, the place will merely be the fertile ground in which to plant the dream.

"And, Gene, whatever it is, it will take hard work. The idea that's circulating back East is 'go out West and get rich quick.' There is no such thing. Building your dream takes hard work, and even more hard work to sustain it, no matter what it is."

"What's it like living here in Nampa?"

"The people who live here are salt of the earth. You won't find better anywhere. They embraced us from the very first day and welcomed us into their town. But at the same time, I have to tell you, it's not home. It's not Cleveland. It's not where our family is or where all our pleasant memories are. I wouldn't trade places for anything. It's where I am supposed to be. But it will never replace where I was; it is just something different.

"One other thing I need to tell you—chasing your dream can be a lonely pursuit. I'm not married. I don't even have a boyfriend. When I'm not working, I'm resting to gather the strength to work. I've never been able to figure out how to make a relationship fit in. Sometimes I wonder if achieving my dream, but not having someone to share it with, is worth it. Some days I think it is; others, I don't."

I never expected my stay in Nampa to yield such wise counsel. I had thought I would be killing time. Instead, I had gleaned some of the best advice I'd received on my trip thus far. As I stood up to settle my bill, I thanked Sarah for the good food and the excellent service. But most importantly, I thanked her for the investment she had made in me.

"I ask only two things in return," she said. "One, I want you to write me after you get settled, and tell me how everything worked out. I'll be waiting to hear. And two, once you are ten to fifteen years into pursuing your dream, be sure to encourage someone else who is chasing theirs. I like to call it 'paying it forward.'"

It didn't take long to explore Nampa and see all the sights. It's a vibrant, close-knit community nestled in the beautiful Treasure Valley. But my take-away from this city will always be a woman named Sadie who invested in my life that day.

That afternoon, the Oregon Short Line Train #5 pulled out of Nampa en route to Portland. Seated next to me was the Rev. Graham Cooper of St. Peter's Methodist Episcopal Church in Portland. I wasn't very excited about traveling seated next to a minister—or anyone who was interested in saving my soul. So I lay my head back and closed my eyes to avoid any unwanted conversation.

∾

12

SATURDAY EVENING, APRIL 13 – SUNDAY MORNING, APRIL 14

~

I decided not to pay the additional fare for a sleeping berth on this leg of the trip. I had already spent too much of my seed money on extra expenses along the way. But now I was second-guessing my decision. Rev. Cooper had not stopped talking since I awoke from my nap. I felt like I was a congregation of one trapped in a "pew" as he continued to preach his never-ending sermon.

"Mr. Fearsithe, is it not essential for us to anchor ourselves in the unchanging truths of the Holy Scriptures in this modern era of rapid progress and ever-changing circumstances? Our faith is the rock upon which we must build our lives, and it must be the compass we use to guide us through the storms of uncertainty. We must cling to the teachings of our Savior with unwavering devotion. Do you not agree?"

I started to answer, but just like each time before, he did not wait for a reply.

"We must hold fast to the power of personal piety as we cultivate our relationship with God. In our daily lives, our actions must reflect our faith. Whether we are at home, in the workplace, or in the community, our conduct must be a testament to the love and compassion of our Heavenly Father. I know you must agree with me, Mr. Fearsithe!"

Having endured this ongoing litany for over an hour, I finally reached my limit.

"Reverend Cooper, I thank you for your concern for my welfare and my soul," I interrupted, "but you have already provided me with more of a sermon than I could ever possibly absorb. I fear you must now stop and allow me time to ponder all you have said."

"Forgive me, Mr. Fearsithe," he replied. "I just get so excited about the hope rooted in the Holy Scriptures, I can't help but share that message with everyone I encounter. I was only going to add the truths from the writings of Hebrews chapter eleven that says—"

"Yes, Reverend," I interrupted again. "I am very familiar with that passage, so I will certainly apply those truths to all you've told me. Again, I thank you for your concern, but now I must stretch my legs and go for a walk through the train."

"Perhaps, I could join you," he suggested. "I could do with a walk myself—"

"No, Reverend," I interrupted once more, "I am certain I will be walking in a different direction."

"But I haven't told you which direction I plan to go," the clergyman said in surprise.

"Perhaps not," I replied. "But I fear that whatever direction you choose, I will have chosen the other. Good evening, Reverend, and enjoy the rest of your journey."

I decided to head for the dining car. Though I knew it was too late to make dinner reservations, I thought I would splurge for a sandwich and a cup of coffee. When I asked the steward if there was any space available, he checked his list and told me there was one spot.

I followed him halfway down the car to a table set for two with one vacant seat.

"Miss, would you permit me to seat this guest at your table?" the steward asked.

"Of course, Monsieur," the fashionably dressed young woman said in an unmistakably French accent. "This table does not belong to me. I am merely its temporary occupant. By all means, please seat the gentleman here."

I reached out to shake her hand. "Mademoiselle, thank you for your kindness. My name is Gene Fearsithe."

"Monsieur, it is a pleasure to make your acquaintance," she said as she extended the back of her hand for me to kiss. "My name is Sarah Bernhardt. It is a delight to have such a handsome companion join me for my evening meal. Please take your seat."

I ordered a turkey sandwich and a cup of coffee from the waiter, then turned my attention to my lovely tablemate.

"Where are you traveling from Miss Bernhardt?"

"Originally from Paris," she replied. "But most recently, I have been performing in New York City. I am traveling to Portland to perform in *Hamlet* at the Majestic Theater."

"I had no idea that someone with your notoriety would travel all the way to Portland to perform onstage," I remarked. "I imagine having such a renowned actress in town will cause quite a hullabaloo. What part will you be playing?"

"Why Hamlet, of course!" she answered with a degree of surprise. "I am one of the few actresses who has dared to play that role."

"I am well aware of your great acclaim," I said. "My friend back in Pennsylvania, whose name is also Sara, is a great admirer and has followed your career closely."

"Are you an admirer as well, Monsieur Fearsithe?" she asked with a demure smile.

"I am most certainly an admirer of your great talent, and if I can be so bold, your grace and beauty," I replied. "I count it a rare privilege to share your table."

I hesitated before I added with a smile, "And I never envisioned that one so accomplished in her career could be so young. I thought you would be middle-aged by now, and yet you look close to my age. Either you have truly discovered the fountain of youth, or the reports I have heard about you were grossly overstated."

I watched as her expression transformed from ladylike charm to an impish grin.

"Well, you have found me out, Mr. Fearsithe," she said, the French accent now replaced with a Midwestern one. "Forgive me for misleading you, but I was attempting to play the role of a French actress. I obviously should have chosen a persona less well known than Miss Bernhardt."

"It was your age that gave you away," I confessed, returning her smile. "As I recall, Miss Bernhardt is over sixty years old. And though I would never ask a woman her age, I expect you are less than half that. But your accent and manner were exemplary. You would have had me completely fooled otherwise!"

At that moment, the waiter arrived with my sandwich and coffee. "Let's start over," I declared to my dining companion. "My name is Gene Fearsithe, and it is a pleasure to meet you. What is your name?"

"My name is Margaret Reed," she replied. "But please call me Maggie, Gene."

"Where are you from, Maggie?" I asked. "I presume you're not from Paris. And where are you headed?"

"I'm an actress—at least I want to be," she confessed. "That part was true. I've spent all my life in Cincinnati. But I hear there are countless opportunities for actresses on the West Coast, between the emerging film industry and the growing number of legitimate theaters in cities like Portland, Seattle, and Los Angeles. Since most actresses I know are headed to Hollywood and Los Angeles, I decided to try my luck in Portland."

"Well, Maggie," I declared, "if your performance here in the dining car is any indication of your talent, my money's on you to do well in your acting career! Do you have a role already lined up?"

"No," she confessed. "I'm headed there on a wing and a prayer. How about you, Gene? Where are you headed?"

"You and I actually have a lot in common," I told her. "I'm headed from Pennsylvania to Portland to pursue my dream. I've stopped at other cities along the way, but each time I felt like I needed to continue my journey to Portland. So I'm not stopping anywhere else!"

"Do you have a job waiting for you?" Maggie asked.

"No," I admitted, "I'm also headed there on a wing and a . . . well, I guess I'm not really with you on the 'prayer' part. But, other than that, it sounds like we're in the same boat."

"It sounds like we have a lot in common with the people who left on the RMS Titanic the other day," Maggie stated. "We're making history on this exciting new voyage, with a lot to look forward to once we reach our destination. And in the meantime, we need to enjoy the journey—the sights we see, and the people we meet along the way!"

"Well said, Maggie!" I acknowledged. "I hadn't really thought of my journey like that, but you are most certainly correct. And we are fellow passengers."

"Well, Monsieur Fearsithe," Maggie replied, returning to her French accent, "it is a pleasure to be on the voyage with you!"

I noticed there were few passengers remaining in the dining car. I was enjoying my conversation with Maggie, and I had absolutely no interest in returning to my seat next to Rev. Cooper. I called the steward over and asked, "Do we need to leave our table by any certain time?"

"No," he replied, "you are welcome to stay as long as you like. Would you permit us to go ahead and clear the table?"

"By all means," I answered. Then turning to Maggie, I said, "I'm in no hurry to leave, but if you want to return to your seat, please don't let me keep you. I just know I'm not in any hurry to return to mine."

"*Moi non plus* (me neither), monsieur," she said with a slight twinkle in her eye.

"Please don't think me intrusive, but are you married?"

I could tell my question surprised her, so I quickly explained about Ethel and how I had discovered she was married. Although I did not see my time with Maggie leading to a relationship, I still did not want any surprises. After hearing my explanation, she answered with a laugh, "No, at least not yet!" with a glint in her eye.

We talked for hours, sharing details about our pasts and more about our dreams for the future. Eventually, I noticed it was getting cold in the dining car. I asked the steward if they turned off the heat after a certain hour.

"No," he replied, "it is not only in this car. The heat is not working in any of the train."

"Why is that?" I questioned.

"The engineer says one of the steam valves is faulty, and he's not able to spare the brakeman to make the repair. Besides, the engineer told me, 'it's April, surely it can't be that cold!'"

I decided to remedy the problem myself. I told Maggie the situation and excused myself. "I'll be right back," I told her after putting my coat around her shoulders.

As I made my way to the train engine, I heard other passengers complaining about the cold, which just made me more determined. The engineer was agitated that a passenger was invading his space, even after I told him the purpose of my visit. He attempted to put me off with the same excuse he had given the train employees. However, I was not about to be dissuaded.

I told the engineer I was scheduled to meet with one of the railway executives after we arrived in Portland—and I would be sure to mention how he had responded to our plight. I must admit that I failed to mention the one detail that the executive I would be meeting with worked for a *different* railway company! But since the engineer never asked, I decided the detail was inconsequential. Eventually my determination prevailed and the engineer told his brakeman to go make the necessary repairs.

Heat was already coming out of the radiators before I made it back to the dining car. Several passengers expressed their appreciation as I walked past. As I arrived at my seat across from Maggie, she announced, "*Tu es mon chevalier en armure brillante.*"

"What does that mean in English?"

"It means, 'you are my knight in shining armor!'" she replied with an appreciative smile.

The time raced by as Maggie and I continued to talk through the night. Before long, the darkness outside was beginning to fade. We both sipped a fresh cup of coffee as we admired the beautiful sunrise. About thirty minutes outside of Portland, we passed the cascading waterfall at Bridal

Veil Falls. The sun's reflection made it appear as if a stream of light was pouring out of the rocks. It was truly an incredible sight.

About half past seven Sunday morning, the train came to a stop on the east side of the Willamette River. The waterway divides East Portland from the rest of the city. We could see the train station on the other side of the river, so I was wondering if the engineer had missed a turn. Or perhaps he was planning for all of us to swim to our final destination! Maggie didn't think my suggestion was funny since she couldn't swim.

I called the steward over to our table and asked what was happening. "Oh, we're just waiting for the donkey engine," he replied.

"What's a donkey engine?"

"The cars are uncoupled from the main engine at the front of the train," he explained. "The donkey engine is then attached to the rear car so it can pull the cars in reverse across the railroad bridge into the station."

I understand," I replied.

"Well I sure don't," Maggie interjected. "Why doesn't the main train engine just take us across?"

"I would venture to guess the bridge was not designed to accommodate the weight of the main engine and a fully loaded train," I told her. "By downsizing to the donkey engine, we can safely cross the bridge."

"I couldn't have said it better myself," the steward added.

"Oh, I know the reason," I replied, "but after having crossed most of these United States going forward, it still seems strange going in reverse for the last few hundred feet. It almost feels like a bad omen."

The steward just shrugged and walked away. Maggie, on the other hand, seemed to be more concerned about whether we were going to be too heavy for the bridge than she was about which direction we were headed.

I think Maggie decided it was time to pray because she kept her eyes closed until we came to a stop on the other side of the river. It was eight o'clock when we pulled into Union Station. Maggie and I exited the train together after retrieving our suitcases. I was impressed she had only one bag, just like I did. As I carried both bags, though, I quickly discovered she had clearly packed more in her luggage!

Rev. Cooper passed by as we made our way out of the station.

"Mr. Fearsithe, please know you are always welcome at St. Peter's on Twelfth Street. As a matter-of-fact, our Sunday service starts in a couple hours. Please come join us."

I tipped my hat at him, and we both continued on our separate ways. I needn't bother telling him it was unlikely he would ever see me again. Maggie laughed at my expression.

I had decided I would check into a hotel for one night and then search for a boarding house. Since Maggie had no idea where she was going to stay, she decided to do the same.

As we passed the Hotel Portland, I could tell it was beyond my budget, so I kept walking. The same was obviously true of the Multnomah Hotel. But when I spotted the Imperial Hotel, I knew it was just what I was looking for—a no-frills place to rest my head for one night.

When we approached the front desk, the clerk called out, "Welcome to the Imperial Hotel. Is this your first time with us?"

"Why yes, it is," I replied. "Actually, it is the first time for both of us to visit your fair city. We plan to make it our home."

"Well, welcome to Portland!" he declared. "It is always a delight to accept new residents to our city. Do you need a room?"

"We'll be needing *two* rooms," I answered. "My name is Mr. Gene Fearsithe, and this is Miss Margaret Reed, the famous actress from Cincinnati."

"Oh, I'm sorry. I thought the two of you were together," the clerk said, somewhat embarrassed.

"No problem, my friend, an easy mistake to make," I told him. "We've only recently met. We shared a dinner table on the train last night."

We would have been fine if Maggie hadn't batted her eyes and added in her French accent, "*Oui*, it was a delightful dinner that lasted until this morning."

Seeing the clerk's reaction, I hastily blurted out, "Yes, now about those two rooms!"

∾

13

SUNDAY AFTERNOON AND EVENING, APRIL 14

∼

I decided to be chivalrous and let Maggie have the room on the second floor, while I took the one on the third floor. She told me she needed to take a nap since we had sat up all night on the train. We agreed to meet for dinner.

I took a few minutes to wash up and change my shirt before setting out to explore my new city and look up my friend who had moved here from Williamsport. As I strolled down the streets of Portland, I sensed an air of tranquility. The city's architecture stood proudly, showcasing a blend of styles from its sixty-year history. Ornate commercial buildings—constructed with brick and stone—lined the streets, their facades adorned with intricate details.

Though the streets were less busy since it was a Sunday, there was still a gentle flow of people going about their day. Men and women, adorned in their Sunday best, strolled leisurely toward nearby churches. I was grateful I had attended a church service the prior week, but I wasn't inclined to go today. After all, Rev. Cooper's sermonizing would last me a lifetime . . . or at least until next Easter.

Amidst the occasional clatter of horse-drawn carriages, wagons, and carts, the streets exuded an old-world charm. The steady clip-clop of hooves created a rhythmic melody that added to the morning atmosphere.

Although the automobile has made its way to Portland, its presence seems to be limited. I spotted only a handful as their gleaming surfaces reflected the morning sun. Their sleek forms stood in stark contrast to the horse-drawn vehicles still dominating the streets.

As I continued my tour, I couldn't help but appreciate the buildings and landmarks that punctuated the cityscape. The Portland City Hall clearly stands as a symbol of civic pride, its grandeur an architectural testament to the aspirations of this growing city. The nearby Portland Art Museum promises inspiration and cultural immersion to the area's art enthusiasts.

Parks and green spaces, such as Lownsdale Square and Chapman Square, offer pockets of respite amid the growing urban landscape. These are places residents can obviously find solace in nature's embrace. I was pleased to discover the city was living up to all I had heard.

It appears Sunday here is a day of rest and religious reflection, just as it is in other cities across the U.S. Most businesses apparently close or operate with reduced hours, allowing families to spend the day together.

As I concluded my walk, I couldn't help but feel the palpable history embedded within the streets of downtown Portland. The amalgamation of architectural wonders, the harmonious coexistence of old and new transportation, and the unique atmosphere of a Sunday morning whispered tales of a bygone era.

At the corner of Southwest Fifth and Yamhill streets, I happened upon the offices of the *Oregon Journal*. I later learned this newspaper had already made its mark by becoming the loudest voice for better protection of natural resources and greater social responsibility.

The newspaper is housed in the Goodnough Building, along with several other businesses. As it turns out, the building also contains a rooming house, which operates out of the remains of a hotel that was part of the original structure built in 1891. There I was to find my good friend, Clyde Sheets. He had made the journey here from Williamsport over a year ago and was living in this rooming house.

Clyde and I are the same age and have been chums since grade school. We have always shared common interests in just about everything. After he graduated from Dickinson Seminary, he went to work for J.C. Winter at the Vallamont Building and Planing Mill Company in Williamsport. It is a successful general contracting and lumber business, producing its own building materials. Clyde is a capable draftsman, and in a short time he became proficient at designing intricate, decorative moldings for the interior and exterior of homes.

Though the lumber and building business was still prospering in Williamsport, Clyde was hearing about opportunities in his field out West, and in Portland, specifically. He believed he could make his fortune faster here, so he had set off on his journey.

The main entry and reception of the rooming house within the Goodnough Building harkened back to its use as a hotel. Thus I came face to face with a reception desk upon entry. A man who appeared to be forty years my senior greeted me with a scowl as I approached the desk.

"What's your business here, young man?" he asked without a hint of cordiality.

"I have come to visit a friend."

"Is he expecting you?" the man countered abruptly.

"He knows of my planned arrival, but he does not know I am already here. We are friends from back home in Pennsylvania," I added, as if it was any of the man's business.

"What's your friend's name?" he asked with a raised eyebrow, as if I were about to speak the name of some notorious scallywag.

"Mr. Clyde Sheets," I replied tersely.

"Oh yes, Mr. Sheets. A fine gentleman. And you say you are a friend?"

"Yes, a lifelong friend," I said. "Can you get a message to him that I am here in the lobby?"

"Oh, I can do better than that," he answered. "Do you see this contraption right here? It has just recently been installed. I can press a button and a bell will sound in whichever room I select to let the tenant know he has a visitor. Let me just see—Mr. Sheets is in room 404.

"You can be seated right over there," he said, pointing toward several chairs against the wall. I was grateful for a chance to sit after my morning walk.

Time seems to move at a snail's pace when you are waiting. Five minutes seems like twenty. I was about to tell the desk clerk I would just leave a message for Clyde when he appeared around the corner.

"Gene Fearsithe!" Clyde shouted. "You really did come. I thought you were going to lose your nerve or settle for something else before you ever made it here. But here you are—in the flesh!"

"How could I settle for something else after the picture you painted of Portland?" I asked as the two of us shook hands.

"You won't be disappointed, Gene. It is all that and more! I see you have already met Reginald," he said with a broad smile motioning at the clerk. "Reginald is the finest doorkeeper in the city. We all know our privacy will never be disturbed as long as he is on watch."

Reginald's expression only slightly relaxed from the scowl that apparently was permanently affixed to his face. He did, however, acknowledge the compliment by saying, "Mr. Sheets, you are most kind as always."

"Reginald, I expect Mr. Fearsithe may want to inquire about the availability of a room," Clyde remarked. "Is there one immediately available?"

"Since he is a friend of yours, Mr. Sheets, I am confident we can accommodate him," Reginald replied.

"I'm going to take him upstairs and show him around," Clyde said before turning to me to ask, "Where is your luggage, Gene?"

"I got a room at the Imperial Hotel for the night," I replied, "so my luggage is there."

"Well, if you like this place, we can get you moved in today, and you won't have to pay for a night at the hotel," Clyde responded.

I hesitated. "Actually, I feel obligated to remain there for the night. I checked into the hotel with a friend, and I don't want her to feel that I've abandoned her."

"Did Sara come with you from Williamsport?" Clyde asked excitedly.

"No, it's not Sara," I replied. "She would not leave her family. This is another young woman I met last night on the train."

"And you invited her to stay at the hotel with you?" Clyde asked, astonished.

"Oh, it's nothing like that!" I hastily explained. "She is a cute kid who has traveled here by herself from Cincinnati looking for an acting job—and I have kind of taken her under my wing. She has her own room at the hotel. I can assure you there is nothing untoward about our relationship. I just don't want to desert her on our first night here.

"I told her we would meet back up for dinner, and I was hoping you would join us."

"If you say so, Gene," Clyde chuckled with a devious wink. "I always knew you were smooth with the ladies. And you say you just met her last night? I've been in Portland for a year, and I have yet to meet a woman I can invite to dinner."

"Well, you know, Clyde," I said with a glint in my eye, "like I told you when we were in school together, some of us have it—and some of us don't." I laughed, then added, "So show me the rooming house."

Clyde told me all the rooms looked the same. Each was furnished like a basic hotel room with a bed, a table, a small clothing rack and a basin. The furnishings were obviously left over from the days it served as a hotel. A larger enclosed room on the main floor served as a communal sitting room for tenants to socialize with one another or to entertain guests. Clyde told me guests were absolutely forbidden in the individual rooms. He also said women were permitted only in the reception area.

Next, we went to the dining room, and then he took me for a tour of the kitchen.

"Breakfast and dinner are included in our rent," he reported. "The food is nothing fancy; it's your basic meat and potatoes. But it does the job. Each man is responsible to keep his room clean. They wash our linens and towels once a week if we get them turned in on time."

Rent, he clarified, was twelve dollars per week, which seemed reasonable compared to every place I had stayed since leaving Williamsport. Given the money I had spent getting here, I had enough left over to cover three weeks' rent—if I didn't spend it on anything else. I started to reconsider staying in the hotel that night but reminded myself it was the right thing to do for Maggie.

Clyde and I returned to the reception desk, and I arranged with Reginald to rent a room starting the next night.

"That will be one week in advance, Mr. Fearsithe," Reginald said as he reached out his hand. Once I handed over the twelve one-dollar bills, I realized I was now officially a Portlander. I had my own room and everything. Now all I needed was a job.

While we were together that afternoon, Clyde told me he was working for Eilers and Company, a prominent wood manufacturing business.

"We produce high-quality furniture, cabinetry, and interior millwork," he explained. "The company has a reputation for exquisite craftsmanship. The owners have been impressed with my work and have allowed me to create innovative designs, which have been well-received by our customers. There is already talk about my becoming a partner in the company one day soon."

"I'm happy for you, Clyde. You are beginning to achieve what you came out here to do. Well done! I hope I can be that lucky!"

By now it was late in the afternoon, so we walked back to the Imperial Hotel. Maggie was already in the lobby waiting for me. After introductions, I asked Clyde if he had a recommendation where we might eat dinner.

"I know a great little Chinese restaurant in Chinatown, if the two of you are willing to give it a try," he replied.

Until that night, I had never tried Chinese food, but after Maggie enthusiastically agreed to the suggestion, I could not turn it down.

When we arrived, the restaurant owner immediately showed us to a table. Clyde was obviously a regular customer. I don't normally let other people make my food selections, but since I had no idea about any of the items on the menu, I decided I had nothing to lose. Maggie and Clyde seemed to revel in the moment and did a wonderful job choosing my meal.

While we ate, I told Maggie about my day. I recounted all the sights I had seen and gradually worked my way up to telling her about taking a room in the rooming house. Rather than feeling abandoned, Maggie was genuinely happy for me.

"But Maggie," I said, "they do not allow women in the rooming house, so we will need to find something else for you."

"Don't you worry about that, mon *chéri*," she said with a mischievous grin. "While you were out, so was I. A production of *The Merry Widow* is starting its run in two weeks at the Majestic Theater. The directors were looking to fill the part of the young wife, Valencienne, who carries on a flirtation with the Frenchman, Camille de Rosillon. When they heard this unassuming French actress, they could not resist. I got the part!"

"You what? You got a part your very first day in Portland! That is tremendous, Maggie. I couldn't be happier for you."

"Rehearsals start first thing in the morning. They have a block of rooms at the Multnomah Hotel, so I will be moving in there tomorrow," she continued. "I was worried I would be abandoning you, but it appears that tonight is a celebration. *Célébrons!*"

I did my best to share in her enthusiastic joy, but I couldn't help thinking, *I hope my job search is as equally productive.*

∽

14

MONDAY MORNING AND AFTERNOON, APRIL 15

~

*A*s I looked over Emmett Hall's business card, I reread the address for Oregon-Washington Railroad and Navigation Company, or OWR&N for short. The offices were located in the North Bank Depot Building at the corner of Eleventh Avenue and Hoyt Street. It turned out to be a twenty-minute walk from the hotel—and that included a brief stop at the rooming house to drop off my suitcase. I arrived at the office a few minutes before nine o'clock.

The streets were bustling with activity. There was no question that the workweek was off to a busy start. It was a sharp contrast from the tranquil scene I had witnessed the day before. Even the office's reception area appeared to need a constable to direct traffic—though I'll admit the matronly woman behind the desk appeared to have everything well in hand.

"What can I do for you, young man?" she asked politely and succinctly.

"I'm here to see Mr. Emmett Hall," I nervously replied. I showed her his business card as if it were an engraved invitation. She looked at the card and asked, "Do you have an appointment, Mr. . . .?"

"My name's Fearsithe, Eugene Fearsithe. No, I do not have an appointment, but we traveled together last week, and he told me to look him up when I arrived in Portland."

"Please take a seat, and I will see when he might be available," she replied.

I looked around and noticed a collection of pictures on the wall, conveying a visual history of the company. OWR&N was established in 1906 by Union Pacific Railway with the infamous E.H. Harriman—whose picture was prominently displayed on the wall—as chairman. I was beginning to understand that every time tracks were laid from one city to another, a new company was formed for that express purpose. What was now a massive spider's web of companies was created to limit Union Pacific's financial exposure in the event of catastrophic loss.

OWR&N had initially been formed to connect Portland to Seattle. Another photograph showed Mr. Harriman and several other men standing with shovels around what was evidently the first piece of track laid for that line. As I studied the picture more closely, I identified Emmett Hall standing in the back of the group.

Another picture featured a riverboat barge transporting freight down the Willamette River. Beside that photo was one of a recently commissioned electric streetcar used to carry people from Union Station to the southern portion of the city. The company was undoubtedly expanding to include every possible means of transportation for this region. Though I had learned in Boise that the streetcar may soon undergo significant change, I felt confident that OWR&N—and even more, Union Pacific—was a force to be reckoned with and a powerhouse of industry. It seemed to be a safe rising star on which to build my future.

I was lost in thought when the receptionist called out, "Mr. Fearsithe . . . Mr. Fearsithe, Mr. Hall will see you now!" I made my way to the reception desk and she continued, "Mr. Fearsithe, please follow this young woman to Mr. Hall's office."

I tried unsuccessfully to engage my guide in conversation. Everyone seemed so focused on their tasks, they didn't have time for chitchat. However, when I realized how circuitous our path was to Emmett's office, I was grateful for a guide. Otherwise, I probably would have gotten lost in the maze.

My guide stopped and pointed for me to enter a door. I found myself in an anteroom where a young woman greeted me with a smile. "Mr. Fearsithe, welcome. Mr. Hall is expecting you."

I was dumbfounded as I walked into Emmett's office. It was the largest I had ever seen. Every other office I had visited paled in comparison—not only in size, but also in appointment. I decided the décor and furnishings would make Clyde jealous!

Emmett Hall stepped out from behind his desk and extended his hand.

"Gene, it is so good to see you! I am glad you made it to Portland. I presume, based on your presence, you decided you were seeking more than Boise had to offer."

"You would be correct," I replied as we shook hands. "And my preconceptions of your fair city have already been confirmed!"

"I am so glad to hear that," Emmett smiled, directing me to take a chair. "When did you arrive?"

"Yesterday morning," I answered, "which gave me the day to wander about the city and find a more permanent place to stay."

"Where is that?" Emmett asked.

"I've taken a room at the rooming house in the Goodnough building. One of my chums from my hometown lives there and recommended it."

"Good choice, Gene," Emmett affirmed. "It is centrally located and known for being the place where up-and-coming young men initially land until they are able to better establish themselves. Bravo! So now you are officially a resident of Portland."

"Yes, I guess I am," I agreed with a smile.

"I imagine you are looking for work then?"

"Yes!" I replied. "I've had enough vacation these past two weeks traveling out here. I am definitely ready to get to work!"

"Well, good! Let's get you to the personnel office and see what might be available. How does that sound?"

"That would be great," I replied, though I had hoped Emmett would actually have something in mind for me. "Are there any openings you might point me to, Emmett?"

"It might be premature for me to make any such recommendations," Emmett answered, a little abruptly. "The people in personnel know the questions to ask and the suggestions to make."

Realizing this conversation was not going any further, I responded, "Then I look forward to hearing what they have to say."

"Good . . . very good," Emmett said. "I am always happy to assist young men I meet along the way. My secretary, Miss Adams, will show you to the personnel office." As he stood to shake my hand, he added, "And please let me know if anything works out."

"I sure will," I replied with more enthusiasm than I felt. His words "if anything works out" were ringing in my ears. I had come this morning thinking Emmett would already have a job selected for me—one I could start today. But now it seemed I was no closer to employment than when I started this journey. I had clearly misread Emmett's intentions when we talked on the train.

Miss Adams led me through the maze to the personnel office and politely wished me luck.

"I hope you find something along the lines you're looking for," she said before hurrying back to her desk. I walked up to the receptionist and announced, "Mr. Hall suggested I come here and speak with someone about employment."

"Did he suggest you speak with anyone in particular?" the woman asked.

"No, he did not," I hesitated, suddenly realizing how telling that fact was.

"Well, in that case, let's get you started by filling this out," she said, handing me an employment application. It reinforced the harsh reality I had traveled 3,000 miles to start all over again at the bottom rung of the ladder.

I quickly filled out the application, trying my best to convince whoever was going to read my answers that OWR&N needed to hire me. I confidently pointed out I was the best possible candidate for any of their important roles. But I must confess, my heart wasn't in it. I felt as if I had been sucker punched in the last round of a fight—and I had no prospects of winning. At that moment, I made a decision.

I got up from my seat and walked over to the receptionist.

"Are you done with your application already?" she asked.

"No, I changed my mind," I replied. "I've traveled 3,000 miles to do something more than fill out an application. I came in pursuit of my dream. A friend of mine got off the train yesterday and today is starring in an upcoming play. Another friend came here a year ago and is now being offered a partnership. I didn't come all this way to apply for any old job. I think my dream must be elsewhere."

I tore up the application and threw it into the trash can. "You have a wonderful day," I said as I walked out the door.

"You as well, sir," she called out. "And I hope you find that dream!"

Everything looked different to me when I stepped outside. I had arrived in Portland thinking my dream was here just waiting for me to seize it. But the reality is, my dream must come from within. Maggie didn't discover her dream to act when she arrived. She came with that dream, and that dream led her to a position. The same was true for Clyde, and the same would be true for me.

I had some work to do before I could walk into another office for an interview. But in the meantime, I needed to find some gainful employment that would cover my rent. Not knowing where else to go, I returned to the rooming house to unpack.

On my way, I passed the office of the *Oregon Journal*. A notice board caught my eye, so I stopped to look at it. One ad in particular stood out:

SPECIAL COLLECTOR WANTED!
Collect delinquent accounts from advertisers.
Not for the faint of heart.
Work on commission.
Apply with Jake in the advertisement office.

No, it was definitely not my dream job, but it could put money in my pocket in the interim. I went inside to find Jake, who turned out to be a crusty fellow in his fifties. He was only too happy to let me try my luck.

"No sweat off my back," he shrugged. "If you don't collect, you don't get paid. And if you do, it's money we probably wouldn't have otherwise received. You earn twenty percent of whatever you bring in. All you have to do is sign here and here, then I'll give you your first batch of names."

I had traveled all this way to collect money from deadbeats! Oh well, I guess even tycoons had to start somewhere! I signed his papers and put the list of ten names and addresses in my pocket. If I collected them all, I'd make fifteen dollars. At least it was a start.

I went up to my room and unpacked before I set out to visit the names on my list. The first two people were embarrassed that someone had come to collect their debts. They immediately pulled out money and paid me. I decided if it was going to be this easy, maybe this *was* my dream job! But that was before I went to see the third guy on the list.

He was a plumber who had been advertising his services. From the looks of him, I wondered if he knew one end of a pipe wrench from another. When I told him I was there to collect his bill, he picked up an iron pipe and started tapping it into his left palm. I guess he thought he was intimidating me.

"Mister, I'm not here to get into a ruckus with you," I told him. "I'm just trying to earn a living, same as you. If you don't pay me, I don't get paid. So how about you give me a break and pay the money you owe?"

"That thieving newspaper told me if I put an ad in the paper, I would get more work than I would know what to do with," he snarled. "All I got was four measly jobs!"

"Did they pay you?" I asked.

"Well, yes," he replied.

"Did you receive more money for the jobs than you owe for the ad?" I pressed.

"Sure," he grudgingly acknowledged.

"Then you're money ahead—unlike me, whom you're threatening to send away with *bupkes*. Doesn't seem very fair to me! What do you think?"

The plumber ruminated for a minute before he grudgingly replied, "Well, I never thought about it like that. I'll pay you your money, but only because I don't want some working stiff like you getting the wrong end of the stick. I don't much care about that newspaper, but you seem like a good guy. Here you go."

Three down, seven to go! By that afternoon, nine had paid me, and one had promised to pay me on Friday. I delivered my $65 in collections to Jake before his office closed. He reacted as if I'd brought him ten times that amount.

"I have never had a collector do that well on their first day!" he declared as he paid me the $13 he owed me. "You must be a natural. Here's $2 more, because I'm feeling generous. Do you want to keep doing this?"

"For now," I said. "I'll be back tomorrow morning to get more names from you."

I stopped by Clyde's room to see if he wanted to join me for dinner. For some reason I felt like celebrating. Of course, when he asked me if I got the job, I said, "Yes." I just never told him what job!

We walked over to the Multnomah Hotel to see if Maggie wanted to join us as well. When she arrived in the lobby, I could tell her head was in the clouds with excitement.

"I can't wait to tell you all about my first day," she said. "Yes, give me a minute to get ready, and I'll join you. And I met a new friend today. Can she come, too?"

"Sure, the more the merrier," I replied. "We'll make it a celebration!"

Because deep inside, I desperately needed to celebrate something.

∾

15

MONDAY EVENING, APRIL 15 – TUESDAY AFTERNOON, APRIL 16

~

*W*ith my newly earned dollars in my pocket, I was hungry to try some fresh seafood from the Pacific Coast. Clyde suggested the best place to go was Lou's Oyster Bar, located in the basement of the Merchants Exchange Building at the corner of Southwest Fourth and Southwest Stark avenues. He did not steer us wrong! Those were the best oysters I had ever eaten. Plus, the restaurant didn't cater to swells. It was reasonably priced and full of working folks like us.

As it turned out, Maggie's new friend was a fellow actress with a small part in *The Merry Widow*.

"I want you to meet my new friend, Elenore Schroeder," Maggie said as she introduced the young woman to Clyde and me. All three of us looked at each other in astonishment.

"Am I missing something?" Maggie asked. "Have the three of you already met?"

Elenore was the first to speak.

"Clyde, Gene, and I all graduated from the same high school in Williamsport, Pennsylvania, class of '07. I have always heard it is a small world, but this proves it!"

The truth was I'd never really known Elenore in high school. I knew who she was, but I hadn't paid much attention to her. Somehow, she looked different now, and based upon the way Clyde was staring at her, he must have thought so as well.

"Elenore, it is such a surprise to see you!" I declared. "Who would ever imagine we would run into one another 3,000 miles away from home?"

Since all four of us had traveled across the country to explore new possibilities, we decided to celebrate our common purpose. Elenore told us she left Williamsport two years prior, having spent a year onstage in Cleveland and a year acting in Chicago before her recent arrival in Portland.

"I enjoy not being tied down to any one position or any one place," she expressed. "When a show is over, I either seek out another or move on. Each day remains fresh and new for me that way, with no long-term commitments and nothing to weigh me down."

"What did your parents think about your decision to travel the country as a single woman?" I asked.

"My father was opposed," she replied. "In some ways, he still is. But my mother supported my decision and convinced him to grudgingly give me his blessing. She taught me to admire the likes of Mary Pickford and Lillian Gish—women who have made a name for themselves onstage and now in film. She told me if I did not pursue the passion in my heart, I would always regret it."

"But are they not concerned for your safety or welfare?" Clyde asked.

"Of course they are," she assured us. "Probably the same way your parents all worry about you. But they know if we allowed those concerns to keep us from stepping out, we would be sentencing ourselves to lives of imprisonment behind walls built by our own fears. Isn't the same true for each of you?"

Maggie and Clyde slowly nodded in agreement. They both had received the blessing from their families to pursue their dreams, albeit a bit grudgingly. I was the only one who had left family and friends behind without a solitary word of encouragement.

It was Elenore who abruptly changed the subject.

"Gene, whatever happened to that girl I often saw you with in high school? Wasn't her name Sara?"

"Yes, that's her name. She and I continued to date up until I decided to make this journey. She's one of those I left behind," I added softly as my thoughts turned to her.

While the other three enjoyed our night of celebration, I was too melancholy. I kept revisiting the conversations that took place in Williamsport before I left and the emptiness I had felt began to return. Of course, the reception I received from Emmett didn't help my mood. After dinner, I walked back to the rooming house for my first night's sleep in my new bed.

~

Tuesday morning dawned with the sky completely covered in storm clouds. I should have taken it as a bad omen and pulled the covers back over my head. Instead, I decided to seize the day. Jake was already behind his desk when I arrived at his office. He had a fresh list of ten accounts for me to collect. He sent me on my way with a cheerful, "I've given you some of the harder ones today. Try to make it back alive!"

This day's collections took me all over town. A few of my stops were in the old section of town around the waterfront and along the railway yards. I think it's ironic that the first place people see when they arrive in Portland by train or boat is the most rundown portion of the city. Those who never journey beyond their hotel must be left with a poor—and not wholly accurate—impression of Portland.

The money owed on bills in this particular area was less than most, I assumed because of their means. But the debtors were all respectful and cordial toward me. One promised to pay at the end of the week, so I told him I would return. The others all paid in full.

From there I worked my way back into town. I visited a number of fine office buildings and hotels that otherwise I may have never seen. Interestingly, the people I tried to collect from in this area looked at me as if I were the one in the wrong.

Each would say something like, "Who are you to interrupt me with this trivial matter during my busy day? Doesn't the newspaper know I'm good for it? Who do they think I am? How dare they presume to infer that I do not pay my debts!" And it most often ended with, "If that's what they think of me, I will never do business with them again!"

On more than one occasion I told them I had no intention of leaving their premises until I had collected their debt. Furthermore, I would not hesitate to share the reason for my presence with anyone who walked into their place of business. That tactic worked. As for never doing business with the *Journal* again, I knew they were just blowing smoke. The *Journal* is the most read newspaper in the region. Of course, they would advertise again!

My last stop for the day was in the west end of the city, which is comprised of the finer residential sections of town. It was in the Kings Heights neighborhood where I observed crews tearing away a hill with hydraulic hammers and scoops to ready the land for new construction.

I was surprised the address on my list was one of those posh houses in the rolling hills of a section called Portland Heights. This bill was the largest I had been given to collect so far—a whopping twenty dollars. When I knocked on the front door, the man who answered looked like a penguin dressed in livery. When I told him my business, he immediately reprimanded me for presenting myself at the main entrance.

"Tradesmen," he said with an air of superiority, "are only received at the rear delivery entrance. Present yourself back there, and we'll sort out whatever error your employer has made." Then he abruptly shut the door in my face. I had no choice but to abide by this hoity-toity's instructions, so I walked around to the rear entry.

Imagine my annoyance when the same man greeted me at the rear door demanding, "State your business here."

"You know exactly what my business is," I replied. "I just told you at the front door not two minutes ago! A Mr. Archer Winslow owes my employer twenty dollars for advertisements placed in the *Oregon Journal*. Since the debt has not been paid in a timely manner, I have been sent to collect it. So if you will attend to paying me, I'll be on my way and no longer standing on your doorstep."

"I'm sure there has been some kind of error on your employer's part, young man," the penguin said. "Go back and instruct them to correct their records immediately and never send anyone like you to this home again."

There were a number of things I wanted to say to this man, but I realized the brain needed to prevail over brawn.

"My good fellow," I replied using a different tact, "I do understand that errors can occur. And it is possible that my employer failed to record Mr. Winslow's timely payment. That being the case, allow me to offer my sincere apologies for our error and this interruption.

"But having acknowledged the possibility of our mistake, might I also suggest that in the midst of Mr. Winslow's important activities that this bill was inadvertently overlooked and remains unpaid. We can quickly root out which is the case if someone here can tell me when the bill was satisfied. Would you be so kind as to assist me in that regard? I do not wish to take up any more of your valuable time."

I decided I had made some headway when he did not immediately shut the door in my face.

"Yes, that is a reasonable request," he conceded. "Wait here while I go check with Mr. Winslow and see if he might be able to provide that answer."

It was nearing fifteen minutes that I had been standing at the door awaiting an answer. My patience was beginning to wear thin when the penguin returned with a twenty-dollar bill in hand.

"It appears that Mr. Winslow did overlook paying the bill. He extends his deepest apologies for any inconvenience he has caused, and asks that you provide him with a written receipt for this payment." I supplied the receipt and bade the man a good day.

It had been a profitable day. I had $100 in my jacket pocket to turn into Jake. Perhaps my friends and I should go out for oysters again tonight! And maybe I should consider going into this line of work on a permanent basis. I appeared to have a knack for it, and I was learning new approaches each time I made a call.

All those thoughts were rolling around in my head as I strolled back to the newspaper. I decided to cut through the alley leading to the Goodnough Building to shorten my walk. Unfortunately, I failed to hear the footsteps quickly approaching me from the rear. Suddenly, everything went dark.

I opened my eyes, and everything was fuzzy. At first, I didn't know where I was. Slowly, things began to come into focus. I was lying on what was presumably a bed with my head resting on a pillow. As I scanned my surroundings, I realized I was in a sea of white—the sheets, the walls, the ceiling . . . everything!

That was when I saw someone stirring beside me.

"Mr. Fearsithe, I am Nurse Miller. You are in the Good Samaritan Hospital. You've had a nasty blow to your head. I'm going to call for the doctor so he can come examine you. I will be right back."

She wasn't kidding. I *had* sustained a nasty blow; my head had never hurt this bad. It felt as if someone had split it open like a watermelon. I tried to raise my head off the pillow, but everything in the room began to spin. I instantly decided it was best to lay my head back down.

The doctor entered my room and said, "Yes, Mr. Fearsithe, just keep your head resting on that pillow. You are not in any condition to raise yourself up." He then proceeded to look me over.

"Mr. Fearsithe," the doctor continued, "you have sustained a concussion as a result of a blunt force trauma to your skull. It appears you were hit with some type of metal object. A police officer brought you to the hospital several hours ago. You have been unconscious until now.

"What happened?" I asked. "Who did this to me?"

"There is a constable here who is going to help you with all of that," the doctor replied. "But first, I need to ask you a few questions. What is your full name?"

"Robert Eugene Fearsithe."

"What city are you in?"

"Portland."

"What year is it?"

"1912."

"What day of the week is it?"

"I think it's Tuesday. But that all depends on how long I was out."

"You are correct, Mr. Fearsithe. It is still Tuesday. And your memory seems to be functioning well. We're going to keep you in the hospital overnight for observation. In the meantime, we'll continue to give you something for the pain and make sure the dizziness settles down. Do you have any questions for me?"

"Yes. I see I'm wearing a hospital gown. Where are my clothes?"

Nurse Miller spoke up. "We have them all right here. Don't you worry, Mr. Fearsithe."

The doctor spoke again. "Mr. Fearsithe, I will come back and look in on you a little later this evening. Be sure and let the nurse know if you need anything. In the meantime, a constable is waiting just outside the door to talk to you. I'm going to tell him he can come in if that's okay with you. He might be able to answer some of your other questions."

"Thank you, doctor," I said. "Thank you for everything."

The next voice I heard belonged to the policeman who identified himself as Constable Burton. After introductions, he jumped right in with his questions.

"Mr. Fearsithe, do you have any idea who hit you over the head?"

"None, whatsoever," I replied. "All I know is that right after I turned into the alley, I heard footsteps coming up quickly behind me. And then bam— I was struck on the head. I didn't see who it was. I think it was a man because of the heavy footsteps and the strength of the wallop I got. How did someone find me to bring me here?"

"We don't know how long you were unconscious until you were found. About ten minutes after four, a pedestrian was walking down the alley from Morrison Street and saw you lying there. He ran and found an officer on the street."

"Then I must have been lying there for about ten minutes," I said, "because I remember looking at my watch as I turned down the alley and it was four o'clock. I was pleased that my day was ending early."

"What do you do?" the officer asked. "Where were you coming from, and where were you going?"

"I started working for the *Oregon Journal* yesterday as a collector," I told him. "I collect delinquent accounts. I had completed that day's collections and was headed to the office to turn the money in to my boss—a fellow by the name of Jake."

"How much cash did you have on you, Mr. Fearsithe?"

"It was a good day," I answered. "I collected $100."

A chill suddenly ran down my spine. "It should be right there in my inside jacket pocket. Please hand me my coat so I can check."

"There's no money in your coat, Mr. Fearsithe. It appears that whoever hit you over the head took the money. Did you have any money in your wallet?"

"I had thirty-five dollars of my own money in my wallet. Please don't tell me that's gone, too!"

"I'm afraid so, Mr. Fearsithe. We didn't find any cash in your jacket or your pants. Whoever took your money left your wallet though. That's how we were able to identify you."

∼

16

TUESDAY EVENING, APRIL 16 –
WEDNESDAY AFTERNOON, APRIL 17

~

*C*onstable Burton told me he had taken my wallet to the police station to be dusted for fingerprints in hopes they could identify a suspect. He told me I would need to come to the station to be fingerprinted so they could rule out my prints, and my wallet would be returned to me at the same time. He continued to ask me questions for about thirty more minutes. When he was done, I asked if he could get a message to Clyde Sheets at the rooming house. He assured me he would and promised to keep me informed about my case if there were any developments.

But I doubted there would be any further progress. I had lain on the ground for ten minutes before anyone saw me—at least, anyone who had come forward. So the odds were either no one else saw it happen, or if they did, they had no interest in getting involved. The money taken was all cash, so there was no way to identify it. Woefully, it was every penny I had; I was now flat broke! To make matters worse, I now owed a hospital bill.

It was about nine o'clock when the constable left. I was starting to get hungry, so I asked Nurse Miller if I could get some food. She told me she was sure the kitchen could rustle up something for me.

The nurse returned a short time later with a cheese sandwich and a cup of tea. Nothing had ever looked so good! But she surprised me when she said I had a visitor. She motioned for the person to come into the room.

It was Maggie!

"Visiting hours are long passed," Nurse Miller explained, "but I told the head nurse your fiancée had just received news about your injury. She agreed to allow Miss Reed to see you for a short while. I'll leave the two of you to talk in private. I'll return in about thirty minutes or so to retrieve you, Miss Reed."

"Thank you, nurse, for your kindness and understanding," Maggie replied.

After the nurse left, I looked at Maggie quizzically. "I must have been unconscious a whole lot longer than they told me! I had no idea we were engaged. When I'm feeling better, you'll have to tell me how I proposed."

It was the first time I'd had anything to smile about all night.

"Well, Gene, they wouldn't let me come in to see you until I told them I was your fiancée. What else was I to do?" she added with a naughty grin.

"Tonight you are my maiden in shining armor coming to *my* rescue," I replied. "You are a welcome sight. Thank you so much for coming. How did you find out I was here?"

"Clyde and I have been worried about you all night," Maggie responded. "We were waiting for you so we could have dinner together. But when you didn't return to the rooming house, we became worried. We were just about to go to the police station to report you missing when the constable arrived looking for Clyde. He came to the hospital with me, by the way, but they would not let both of us come up to see you. That's when I got the idea to tell them I was your fiancée."

"They took everything, Maggie," I uttered in despair. "They took all the money I collected today as well as all of my personal money. I don't have a penny to my name."

"Yes, but at least you're alive," Maggie replied anxiously. "It could have been much worse. In a few days, your bumps and bruises will heal. And you're a resourceful man, Gene. You'll be back on your feet in no time."

"I guess this Sunday, I'm going to have to attend Rev. Cooper's church and thank him," I conceded.

"Thank him? Why is that?" Maggie replied, looking confused.

"Well, because if he hadn't talked my ear off, I probably wouldn't have made my way to the dining car. And if I hadn't gone to the dining car, I never would have met a certain French actress who seems to know just what to say to cheer me up. Besides that, I wouldn't be sitting here talking to my fiancée right now," I added with a smile.

Maggie told me Clyde wanted to know if there was anything he could do.

"Ask him to tell Reginald at the rooming house what has happened. I expect I'll get out of this place tomorrow, but they haven't yet told me."

"Reginald already knows. He was standing with us when the constable gave us the news. He said not to worry about your room. Everything will be there just like you left it when you return."

"That's most kind," I sighed with relief. "One more thing. Please ask Clyde to stop by the *Oregon Journal* and tell my boss, Jake, I will be there as soon as the hospital discharges me. I'm sure Constable Burton will already have told him the news about the theft, but I don't want him to think I'm not coming back. I need that job now more than ever."

"But Gene," Maggie replied anxiously, "is it safe? Aren't you concerned the same thing could happen again?"

"This time I'll keep my wits about me," I promised her. "Hopefully, the police will catch whoever did it; but if not, I can't let it keep me from earning a living. And right now that's the only thing open to me. With any luck, I'll be doing something else soon. But for now, that will have to do."

As I took a few bites of my sandwich, Maggie changed the subject.

"Gene, did you hear about the Titanic?"

"No, what about it?"

"It sank!" she exclaimed. She handed me the newspaper she had brought with her. The headline read:

STEAMSHIP TITANIC SINKS--DEATH LIST EXPECTED TO REACH TWELVE HUNDRED--WORST MARINE DISASTER IN HISTORY.

"How could that be?" I asked. "What does the article say? That ship was supposed to be unsinkable!"

"The newspaper reports, '*The ship hit an iceberg at twenty-five minutes past ten on Sunday night and sank at twenty minutes past two on Monday morning*,'" Maggie read. "'*The ship sank long before the vessels hurrying to her rescue reached the spot*.'"

The tragedy of the disaster weighed heavily on me. I thought about Ethel and her husband—and how grateful I was they were not on board. But then I thought of all the souls who had been, and the families and friends who were grieving their loss. Just two weeks ago, when I set out on my own journey, I had compared it to that of the Titanic. Both were maiden voyages setting out to make history. Neither journey was supposed to have any risk of failure.

But now it was estimated that over 1,200 souls lay at the bottom of the Atlantic—and here I was lying in a hospital bed. I knew my injuries did not equate to the loss of life on that ship, but still I could not ignore the unexpected outcomes in both journeys.

But my journey is not over! I thought. *I will weather this storm and get back on my feet. I will not be defeated by this.* I must have said that last part out loud, because Maggie declared, "No, Gene, you will *not* be defeated by this!"

Right then Nurse Miller entered my room to remind us our thirty minutes were over. Maggie leaned down to kiss my forehead and told me to rest.

"Tomorrow will be a new day with new possibilities," she told me confidently.

"Nurse Miller, do you expect me to be discharged tomorrow?"

"That will be up to the doctor," she replied. "But if you continue to improve as you have, he probably will release you in the afternoon."

"Gene, I will be back here at noon tomorrow, one way or the other—to either pay you a visit or help you get back to your rooming house," Maggie declared.

"You don't need to do that," I protested. "I don't want you to miss your rehearsal. I'm a big boy, I can make my way home."

"Well, of course you are," Maggie countered with her French accent and mischievous smile, "but if I didn't come, what kind of a fiancée would that make me, *mon chéri*?"

～

I woke up several times during the night when Nurse Miller checked on me. However, I still was able to get some rest, when I wasn't thinking about what I might have done differently to avoid being robbed. One thing I knew for certain—I would never again take the shortcut through the alley.

The sun flooded my room early the next morning. The bump on my head still hurt whenever the pain medicine began to wear off. Fortunately, the nurses seemed to arrive right on time. Nurse Miller's shift had ended at six o'clock. Her replacement, Nurse Davis, did not seem to be quite as concerned about my welfare, though I admit she appeared to be very efficient.

The morning seemed to drag on as I sat waiting to be released. Nurse Davis made it clear—to the point she threatened to lock me in my room—I could not leave until the doctor gave his approval. So I continued to count the minutes until he arrived.

He and Maggie arrived at the exact same time—a few minutes before noon. The doctor rattled off his long list of questions, and apparently my answers were satisfactory, because he announced I was free to go. He did, however, warn me to take it easy for the next several days and not do anything physically exerting. Maggie assured him she would make sure I did not, even before I had the chance to reply.

When we arrived at the Goodnough Building, I told Maggie I needed to go to the newspaper to see Jake before I did anything else. I insisted she return to her rehearsal and not miss any more time on my account. She was not pleased with my decision, but I vowed to spend the rest of the afternoon resting after I finished meeting with Jake. Though she looked doubtful, she ultimately agreed to return to the theater.

"But I will be back here by six o'clock to check on you," she said before she left, "and you had better be resting . . . *mon chéri!*" adding the last part for emphasis.

Jake didn't seem the least concerned about me when I walked into his office.

"So I hear you lost $100 of our money," he stated, as if I had been negligent in my duties. "How do you plan to repay us?"

"Repay you!" I practically bellowed. "I got my skull cracked working for you! How dare you even suggest I owe you for the money that was stolen. After all, you're the one who told me it was money the paper would never receive."

"Yes, but you did collect it. So it was received—and it was the *Journal's* money. And you are responsible for the money you collect from the time you receive it until the moment you turn it in to me. That's what the lawyers call a fiduciary responsibility. It was all spelled out in those papers you signed the day you took the job."

"But Jake, I don't have any money with which to pay you. So, you're telling me not only did that thief take all your money and my own money, but now I owe you in addition to my hospital bill. I am in debt past my eyeballs!"

"Yeah, that's what I'm saying," Jake replied. "And if you don't pay us, our lawyers will take you to court!"

"But there's nothing for them to collect from me. That just isn't right, Jake!" I insisted indignantly.

"I understand how you might think that way, Gene," Jake said. "But it's what you agreed to when you took the job. The lawyers will get an order from the court to seize any of your future earnings if you don't pay."

"As spelled out in all that legal mumbo jumbo that you had me sign," I retorted angrily.

"Yeah, that's true," he replied begrudgingly. "But contrary to what you might think, I do have a heart. I know you're in a tough spot, so here is what I am willing to do. You're one of the best collectors I've ever had. The fact you collected $100 yesterday is proof of that. You owe the *Journal* eighty dollars since twenty of that money was your commission. I'll give you more accounts to collect. But instead of paying you 20 percent, I'll pay you 15 percent. The 5 percent difference will go to repay the paper. Once you've repaid the eighty dollars, you'll again get to keep the full 20 percent.

"That way you'll work off your debt but still be earning some income as you do. I wouldn't give you a better offer if you were one of my kin. How 'bout it, Gene? Do we have a deal?"

I didn't have much choice. I had no other employment prospects, and given my current financial state, I needed to earn some money fast.

Jake could see I had made up my mind to accept his offer, so he asked, "When can you start?"

"Right now," I replied.

"Your friend Clyde told me this morning your doctor was probably going to want you to rest for a few days. Are you sure you can start today?"

"Well, the doctor isn't in my financial predicament, so I don't reckon he truly knows what I need to do," I replied. "Give me some names. I'll start this afternoon."

Just then my eye caught a glimpse of something sitting on a shelf behind him.

"But, Jake, I have one condition," I added.

"What's that?"

"I want to carry that billy club on your shelf while I'm working," I replied.

"I think we can allow that," Jake said, smiling briefly.

I looked through the list he gave me and decided to call on the five closest addresses. I was able to collect from all five people, though two took a little extra convincing. I will confess that seeing the billy club I was carrying probably had something to do with their decision.

It was half past five when I returned to Jake with my collections. I was on high alert as I returned to the Goodnough Building, staying on the main streets and keeping a watchful eye for anyone who looked suspicious. I had collected forty dollars. Jake returned six to me, and now I only owed the *Journal* seventy-eight dollars. At this rate, it would be a long time before I settled my debt.

I was able to slip up to my room without Reginald seeing me, so he would be none the wiser as to when I arrived. I had just finished washing up and doing my best to look like I had been home resting all afternoon when the bell rang in my room. Maggie must be downstairs waiting.

~

17

WEDNESDAY LATE AFTERNOON, APRIL 17 – THURSDAY, APRIL 18

∼

*W*hen I reached the lobby, I was surprised to find that Maggie was nowhere in sight; rather, it was Constable Burton who was waiting at the front desk to see me.

"Good afternoon, Mr. Fearsithe. I'm glad to see you are well enough to have been released from the hospital," the constable greeted me.

"You and me both," I replied. "I couldn't stay confined in that bed a moment longer. It has made all the difference just getting up and about."

"Oh? I assumed the doctor would want you on bed rest before doing much of that 'getting up and about.'"

"That's exactly what he told him," Maggie declared as she approached us, obviously overhearing the constable. "And I am certain he has been a good patient and rested in his room just like his doctor ordered. Isn't that right, Gene?"

"Good afternoon, Miss Reed," the constable nodded to Maggie. "It is a pleasure to see you again. I see you are checking up on the patient."

"Presumably, you are as well," I addressed the constable, "unless you have come to give me an update on my case. Have you arrested the scoundrel and recovered my money?"

"Regrettably, no," he replied. "We do not have any suspects at this point. I'm afraid the trail is cold. But hopefully we will get a lead tomorrow after you come by the station so we can take your fingerprints. We have pulled several prints off of your wallet, so we need to eliminate yours and identify any others."

"The doctor did tell him to rest, constable," Maggie interjected, "but I suppose a walk to the police station would not be too overtaxing."

"Oh, I think it would be less strenuous than going door to door to collect debts, don't you, Mr. Fearsithe?" the constable asked.

"I'm sure you're correct, sir," I replied. "Why do you ask?"

"Well, that's why I'm here to see you, Mr. Fearsithe," he replied. "We received two complaints today from individuals who said a man fitting your description came to their homes to collect money on behalf of the *Journal*. And they told us the man was brandishing a billy club."

Reginald, still wearing his scowl, began to inch closer so he could hear the conversation more clearly. Maggie turned and looked at me in shock.

"Surely that wasn't you, Gene! You promised me you would rest this afternoon."

"Well, I, uh," I stammered. Then, electing to take control of the conversation, I continued, "Yes, constable, I'm sure those individuals were talking about me. But I can assure you I did not threaten anyone. And I most certainly did not carry it to intimidate anyone—except for would-be thieves. My employer gave it to me for protection. I am certain there is no law against that."

"There is no law against it," the constable agreed, "unless you use it to threaten or cause unprovoked injury. In that instance, it would be deemed a lethal weapon, and I would have to arrest you."

"I can assure you that is not the case, constable," I reiterated. "But should anyone attempt to do me harm, I promise you I will not hesitate to defend myself."

"Mr. Fearsithe, knowing the two individuals who issued the complaints, I am inclined to take you at your word," Constable Burton declared. "But please be careful how you wield it in the future. We don't need law-abiding citizens thinking you intend to do them bodily harm. Do we understand one another?"

"Yes, we do."

"And can we expect to see you at the station tomorrow?"

"Yes, I will be there," I said. "And please let me know if there is anything else I can do to assist you in your investigation. I have the utmost faith you will stay focused on the real crimes that have been committed and not allow spurious complaints to distract you. Good day to you, sir!"

As the officer left, I knew I had successfully defended myself against his accusations. However, I doubted I would have the same result with the prosecutor left standing before me. Even Reginald began to back away.

But surprisingly, Maggie did not say a word. Instead, she stared at me, slowly shook her head, and stormed off. I would have preferred her to berate me rather than leave me in silence.

"Maggie!" I called after her, but she never looked back. I decided to let her have the night to cool off. I headed to the dining room; this would be the first evening meal I had eaten there, and given my limited financial resources, it seemed the prudent choice.

I can't say the meal was delicious, but it was better than hospital food. Plus, it was the right price since it came with my room and board! Truth be told, I had overdone it that afternoon. So after dinner, I took some more aspirin and went straight to bed.

I updated Jake the next morning about the false accusations made against me regarding the billy club. I wanted him to know how I had responded in the event some of those same disgruntled customers decided to "report" me to the paper. Not only did Jake not take the complaints seriously, but he also laughed—which I knew he did sparingly.

After getting my list of ten delinquent customers, I stopped at the police station before starting my collections. During my walk over, I pondered what I should say to Maggie that evening. I hoped her temper had cooled by then. If I had a profitable day, I considered asking her out for a good meal.

Constable Burton arranged for an officer to take my fingerprints right away. When they compared them to those on my wallet, they found two prints that did not match mine. Their next step was the tedious job of checking those prints against any on file of criminals arrested in the past. After listening to the officer, I didn't hold out much hope they would find a match. But, at least, it was a possibility to pursue.

I was glad to have my wallet back; I double-checked to make sure nothing else was missing. The first thing I saw was the faded picture of Sara. The photograph had been taken four years ago and had gotten pretty dog-eared in my wallet. It no longer did her justice. Sara is an attractive woman. She doesn't necessarily have the dazzle of an Ethel or Maggie, but she is just as beautiful in a less showy way.

Until that moment, I had forgotten just how beautiful she is. I wondered what she had been doing since I left Williamsport. Did she miss me or had she quickly moved on? If I was being honest, a part of me hoped she missed me; there was a part of me that was most definitely missing her.

My collections for the day took me to East Portland, a separate munici-pality on the eastern side of the Willamette River. As I crossed the river on the Hawthorne Bridge, I realized the cityscape around me was undergoing a subtle transformation. Portland was giving way to a more tranquil and residential setting with a distinct charm all its own.

Instead of the tall buildings and crowded streets that had become the setting for my weekday travels, I found East Portland to be a collection of neighborhoods characterized by a sense of community that enjoyed a much slower pace.

Even the downtown was different. Instead of six- to eight-story office buildings and storefronts rising up on each side of the streets, this side of the river was a patchwork of local shops, quaint storefronts, and markets. There was a sense of familiarity as residents greeted one another and exchanged pleasantries.

Though East Portland doesn't have the grandeur and sophistication of its counterpart, it does possess a unique character. People greeted me warmly as I walked by, but I could tell they were watching me warily. I soon realized it was the billy club in my hand that was putting them off. I quickly tucked it into my belt underneath my jacket.

As I crossed back over the bridge later that afternoon, I was feeling pretty good about my productive day. I was unable to contact two of the people on my list; but of the remaining eight, six paid me a total of forty dollars and the other two promised full payment the following week.

Since it was midafternoon, I decided to stop by the Majestic Theater to see if I could talk to Maggie. I was met at the stage door by an Irishman about ten years my senior—who was carrying about fifty more pounds than I was, all of which was muscle. It quickly became obvious that no one got past this guy unless he had permission.

"What's your business here?" he asked, noticing the protrusion underneath my jacket.

"I am a debt collector, and I carry a billy club to ward off unsavory characters. I'm a friend of Miss Margaret Reed, and I wondered if I might be able to see her."

Though he seemed satisfied with my explanation, he still kept a watchful eye on me.

"They are in rehearsal now and cannot be disturbed."

"Is there any possibility I could sit and watch their rehearsal while I wait for her?"

"No one is permitted to watch rehearsals without the permission of the director," he replied. "And before you ask, I cannot interrupt him to see if he will allow you to come in. If you want to wait for Miss Reed, you'll have to do so out here."

"How much longer do you expect their rehearsal will last?"

"I really don't have any idea," he answered as he started to close the door in my face.

Instinctively, I placed my foot in the door to keep it from closing all the way.

"Can you at least give her a message for me?"

"Sure," he said. "What is it?"

"Tell her Gene stopped by to ask her out for dinner," I replied. I removed my foot and the door closed with a loud thud.

I stopped by the newspaper to see Jake and settle up that day's collections. By the time I arrived back in my room it was four o'clock. I suddenly realized just how tired I was. I decided to take a short nap while I waited for Maggie to arrive. As soon as I stretched out on the bed, I was fast sleep.

Sometime later, I awoke with a start. The room was dark, and I could tell it was well past sunset. I looked at my pocket watch, which showed a few minutes past eight. Had I slept through the bell announcing Maggie's arrival? I quickly made my way down to reception.

"Reginald, did you ring the bell when Miss Reed arrived?"

"I didn't ring your room, Mr. Fearsithe," Reginald replied. "And I can assure you no one has come by inquiring after you."

"But Miss Reed was to come by so we could dine together."

"That may be, sir," Reginald replied, "but I have not seen her since she left last evening."

Had the stagehand not given her my message? Did she even know I had come to the theater to see her? I decided right then I needed to go to the Multnomah Hotel. After making myself more presentable, I hopped on a streetcar and headed to Maggie's hotel.

The Multnomah desk clerk told me he did not know whether Maggie was in or out. He had no way to contact her room, and he was unwilling to tell me her room number.

"You can, however, leave her a message and I will see that she receives it," he told me.

I wrote a note telling her I had been by the theater earlier in the afternoon but feared she had not received my message about meeting for dinner. I told her I was sorry for misleading her yesterday and wanted to make it up to her. "Would you have breakfast with me tomorrow?" I wrote. "I'll come by at half past seven in the morning to get you."

I sealed the message in an envelope and tipped the desk clerk fifty cents to deliver it to her tonight. But as I turned to go, I realized the note wouldn't be necessary. Maggie was passing through the entrance doors walking straight toward me—on the arm of another man.

We saw each other at the same time, but I was more startled to see her with another man than she was to see me.

"Good evening, Gene," she greeted me as she approached. "It is so good to see you up and about. I am glad you don't appear to have any lingering effects from your injury. I was concerned at first, but after seeing you last evening, I realized you had everything well in hand."

"Maggie, that's why I've come. I want to apologize for last evening."

There was an awkward silence as the gentleman with her just stood there.

"Samuel, please forgive my lack of courtesy," Maggie said. "And please allow me to introduce Mr. Eugene Fearsithe. He and I met on the train the night before we arrived here in Portland. And Gene, this is Mr. Samuel Jacobs, the director of our theatrical production of *The Merry Widow*."

Samuel and I exchanged pleasantries before he excused himself, saying it had been a long day and he needed to get some rest. Maggie and I stood there, waiting for the other to speak.

Finally, I asked, "Did you get my message at the theater today?"

"Yes, I did," Maggie replied, "but by then I had already accepted Samuel's invitation to join him for dinner. I hope you weren't waiting for me."

"No," I answered, "I actually fell asleep once I got back to my room. When I awoke a little while ago, I berated Reginald for not waking me when you arrived. I will have to apologize to him when I return."

The tension between us was still palpable, so I plunged ahead.

"Maggie, I am truly sorry for working yesterday after I promised you I would rest. But I needed the money! Not only have things not gone as planned since I arrived here, but frankly I am worse off. I have no permanent job and no employment prospects, and now I have no money and I'm in debt. I couldn't just lie in bed and worry all afternoon."

"I know things have not gone well, Gene," Maggie said, "but I had hoped some of the good things—like the two of us meeting—would make up for at least some of the bad. Even though we have known each other only a few days, I thought we could count on one another. And that includes being honest with each other. But Gene, you deliberately lied to me. You never intended to follow your doctor's orders. You just wanted me to return to my rehearsal so you could go to work.

"It was the fact you lied to me that hurt me most. A relationship needs to be built on trust and honesty—and yesterday, you destroyed that between us."

"Maggie, I am so sorry."

"Gene, I know you are sorry you hurt me, but I don't believe you're sorry you lied to me. I think you're a man who will say and do whatever you need to in order to get what you want. And that tells me you will do it again if you believe it's necessary. So I could never really be sure if you were being honest with me."

I tried to speak, but she held her gloved hand to my lips as she continued.

"Gene, I am glad I met you. Your strength helped me take the steps I needed to when I arrived here. And for that, I will always be grateful. But I think the time has come for us to establish separate lives here. I'm sure we will see each other on occasion; Portland is not that big. But when we do, it will be as friendly acquaintances.

"I wish you all the best, *mon chéri*. I hope you find your dream."

She held out her hand for me to kiss. I wanted to say something to change her mind. Though we had not known each other long, I could not imagine a life in Portland without her. But the words didn't come. So I reached out and drew her hand to my lips.

And with that, she turned and walked away. I stood there watching her until she disappeared from sight. I realized the expression on her face was similar to one I had seen before. Then it struck me: Sara had that same expression the night we parted.

I decided to walk back to the rooming house. I wasn't in any hurry to get back there. There wasn't anyone there to get back and see. There wasn't anyone I was looking forward to seeing tomorrow—or the next day. Portland now seemed like a very lonely place. I may have felt bad yesterday— but it didn't compare to how I was feeling now.

As I entered the lobby of the rooming house, Reginald handed me a sealed envelope with my name written on it.

"Who is it from?" I asked.

"I have no idea," Reginald replied. "I didn't recognize him. But I will tell you he was dressed like a swell."

≈

18

FRIDAY MORNING, APRIL 19

~

The message read:

Dear Mr. Fearsithe,
Please come to my home in Portland Heights at 9:00 a.m.
tomorrow morning.
I have a business venture I would like to discuss
with you.
Sincerely,
Archer Winslow

It took only a moment for me to recognize the name. He was the swell on my Tuesday collection list who lived in that posh house. I had no idea what kind of business venture he could possibly want to discuss with me. But since his was the only job invitation I had received, I decided to at least hear what the man had to say.

The next morning, I arrived at Jake's office at 8:00 a.m. sharp. I wanted to pick his brain about Mr. Archer Winslow.

"He is the majority owner of the Pacific Steamship Company," Jake began. "He's one of the big swells in the city—but he wasn't always so posh. He came to Portland from back East about twenty-five years ago. He was a smooth talker and had a little bit of money. The steamship shipping business was growing just like everything else here in Portland. But it was clear that some of the big railway companies like Union Pacific had their eyes on taking over that business.

"The small, family-owned shipping companies were worried the railroads were going to take over all the routes and beat their prices. Archer convinced them that if they consolidated and formed one larger company, they could eliminate duplicate costs and provide even more reliable and efficient services for both cargo and passengers along the West Coast.

"And he was right. Since most of the owners of those smaller companies were advanced in years, they chose Archer to lead the consolidated company—and he did all he promised them he would do. Pacific Steamship is now one of the largest and most successful in the industry."

"Well, if he's so successful, why did he end up on your debt collection list?" I asked.

"That was a personal bill for a number of ads he was running outside the company," Jake explained. "Since the bills weren't being sent to the bookkeepers at his company, they probably ended up in a desk drawer at home, and he forgot to pay them. So, why all the interest in him anyway?"

"He invited me to come to his house this morning."

"Well, lucky you," Jake declared. "If Archer Winslow offers you a job, you'll do well. I hate losing you, Gene, you're the best collector I've ever had. And if it doesn't work out, come back and see me, I'll always have a list of names for you. But if it does work out, I wish you the best of luck!"

I arrived at Mr. Winslow's home at five minutes before nine. When I presented myself at the front entry, the same butler from before opened the door.

"Have you forgotten that tradesmen are supposed to come to the delivery entrance at the rear of the house?" he asked haughtily, obviously recognizing me.

But before he could close the door in my face, I wedged my shoe into the opening and said, "Yes, but this time I have come at the invitation of Mr. Winslow!"

The butler slowly opened the door and looked at me in disbelief. "What's that you say?"

"Your employer asked me to come meet with him this morning," I said. "Please tell him Mr. Eugene Fearsithe is here for his appointment."

Though obviously befuddled, the butler still maintained his composure.

"My name is Church. Please step inside, Mr. Fearsithe," he said, "and wait here while I go tell Mr. Winslow you have arrived."

Church disappeared for a few minutes before returning to announce, "Mr. Fearsithe, Mr. Winslow will see you now. Please follow me."

I was shown into the library, by far the most impressive room I had ever been in. The rich woodwork and furnishings were of a quality that exceeded anything I had ever seen. Mr. Winslow stood up from his padded leather chair and extended his right hand. His left hand held a lit cigar that was creating quite a pleasant aroma in the room.

"Mr. Fearsithe, thank you for accepting my invitation," he said as we shook hands.

"I must admit I was both surprised and intrigued to receive your invitation," I replied. "How do you even know who I am?"

"We will discuss that in a little while. Please have a seat," he said, pointing at the matching leather chair facing his. "Can we serve you anything? Some coffee or tea, perhaps?"

"Coffee, black, would be nice. Thank you," I replied as I made myself comfortable.

"Church, I'll have the same," Mr. Winslow instructed the butler, who immediately set out to attend to our requests.

"Can I interest you in a cigar, Mr. Fearsithe?" my host asked as he pointed to a wooden humidor on the table to my left. I'd heard of humidors, but I had never actually seen one. "These are imported from Cuba, and I find them to be the best I have ever smoked."

"I don't mind if I do," I replied. He cut away the tip and helped me get it lit. I had to concur that it was the finest cigar I had ever smoked. Church soon returned with our coffee, and we settled into our chairs—and our discussion. I'll admit that between the cigar and the coffee being served by a butler, I decided the life of a swell definitely had its advantages!

"Mr. Fearsithe, or can I call you Gene?"

"Gene is fine."

"Well then, Gene—and by the way you can call me Archer—I have been searching for someone like you for a matter of months. As a matter of fact, the unpaid bill you came to collect earlier in the week was for advertisements I had placed in the *Oregon Journal* for that purpose. Does that surprise you?"

"What surprises me, Mr. Winslow, I mean Archer, is that you don't even know me. So how can you be sure I am a qualified candidate for your opening?"

"Gene, I actually know quite a bit about you. Allow me to explain. I was impressed with the way you handled yourself with Church the other day when you came to collect on my unpaid bill. First, you were not intimidated by your surroundings. You walked right up to my front door and demanded payment.

"Second, you were not intimidated by Church, and I will tell you very few people are not intimidated by him. He is as much my protector as he is my butler.

"Third, you demonstrated you can think on your feet. When you realized Church was about to send you packing, you changed course from trying to intimidate him to positioning yourself as someone who wanted to help solve an obvious mistake on the part of the paper.

"Gene, I have worked with a lot of people in difficult discussions over the years, and very few of them have shown that same keen sense of problem-solving."

"I had no idea you were listening to our conversation," I responded.

Archer chuckled. "I know you didn't. That's what enabled me to see you in action—and caused me to consider you might be the man I have been seeking."

"Why have you been looking for someone like me?"

"You have just demonstrated another characteristic I like about you. You get to the point instead of wasting time talking about frivolous things. As I am sure you are aware, I am the president of the Pacific Steamship Company. We have enjoyed a modicum of success over the years and look forward to that continuing well into the future.

"But there are two factors I am dealing with right now that threaten that continued success. The first is the Union Pacific Railroad. They have expanded into the steamship business through their subsidiary, the Oregon-Washington Railroad and Navigation Company or OWR&N. They aim to operate lines that connect Portland with other cities along the coast —cities, I might point out, that we have had exclusive control of for close to twenty years.

"OWR&N is using their Union Pacific muscle to convince those cities they will save money on shipping by fostering competition. But you and I both know that Union Pacific's end goal is not to establish competition, but rather to destroy it—namely us. And I have no intention of allowing that."

"Archer," I interrupted, "if this conversation is headed in the direction of defeating the Goliath of Union Pacific and OWR&N specifically, you have found a receptive ear."

Archer's eyes brightened. "So you have apparently encountered the good people at OWR&N. I look forward to hearing more about that! We've now identified another characteristic that makes you the right man for the job.

"The second factor I am dealing with is the waterfront workers. We have enjoyed a mutually beneficial relationship for the entire twenty-five years I have been in the business. But now one of the waterfront workers, a fellow named Richard Morgan, is organizing the longshoremen to go on strike against my company if I do not agree to their demands. They want reduced working hours and an unreasonable increase in wages. I am convinced Union Pacific is behind all of this in their attempt to put us out of business—and Morgan is merely their puppet."

"Where do I fit in all this?" I interjected.

"I need someone inside OWR&N to be my eyes and ears so he can relay their plans to me; that way, I will know their next steps before they take them," Archer explained. "The man leading this effort is a long-time employee by the name of Emmett Hall. He is on a lower rung of their upper management team and looks to solidify his position by establishing their steamship business. And he knows the best way to do that is by putting me out of business."

"I know Emmett Hall!" I exclaimed.

Archer looked shocked. "How is it you know him?"

"We met on the train on my way out here," I replied. "In fact, he was one of the people who convinced me that my plan to come to Portland was the right plan. I even thought he had offered me a job."

"He offered you a job?" Archer asked in disbelief.

"Yeah," I answered, "or so I thought. But when I went to see him Monday about the job, he brushed me off and told me to go to their personnel office —as if I was a nobody off the street."

"Very interesting," Archer remarked. "Did he give you any indication as to why he changed his tune?"

"The only thing I could figure was he recruits young men he encounters during his travels and encourages them to come to Portland. When they do, he points them to his company's personnel department and expects them to do the rest. Only in my case, I understood him to say he had a specific job in mind for me. So when he didn't deliver, I lost interest."

"Well, how do you feel about going back to see Mr. Emmett Hall about a job?" Archer inquired, clearly with a plan in mind. "But this time, helping him discover just how invaluable you can be to him!"

"I thought you were offering me a job," I countered. "Why would I go talk to him about employment?"

"Because you would be working for me, Gene," Archer replied with a smile. "And the job I'm hiring you to do is to work for Emmett Hall as his assistant."

"So I would be your inside man in OWR&N?" I asked, beginning to understand.

"Yes, you would," Archer confirmed.

"But why not just enlist someone who is already working for OWR&N?"

"Because I believe I can trust you to be discreet, Gene. And besides, I don't know anyone else working with Mr. Hall who would be as valuable to me."

"Okay. But how do you know he's going to hire me to be his assistant?" I asked.

"Because I'm going to help you!" Archer replied, exhaling a long stream of cigar smoke.

For the next hour, Archer revealed more of his plan to me. Before he was done, I had agreed to work for him. I hadn't had to fill out one form with the company or talk to anyone in personnel, but I was now the vice president of special assignments for the Pacific Steamship Company.

Archer cautioned me not to tell anyone.

"For now, Gene, it will need to remain our secret. Otherwise, you will not be able to do your job effectively. No one can know you work for the Pacific Steamship Company. You will report only to me."

"And for now, you will receive your weekly salary in cash. How does $100 per week sound to you, Gene?" he asked. "Plus, you can keep whatever salary you receive from OWR&N."

That was a lot of money! The combined salaries would be at least three times what I thought I'd be making starting out in my career. Plus, I felt relieved that I could pay off my hospital and newspaper debts quickly. It all sounded good—and I told Archer so! We shook hands to make it official.

Archer reached into his coat pocket and withdrew an envelope.

"Here is a week's pay to help you get started. Consider it a signing bonus!"

I glanced inside the envelope and saw five crisp twenty dollar bills as Archer proceeded to say that my first order of business was to contact Emmett Hall that afternoon. He told me exactly what I should say to get the job as Emmett's assistant. The more he said, the more it made sense.

I had just entered the high-stakes game of big business in this industrial age. Archer assured me I was on my way to becoming a major player. I felt a rush of adrenaline as he unfolded more of his plan. When he was done, he again reminded me I could not tell anyone about our business arrangement, and then he added, "including your girlfriend."

"I don't currently have a girlfriend," I replied.

"Oh, I thought you did. I was certain a good-looking young man like you would surely have a girlfriend."

The clock in the library chimed eleven as Archer led me out of the room.

"Oh, and one more thing: we will have to be careful that we are not seen together," he added. "We will meet here at my home, but make sure you are not followed or seen coming and going from here. And use the tradesman's door at the rear of the house."

We passed a man who was about my age and build as we walked to the rear door. He wasn't dressed in livery like a servant or a butler; rather, he wore a business suit. But Archer did not introduce us. He had a familiar manner about him though, but I couldn't place him. We passed one another without saying a word, simply nodding in acknowledgment.

19

FRIDAY AFTERNOON AND EVENING, APRIL 19

~

J arrived at OWR&N promptly at one o'clock and approached the same woman who had greeted me in the lobby on Monday. This time, however, I knew what to expect.

"My name is Mr. Eugene Fearsithe, and I'm here to see Mr. Emmett Hall."

"Good afternoon, Mr. Fearsithe," she replied. "I recognize you from earlier in the week. Do you have an appointment with Mr. Hall?"

"No, I do not," I answered. "But tell him I have information regarding the Pacific Steamship Company I am confident he will want to hear."

I was prepared for her to press me for more information before she dispatched her messenger to Emmett's office, but she did not. She directed me to take a seat while she awaited a response, but I chose to stand there looking rather impatient. My intention was to convey that any further delay would be a waste of my time.

The messenger quickly returned and said something to the woman. She instructed me to follow the messenger to Mr. Hall's office. Even though I had been through these halls earlier in the week, I never would have found Emmett's office on my own.

Miss Adams was sitting at her desk as I was shown into the anteroom. I believed she was as much a fixture in that room as the furniture. She informed me Mr. Hall was finishing up with another appointment, and I should take a seat.

"How did it go on Monday with our personnel department, Mr. Fearsithe?" she asked. "I hope they were able to help you find a suitable position here at OWR&N."

"They were most instrumental in helping me identify both what I did and did not want to pursue. Thank you for asking."

That question seemed to exhaust her level of curiosity, so she turned back to the letter she was typing. I did notice, however, her occasional glance in my direction, as her fingers continued to glide over the keys with measured precision. Thankfully, Emmett's office door opened within a matter of minutes before the hypnotic sound of the typewriter keys had lulled me to sleep. Emmett stepped through the doorway with an older gentleman who nodded in my direction before exiting the room.

"Gene, it's so good to see you again," Emmett said, as he shook my hand and invited me into his office. Although I was still impressed with the décor of the room, I noted that it didn't quite measure up to Archer's library.

"Have a seat," Emmett continued. "Can I offer you any coffee or tea?"

It appeared Emmett was planning for our conversation to last longer than our previous one. "Yes, coffee, black, would be most kind," I replied.

As he poured coffee, he directed me toward a set of upholstered chairs in the corner of the office—much nicer than the ones in front of his desk. Yes, I had obviously piqued Emmett's interest.

"Our personnel office tells me you never talked to them regarding a position on Monday," Emmett said. "As a matter of fact, they said you never completed an employment application. Why is that, Gene?"

"Because I didn't come here looking for an entry-level position, Emmett. I am in pursuit of a dream, and dreams are not listed among the job openings in your personnel department. I came to see you, expecting you had something of consequence to offer me. Instead, you relegated me to the 'assembly line' through which you put all your rank-and-file employees. To say the least, I was disappointed. At least the other men with us on the train had sincere offers in mind for me."

"Well, I'm sorry to hear you were disappointed and had expected more, Gene," Emmett responded. "That is the process we take all of our new employees through. It gives us an opportunity to know more about them before we offer them a position. I'm sure you understand."

"No, I don't understand, Emmett," I declared. "And I seriously doubt that is the way *all* your new employees are hired. If it was, you would be missing out on some of the best and brightest. And I don't believe OWR&N or Union Pacific have gotten where they are today by missing out. I can assure you Archer Winslow is not missing out."

"Yes, I got your message about the Pacific Steamship Company," Emmett said. "Did you have a meeting with Mr. Winslow?"

"Yes, he was most hospitable—definitely more hospitable than my time here. But then again, he and his company function in a way that is more agile and responsive to changing circumstances. One of the dangers Union Pacific and OWR&N face is functioning like a passenger liner, needing more berth to change directions. Sadly, we have all been reminded this week of the tragedy that can result when a large ship fails to turn in time."

"Perhaps, Gene," Emmett retorted, "but the large ship is typically the most stable in rough seas and can ride out the storms. Our ship has proven that time and again—and I venture we will continue to do so."

"But why not do both?" I countered.

"What do you mean?"

"Why not utilize the resources of the large ship—Union Pacific—but operate OWR&N, or at least the steamship division, more nimbly?" I replied. "You, by far, have more to offer the ports along your planned routes than anyone else. But your greatest obstacle is the fear they have that your size will ultimately cause you to dictate terms that would be harmful to them. They are afraid of what you will do. Give them solid assurances that will alleviate their fears. That's what Winslow is doing."

"Gene, how do you know all this?"

"Because Archer offered me a position as his assistant," I replied. "I actually met him as I was collecting a debt he owed the *Oregon Journal*. He was impressed by the way I conducted myself and subsequently collected the amount he owed. Right then and there, he decided I have the ability to get results in the midst of difficult circumstances."

"So did you take the job?"

"I told him I would think about it. But before I make my decision, I wanted to talk to you one more time. You are one of the reasons I stayed the course in my plans to come to Portland. And I have always believed that you dance with the one who brought you. I figured whatever attributes he saw in me could help you as well. So here I am—offering to be your assistant so I can help you tie up those shipping routes.

"But the thing is, Emmett, I have to give him an answer by this afternoon. So if you want to hire me, you need to do so today. If not, there are no hard feelings. I just felt I owed you the opportunity before I said yes to him. Truth be told, I'd rather work for you. You've demonstrated that you are a gentleman, and Archer . . . well, I'm not so sure.

"During our conversation he disclosed some of his plan to beat your company, which obviously I can't share with you. It would be a breach of trust. Particularly if I end up working for him. But I will tell you, when it comes to business, he's no gentleman. Whether you hire me or not, you're going to have a major fight on your hands."

Emmett abruptly got up from his seat and asked Miss Adams to join us.

"Miss Adams," he said, "I would like to introduce you to my new executive assistant, Mr. Eugene Fearsithe. Please take him to Bob Farley in personnel and have him assist Gene with the necessary paperwork so his employment goes into effect as of this past Monday—the day we should have hired him. And give Bob this envelope with Gene's salary arrangement."

Emmett quickly wrote something on a piece of paper and showed it to me:

Pay Eugene Fearsithe a weekly salary of $80 effective Monday, April 15.

"Is this agreeable to you, Gene?" Emmett asked as he reached to shake my hand.

"Yes, that is agreeable," I replied with a smile as I shook his hand. I was pleasantly surprised because Archer had thought Emmett would offer me a weekly salary of $60. Given the combined income, I was hoping I could keep both of these jobs for a very long time!

"Welcome to the company, Gene," Emmett said. "And thank you for demonstrating that you are more than just another mechanical engineer. We have plenty of those. But this afternoon you expressed what I thought I saw in you on the train."

"What's that, Emmett?"

"That you are a man willing to take appropriate risks to get what he wants —and to help us get what our company wants. I look forward to a long and prosperous journey together as we establish the largest shipping company on the West Coast. I'll see you back here at eight o'clock Monday morning."

As I turned to leave with Miss Adams, Emmett added, "By the way, help yourself to a cigar!" He opened the wooden box on the table between us. As I reached for one, a familiar aroma wafted through the room. It was pleasant—but I knew right away these cigars weren't from Cuba!

It only took an hour to complete the paperwork in the personnel office, so I was back on the street a little before 3:00 p.m. I had the weekend before me. I was now gainfully employed, and I had money in my pocket. There was no question I planned to celebrate.

This was the start of my dream—and things would only go up from here. I was on my way to becoming a tycoon in the steamship shipping business.

I sure couldn't have done that in Williamsport, Pennsylvania. And I never would have earned $180 per week just starting out. On Tuesday I had been a pauper, in debt with no money. Now I didn't have that concern. I decided this weekend I'd look for lodging better suited to my station.

I wanted to run and tell Maggie, but then I remembered I couldn't. Besides, she wouldn't understand what I was doing. She would probably think I was being dishonest again. But I was only doing what a man needs to do in order to make his mark. No, I could never tell Maggie. But I would find Clyde and invite him to celebrate with me.

When I arrived at the Goodnough Building, I decided to go see Jake and let him know I would no longer be able to collect for him.

"I knew this was going to happen," Jake said. "Just when I find someone who is good at the job, he goes and finds himself another one! Though I can't say I blame you, particularly in light of what happened the other day. So, was it Archer Winslow who offered you a job?"

"No," I replied, "I'm now working at OWR&N for Mr. Emmett Hall as his executive assistant."

"Well, what did Winslow want with you?" Jake asked.

"He said he was aware I had been assaulted and robbed after I left his house the other day, and he wanted to make sure I was okay. He told me he somehow felt responsible. He was a nice enough fellow and seemed to really care. He even gave me a fiver for my troubles."

"Doesn't that beat all!" Jake declared.

"Yeah, it does. And Jake, I want to thank you for giving me a job when I really needed one. I know I still owe you seventy-six dollars. Here's six dollars and I'll stop by and pay you ten dollars at the end of each week until the debt is paid."

I knew I was earning enough to pay it off quicker, but I didn't want to make Jake suspicious.

"Somehow, Gene, I wasn't worried about it," Jake replied. "I figured you're good for it. But are you sure you have enough cash to pay me the six dollars now?"

"Yes, I'm fine," I assured him. "Between the fiver I got from Mr. Winslow and the advance OWR&N gave me on my salary to help me get started, I will be all right."

When I arrived at the rooming house, I asked Reginald for a sheet of paper, an envelope, and a stamp. I quickly wrote the message to Archer we had prearranged:

Hall hired me. I start Monday!

I paid Reginald two cents for the stamp and deposited the envelope in the box for the mail carrier. Archer had said we would only meet face to face when necessary. This news didn't require a meeting.

About an hour later, I dropped by Clyde's room to announce my news.

"This requires a celebration!" he asserted. "Where do you want to go?"

"You've lived here longer than I have, Clyde. Which restaurant would you consider to be the finest in Portland?"

"Unquestionably, the restaurant in the Portland Hotel," Clyde answered. "I've never been able to afford to eat there, but the partners at my company celebrated a big business deal there several months ago and said it was the best meal they had ever eaten."

"Well, tonight we're celebrating *my* biggest business deal," I told him, "so that's the place we're going. I've noticed you and Elenore have been together every night since we met up. Do you think she would care to join us?"

"I'm sure she would love to," Clyde replied enthusiastically. "Should I have her see if Maggie wants to join us?"

"I may just be getting started in the steamship business," I answered, "but I'm afraid that particular ship has sailed."

The restaurant lived up to its reputation: the setting was elegant, the food was exquisite, and the service was impeccable. The three of us were definitely dining among the swells of Portland. Clyde even pointed out a few of the biggest names in the room.

"In years to come, people will point us out as two of the most brilliant young men who came here from back East and made our mark," I proclaimed.

"And they'll point to you, Elenore, and declare, 'I remember her when she played her first role in Portland, and now just look at her—she is a famous star of the stage and screen!'

"This may be remembered as the week in April 1912 that the RMS Titanic sank, but it was also the week our ships set sail!"

Then we raised our glasses in a toast. "To us!" I heralded as we excitedly looked toward a bright future.

～

20

SATURDAY, APRIL 20 – SUNDAY, APRIL 21

~

*I*f I was going to work as one of the up-and-coming executives at OWR&N starting Monday, I knew I needed to look the part. And that meant immediately upgrading my wardrobe. I asked Clyde if he had any recommendations.

"Albert Frank is my tailor," he replied. "His shop is nearby on Washington Street, and he does impeccable work. He's not the cheapest in town, but if you want to look the part, he's the man to see. He's made two suits for me, including the one I am wearing right now." I had been admiring Clyde's suit—it was obviously top notch.

After breakfast, I set out for Mr. Frank's shop. When I arrived, there was a customer standing in front of a floor length mirror who was being fitted. The tailor, an older man in his mid-fifties, slightly balding, working with the confidence of a man who knew his craft, called out to me. "Good morning, sir. Welcome to my shop. I will be with you as soon as I finish here."

I was impressed with the craftmanship I observed as I browsed the haberdashery in the shop. I was pleased to see that, in addition to business suits, he also created tailored overcoats and dress shirts. His attention to detail was conspicuous in each and every one. The more I saw, the more convinced I was that I had come to the right place.

"My name is Albert Frank," he said, as he walked over a few minutes later and shook my hand.

"Good morning, sir," I replied. "My name is Eugene Fearsithe, and I am in need of two business suits."

"Are you new to Portland, Mr. Fearsithe?"

"Yes, I've just been here a week. But a good friend of mine, Mr. Clyde Sheets, highly recommended you."

"Oh, yes, Mr. Sheets. He is a fine gentleman. It was so kind of him to recommend me. Have you come to Portland to take a new job?"

"Yes, sir. As a matter of fact, I start the day after tomorrow."

"For whom will you be working?" he inquired.

"OWR&N. That's the Oregon-Washington Railway and Navigation Company."

"Oh, yes," he said. "I am very familiar with OWR&N. They are one of our leading employers. And I have made suits for many of their executives. What will you be doing for the company?"

"I am the executive assistant to the company secretary, specifically relating to the steamship shipping division."

"That must mean you work for Mr. Emmett Hall. Am I correct?"

"Yes, you are! You appear to have an excellent working knowledge of the company."

"In my field, it pays to stay informed about the leading and emerging companies. It helps me know what to recommend to their executives when they come to me for a new suit. And besides, you'll find that Mr. Hall is one of my favorite clients. He, too, is a fine gentleman. So one thing I already know about you, Mr. Fearsithe, is that you keep excellent company."

"And given all you have told me, might I suggest a worsted wool sack suit with a high waistcoat in charcoal gray with minimal ornamentation? I think you will find it durable and entirely appropriate for your position— but also communicate that you are an up-and-comer."

Mr. Frank showed me a sample of what he was suggesting, and I knew right away it was the correct choice.

"How long will it take you to make it?" I asked.

After first looking at his calendar, he said, "I should be able to have it finished for you four weeks from today. Would you like me to go ahead and get started?"

"I have two questions before I say yes," I countered.

"Your first question is, what is the price?" Mr. Frank replied before I even asked. "The suit will cost you sixty dollars—payable half now and the balance when I finish it. You will find my prices are quite competitive. What is your second question?"

I nodded and smiled. "Your price is acceptable. Please go ahead and proceed with the suit. My second question is, do you have any ready-made suits available so I will have one to wear in the meantime?"

"Yes, I certainly do," Mr. Frank replied. "And here is my recommendation," he added, as he pointed to a suit displayed beside us. "Since your custom suit will be charcoal gray, might I suggest this one in dark navy? And before you ask, I normally sell it for twenty-five dollars. But since I am making you a custom suit, I'll sell you this one for twenty dollars and throw in a new tie.

"Go ahead and try on the navy suit so I can make any necessary alterations. I can have it ready for you by the end of today, and then we'll fit you for your new suit."

Thirty minutes later, I walked out of the shop as the proud owner of two new suits and a new pair of shoes with sixty-two dollars less in my wallet. I was grateful Archer had given me that $100 signing bonus!

The next thing on my agenda was to find a more permanent home. The rooming house was considered appropriate for a man just starting out with an entry-level job—but an executive would be expected to live in something a little more upscale.

My research pointed to five apartment buildings in the downtown area that were suitable, but only one had private baths. That building immediately rose to the top of my list! The Marlborough Apartments were located in the heart of downtown, just a block away from my rooming house.

It was a few minutes after eleven when I arrived. I told the rental agent I was looking for a bedroom apartment.

"Those apartments have become our most popular," he replied. "Most of our residents are single men, about your age or perhaps a little older, who are now up and coming executives at the leading companies here in Portland."

When I told him about my position at OWR&N, he seemed very pleased and became more enthusiastic about discussing an apartment with me.

"We have a number of men from your company who live here," he said. "And what's more, you're in luck, Mr. Fearsithe! We have a one-bedroom apartment that has just become available in the basement."

Given my recently acquired fear of building fires, the idea of being located in the basement suited me just fine.

The rental agent took me on a tour of the apartment, where I quickly learned I would need to duck under a few of the interior doorways. I decided that after I had smacked my head against a doorframe once or twice, ducking would become instinctive. The apartment consisted of a small kitchen, a small sitting room, a small dining area, and a small bedroom. The operative word being small; the entire apartment was only 900 square feet. But its greatest selling feature was the private bath—small as it was. I decided immediately the apartment would do nicely.

"How much is the monthly rent?" I asked.

"It is a bargain at $100 per month, payable in advance," the rental agent replied. "We also require a security deposit of $100, of which fifty dollars is payable at signing and the remainder thirty days later. You'll find our terms are comparable to other quality apartments in the city, as is a one-year rental agreement."

The amount seemed reasonable, and with the income I would be earning, it was easily affordable. My only challenge was I didn't have enough money to sign the lease now.

"Go ahead and prepare a rental agreement, and I'll be back next Saturday to sign it and pay you the funds," I said.

"Are you not able to sign it today, Mr. Fearsithe? The reason I ask is that it is very unusual for us to have an apartment available. I normally have multiple inquiries from gentlemen such as yourself looking for an apartment, and I am charged by my employers to keep the accommodations fully rented. If you are not able to sign a lease today, I will be forced to rent it to the next person who comes along."

"That would be most unfortunate for you," I said with conviction.

"For me?" the agent replied, raising his eyebrows. "Don't you mean it would be unfortunate for you to miss out on this splendid apartment?"

"Oh, perhaps it would be unfortunate to miss out on this specific apartment," I replied. "But I know I will be able to find another one. My concern is actually for you. You see, when I inform my employer that you were unwilling to work with one of OWR&N's newest executives, I believe he will feel obligated to tell his senior managers how uncooperative your company has been. I expect they will then tell other existing and new executives at OWR&N to no longer lease from your company—as well as those at Union Pacific's other affiliates.

"And if my information is correct, your employers also own the Portland Apartments and the Cordelia Apartments here in town, which means any boycott of your company would include those properties as well. I just hope for your sake that you don't lose your job because of it."

The smug expression on the rental agent's face had disappeared by the time I was finished.

"Mr. Fearsithe, I fear you may have misunderstood me," he said, suddenly contrite. "We pride ourselves on working with all our tenants, particularly those from your fine company. What I was starting to suggest was we could enter into an agreement today, with a deposit of say twenty-five dollars, calling for you to return next Saturday to sign the lease and pay the remainder of the funds. Would something like that be agreeable to you, Mr. Fearsithe?"

I paused for effect before saying, "Yes, I believe I could see my way clear to do that."

"And I'm trusting you will convey to your employer just how cooperative we have been," he added.

"Oh, yes, most definitely," I replied. "You draw up the agreement, and I'll return to sign the lease and move in next Saturday."

The agent wasted no time in preparing the agreement according to the terms he had outlined. I paid him twenty-five dollars before I departed. Within a matter of a week, I was now gainfully employed and would soon reside in one of the more luxurious apartment buildings in Portland. My dream was beginning to take shape!

Before I returned to the Goodnough Building, I stopped by the tailor's shop and picked up my navy suit. Mr. Frank insisted I try it on while I was there; but, as expected, everything fit perfectly.

When I arrived at the rooming house, I informed Reginald of my plans to move out in a week's time. Surprisingly, his scowl momentarily disappeared as he replied, "I'm going to hate to see you go. You've brought some excitement to the place during the short time you've been here!"

That night, I ran into Clyde in the dining room and asked if he and Elenore would like to join me the next day for an excursion to Vancouver, Washington.

"I hear there's a baseball game there tomorrow afternoon," I said. "The field batters from the Vancouver Barracks are playing the Portland Colts, and I'd like to visit the army barracks in the morning. We could leave from here at nine o'clock."

Clyde accepted my invitation and felt sure Elenore would want to join us.

The next morning, the three of us boarded a streetcar that took us to the ferry landing at the Columbia River. It was a beautiful spring day. The cherry blossoms and tulips were in full bloom creating a vibrant display of color, and the temperature was warmer than normal for this time of year. Everyone appeared to be out of doors enjoying the beauty of the day.

Thus, we ended up having to wait for the ferry to make two round trips before we were able to board. The fifteen-minute crossing was pleasant as we traveled about 1,500 feet across the river to Washington. The Vancouver Barracks was located a relatively short distance from the ferry landing, so we decided to walk.

Clyde and Elenore apparently knew very little about the barracks, so I filled them in on what I knew.

"The base serves as headquarters for the Department of the Columbia, which oversees military operations across the Pacific Northwest. It houses infantry regiments, cavalry units, and several artillery batteries, all of which are stationed here for training and to remain in a state of readiness."

"How is it you know so much about it?" Clyde asked.

"My father was in the Army before I was born," I told him, "and I always thought I would join up as well. He took me to visit military installations throughout the mid-Atlantic from the time I was old enough to walk. I've read up on the barracks around the U.S. for most of my life. That's why I even visited a few on my way here to Portland."

"Gene, why didn't you join up?" Elenore asked.

"By the time I was old enough, my mother had just died. I felt I needed to stay with my father to keep an eye on him. I considered it once again a few months ago, before I decided to come out here, but by then my aspirations had changed. Instead of serving my country in the military, I decided I could better serve by helping shape our nation's future. And now, I'll be doing that by helping establish shipping lines. It's all important."

When we arrived at the main gate, two infantrymen were assigned to show us around. One's name was Jackson and the other was Tyler. Jackson told us he and his entire company were shipping out to Honolulu on May 9. He was looking forward to it. He had grown up on a farm in Iowa and had never traveled farther than ten miles from home.

"Now," he said with a smile, "I'm going to see the world—starting with the girls wearing those grass hula skirts!"

Tyler, however, was just the opposite. "You won't catch me going to a place like that, unless I'm dressed in orange," he said.

Seeing the quizzical expressions on Clyde and Elenore, I explained. "He means unless he's arrested and wearing a prisoner's orange jumpsuit."

"So where do you want to go, Tyler?" I asked.

"I don't much care," he replied, "as long as it's here in the U.S."

The two men did a good job of showing us around the base, then took us to the baseball field where the game was about to get underway.

"So, for whom are we going to cheer?" Elenore asked.

"Well, I don't know about you two," I responded, "but I'm going to root for Army. It almost seems like the patriotic thing to do!"

It was a good game and Army won 6-4. Clyde and Elenore had decided to cheer for the Colts until it became clear they were going to lose—then they switched to my side! We had an uneventful trip back to Portland as we chatted about our day and agreed it had been just the kind of simple, pleasurable excursion we all needed.

The Merry Widow was set to open the next night. It would be a decisive moment in Elenore's acting career. Clyde was scheduled to meet with his company partners in the morning. He was certain it would determine the course of his career. And I was about to embark on my career in industrial espionage. I think we all knew our lives were about to change—just like Jackson's and Tyler's. And I think we realized our lives weren't going to be quite as simple anymore.

21

MONDAY, APRIL 22

~

*W*hen I arrived at the offices of OWR&N at fifteen minutes before eight, Miss Adams was already waiting for me at reception. I realized I would need to arrive much earlier if I ever planned to be at the office before her.

She introduced me to the woman at the front desk.

"Mrs. Brown, I want to let you know that Mr. Eugene Fearsithe has joined the company as the executive assistant to Mr. Hall for the steamship division. His office will be located in the space immediately across the corridor from me, and I will be providing whatever secretarial assistance he requires."

"Mr. Fearsithe, welcome aboard," Mrs. Brown said, as she stood and shook my hand. "If I can ever be of any assistance to you, please do not hesitate to call on me."

"Mrs. Brown, it is truly a pleasure to officially meet you," I told her. "Having observed the magnificent manner in which you carry out your duties, I am already convinced you are the hub of the OWR&N wheel that keeps this company functioning efficiently. I look forward to learning from you in the days ahead."

She acknowledged my comment with a smile as Miss Adams whisked me away to my office.

"Miss Adams, should I be leaving breadcrumbs along the path so I can find my way out at the end of the day?" I asked, as we made our way through the maze of hallways.

"I am most certain a resourceful man like yourself will be more than capable of finding his way out," Miss Adams replied with the slightest of smiles.

When we arrived at my office, I was impressed to see an engraved name-plate had already been installed on my door:

R. Eugene Fearsithe
Executive Assistant, Steamship Division

The room was larger than Miss Adam's work area and had an exterior window that provided natural light. It was furnished with a paneled wooden desk, a leather desk chair and a wooden worktable with four wooden armchairs surrounding it. The office was appointed nicely, and though it was not as grand as Emmett's, it surpassed anything to which I was accustomed.

Everything appeared to be set up and ready for me to begin work. A telephone was situated at the corner of my desk, together with a brass desk lamp. In the middle of the worktable was a carafe of hot coffee sitting on a tray with two cups.

"I have the feeling I have you to thank for getting everything ready for me," I said to Miss Adams. "Since you only learned of my arrival late Friday, you must have worked through the weekend to get everything in place. Thank you for your efforts to make me feel so welcome."

"It was my pleasure, Mr. Fearsithe," she replied. "Your phone extension is working. All incoming calls will be routed through me, so I can keep you from being interrupted at inopportune times."

"I noticed Mrs. Brown does not use a telephone to announce guests," I commented, "but rather the more antiquated method of sending messengers. I wondered if telephones were not used for communication within the office."

"No, that is not the case, Mr. Fearsithe," she replied. "We do rely heavily on our telephones. However, the officers of our company have insisted we not introduce the use of a telephone in the reception area, so guests are not subjected to the ringing of telephones as they enter our building."

"Thank you for the explanation, Miss Adams. I'm certain I will have many more questions before I finally know my way around. One more thing— would you call me Gene when it is just the two of us speaking? If we are going to work so closely together, I do not want us to be so formal."

"Thank you for your thoughtfulness, Mr. Fearsithe," she replied, "but OWR&N has a strict policy that men and women are only to address one another using surnames."

"Oh, I'm so sorry, I did not know about the policy," I responded, somewhat embarrassed.

"Do not be concerned," she replied. "Part of my job is to help you navigate through the many OWR&N policies. Now, Mr. Fearsithe, it is one minute before eight, and I imagine Mr. Hall is ready to see you in his office. Please follow me."

As we arrived in the anteroom, Miss Adams turned toward me and said with a slight smile, "By the way, that's a nice suit, Mr. Fearsithe!"

The clock on Emmett's mantel began to strike the hour as I walked through his door.

"Good morning, Gene, and welcome," he greeted me. "I trust you found your office to be satisfactory?"

"Good morning to you, sir," I replied, "and yes, it was even more than I expected. Thank you for making sure I was welcomed so warmly."

"It is just an example of how much OWR&N values our employees," Emmett added. "You'll find the company also rewards good performance in very tangible ways. I'm sure you will discover that firsthand, as I have no doubt you will be one of our top performers.

"To that end, pour yourself a cup of coffee, and let's get to work."

Emmett led me over to the framed map of the Pacific Northwest hanging on his wall. The ports of Portland, Astoria, and Seattle, plus Victoria and Vancouver in British Columbia, were marked with green flags. The cities of Kalama, Chehalis, and Olympia were marked with yellow flags. Port Madison and Port Townsend were marked with red flags.

"I presume the green flags indicate the ports in which you are currently operating," I said.

"That's correct," Emmett replied. "The ports marked in yellow represent where we are currently in negotiation; those in red designate where negotiations have stalled."

"I regret to inform you that negotiations in the ports marked yellow will also stall."

"How do you know that, Gene?" Emmett asked.

"Because Archer Winslow has promised those port authorities the moon to keep you out," I replied. "He has also tied up Tacoma and Coupeville with similar promises—commitments, I might add, that he has no intention of keeping. His plan is to make good on those promises only to the extent he needs to until you—or I guess it's now "we"—pull out of the running. Once he has eliminated the competition, he'll renegotiate his promises to his advantage."

"How much has he promised those ports?"

"All inclusive to cover dockage, wharfage, pilotage, and tonnage fees. He has offered them fourteen percent of the freight revenue generated through their port," I answered.

"Fourteen percent?!?" Emmett exclaimed. "There is no way he can afford to pay that!"

"Ultimately, he doesn't plan to pay it," I reminded Emmett. "He'll only pay it until he has frozen us out of the deal."

"Gene, are you sure that's correct?" Emmett questioned. "Or was he just providing you with misinformation since he knew you were coming to work for us?"

"Perhaps," I acknowledged. "But while he was out of the room, I looked over some of the invoices from those port cities. They were in a folder on his table, and they confirmed those amounts."

"How do we negotiate against that?"

"We offer two percent more than he has—but only if the cities give us an exclusive use agreement for ten years," I replied.

"Sixteen percent?!?" Emmett practically shouted. "You must be crazier than Archer! There's no way we can afford to pay that! We'd be out of business in a year. Our board will laugh at me if I bring them that proposal!"

"Perhaps, Emmett," I agreed. "But what if that proposal includes an eight percent hike in our freight rate that not only offsets the increased cost but also adds an additional two percent to our bottom line?"

"How could we possibly increase our rates by eight percent?" Emmett looked at me as if I had lost my mind.

"Because we will have exclusive use of those ports," I explained. "Therefore, we will have complete control of scheduling, enabling us to provide our customers with expedited shipping. No longer will they be forced to contend with inconvenient delays while the various steamship companies jockey for access to the docks.

"They will welcome the change and pass along the increased cost to their customers. Soon the other cities will be knocking on our door to make the same arrangement. Overall, I project once it is fully implemented,

OWR&N will yield a twenty-five percent increase in the company's net profit. I don't expect the board would laugh at that proposal."

I stopped talking to let Emmett consider this new information. The silence was almost deafening.

"Gene, if that's all true, I'd say you just earned your salary," Emmett said with a smile.

"Well, Emmett, I'd say I just earned a whole lot more than my salary," I smiled in return.

"Go ahead and write up the plan so I can present it to our board," Emmett directed. "Bring me a first draft at eight in the morning," he added as he stood to his feet. "And like I said earlier, welcome to the OWR&N team!"

I spent the remainder of the day preparing the draft of the plan. I didn't even bother to stop for lunch. I attempted to address every possible question the board might ask. By the time I was done, and Miss Adams had typed it up, I felt pretty positive it was a good proposal.

I exited the office around six o'clock and returned to the rooming house. I stopped by the registration desk and asked Reginald for another piece of paper, an envelope, and a stamp. I wrote on the paper:

First phase complete. I present draft proposal in the morning.

I sealed the envelope and left it for the mail carrier with the feeling that both of my employers should be well pleased with my first day on the job. But I knew ultimately only one would truly be pleased.

I picked up a copy of today's *Oregon Journal* someone left on a table in the dining room. I decided to catch up on the day's news while I enjoyed a dinner of roast beef, mashed potatoes with gravy, and corn. The meal wasn't quite like the one at the Portland Hotel, but it cost a whole lot less!

The main stories in the news included:

A U.S. Senate subcommittee listened in horror during their hearing on Friday as Titanic Second Officer Charles Lightoller testified that the crew had loaded as few as twenty-five people into the lifeboats that were intended to hold sixty-five, because they feared the ropes that were being used to lower the boats could not bear any more weight.

# # #

On Saturday, immediate reforms were ordered by the International Mercantile Marine, requiring all steamers to carry sufficient lifeboats and rafts for all passengers and crew.

# # #

On that same day, the luxury ocean liner, SS France, began its maiden voyage from Le Havre, France, carrying 1,273 passengers. The liner had originally been scheduled to carry its full capacity of 2,026 passengers, but the owner had been forced to accept 753 cancellations in light of the RMS Titanic tragedy. Compagnie Générale Transatlantique, the owner of the liner, reported that the liner was equipped with lifeboats sufficient for all passengers and crew. It is scheduled to arrive in New York City in six days.

The fact that 1,273 people were brave enough to sail across the ocean just five days after the sinking of the Titanic was pretty amazing. I couldn't help but wonder if the company should be paying those passengers to make the voyage instead of the other way around!

The companies were now being held accountable to ensure proper safety measures were taken. No one had envisioned the need for more lifeboats on the Titanic because no one believed it could sink. I'm sure someone in management decided there was no more room for additional lifeboats—the space should be used to accommodate more passengers, which equaled more profits. But they had learned a hard lesson.

In some ways, that was the same game being played by my two employers. Though Archer's practice may be the more despicable of the two—as well as mine, since I have chosen to be complicit in his plan—Emmett and OWR&N are not without some culpability in this cat-and-mouse game of profit and loss. The big companies will never actually pay the cost for their decisions; it is their passengers and the consumers of the goods they carry. In short, we would all pay the price, and in the process some wrong decisions were being made.

But I have come to believe that's what big dreams are made of. Don't misunderstand my sentiment. I am not a socialist; I'm a capitalist. I believe in the law of supply and demand. But that law must be followed in a way that demonstrates moral responsibility. And I'm afraid that underlying principle has been abandoned in our industrial revolution.

I decided it was time to stop philosophizing for the night. Instead, I would find Clyde and see how his meeting had gone this morning. But then I remembered he would be attending Elenore's opening night performance. If Maggie and I hadn't had a falling out, I would have been there as well. But alas, that wasn't the case.

I was again reminded of how much can happen in one week.

22

TUESDAY, APRIL 23 – WEDNESDAY, APRIL 24

⁓

I arrived at the office at half-past seven and somehow managed to find my way to my office. I made only two wrong turns along the way! Miss Adams was already busily working at her desk.

"Good morning, Miss Adams," I greeted her. "My first question for you today is a simple one. Do you ever go home? You were here when I left last night, and you are here before me this morning."

"Oh yes, I go home, Mr. Fearsithe," she replied. "I grew up on a farm in Kansas, and my parents instilled the principle, 'early to bed and early to rise,' in me from a very young age. It has always served me well."

"Well, I must tell you that OWR&N and Mr. Hall, specifically, are very lucky to have you working for them," I said. "And now I, too, share in their luck."

"You are most kind, Mr. Fearsithe," she replied humbly. "Actually, I think I am the one who is blessed to be here."

I could sense my comments were making her uncomfortable, so I retreated to my office, poured myself a cup of coffee, and spent the remaining minutes going over the proposal. At one minute before eight, I walked over to Emmett's office.

I spent the next hour reviewing it with him, responding to his questions, and making note of his suggested revisions. By the time we were done, I could tell he had truly embraced the plan and was prepared to champion it with the board.

That was an important component of Archer's plan.

"It is of utmost importance," Archer had told me, "that Emmett Hall owns this idea as if he came up with it himself. He must demonstrate that kind of ownership and passion if he is going to convince his board to implement the plan."

In the short time I had known Emmett, I had come to appreciate that he was a good man—a moral man. Yes, he was a company man, but he was also a family man. I knew this plan was ultimately going to fail because Archer had designed it that way. If I played my part well, it was going to fail in a big way. But for the first time, I realized a failure of this proportion would cost Emmett his job. It would cost him everything he had worked for over the years.

I didn't mind OWR&N paying a price. After all, this was business. There need to be winners and losers for the game to be played. But knowing it would likely lead to a good man losing his career was a matter I had not considered. I made every effort to push that thought out of my mind as the day went on. But no matter how hard I tried, I couldn't stop thinking about the cost to Emmett.

I spent the day revising the proposal with the suggestions Emmett had made. When six o'clock came around, the updated proposal was on my desk ready for my meeting the next morning. I told Miss Adams good night and made my way to the rooming house in hopes of meeting up with Clyde.

Fortunately, he had received the written message I left for him the night before and was ready to have dinner together.

"How have your first two days at OWR&N gone, Gene?" he asked. "Have they made you president yet?" he added with a chuckle.

"No, not yet," I smiled. "But I wouldn't expect them to promote me to president until my second week! In all seriousness though, everything has gone really well. The people are hard-working and very supportive of one another. It's not the 'dog-eat-dog' environment I had anticipated. But enough about me! How did your meeting with the partners go yesterday?"

"They presented me with a formal offer to become a partner," Clyde told me excitedly. "The agreement calls for me to make a capital contribution, but it is a fair amount and commensurate with the company's current value. I already have a portion of the capital saved up from my earnings, and they have agreed to allow me to invest the remainder on a monthly basis over the course of the next two years."

"So, have you agreed?" I asked.

"Yes," he said with a smile, "we signed the agreement this morning!"

"Well, congratulations!" I exclaimed. "This truly calls for a celebration. Unfortunately, I do not have enough money right now to take you to the Portland Hotel restaurant again. How about the dining room here?"

"That suits me just fine," Clyde replied. "We'll have plenty of opportunities to eat with the swells in the days ahead!" he added with a laugh.

Over dinner, he told me about the opening night of the play.

"Elenore performed admirably. She made our graduating class of '07 proud! And I must confess, I was proud to be there as her guest. The audience gave the cast a standing ovation and demanded three curtain calls. I wish you could have been there. You would have been proud of her—and of Maggie, too! I'm certain Elenore can get you a ticket for another night. Just let me know!"

"It sounds like the two of you may be getting serious," I remarked.

"I know I did not pay her much attention in high school," Clyde replied, "but she has me bewitched now, my friend. I know it's too soon, but I may just ask her to marry me once I'm more established in my new partnership. Who would have thought we had to travel across the country to find each other?"

"You two make a fine couple," I said. "I hope it all works out!"

"What about you, Gene?" Clyde asked. "Do you think you and Maggie could reconcile?"

"I don't think so. For some reason, I don't think our relationship is salvageable. But I have met another young woman who has caught my eye."

"Who is she, and how did you meet her?"

"I'm not saying just yet," I answered. "She reminds me a lot of Sara, so I want to see if anything develops."

We spent the rest of the night reminiscing about high school and how amazing it was to be together during this stage of our lives. 'Who would have imagined?" we both said on more than one occasion that night.

I washed my linen when I got back to my room so I would have a clean shirt for work the next day. Counting the suit I had traveled in, I had only two suits. And it would be another three weeks before Mr. Frank completed the third one. I decided I would need to order another custom-made suit as soon as I could afford it. But I still wanted to look sharp each day. If I was going to be successful, I needed to look the part.

I arrived at the office at 7:20 a.m. Wednesday at the exact same time as Miss Adams.

"I have finally learned how early I must get up if I'm going to beat you here, Miss Adams," I said as I held the door open for her.

"You have indeed, Mr. Fearsithe," she said with a smile, "though I didn't know it had become a competition."

"Oh, not a competition," I replied, "merely a curiosity."

"But now you will have to wait while I get everything prepared for you and Mr. Hall," she said.

"I assure you, it will not be an imposition," I countered. "Besides, I've already had my morning coffee. Why don't you show me where it is made, and I'll brew it this morning?"

"No, I'm afraid that won't do, Mr. Fearsithe," Miss Adams declared. "It's just not the OWR&N way!"

"Oh, well, heaven forbid I should violate another company policy, Miss Adams," I poked fun. "You will have to provide me with a list of these do's and don'ts before I utterly destroy my future with the company!"

"I will endeavor to be your protector in that regard, Mr. Fearsithe," she quipped. "But only if you don't try to run out ahead of me. Now if you'll excuse me, I have some lost time I need to make up."

I, too, wanted to make sure I had everything in order for my eight o'clock presentation to Emmett, so I ensconced myself in my office and started working. My one-hour meeting with him proved to be a repeat of the previous morning. I presented; he probed and made further revisions. Though I agreed his points were legitimate concerns, I wondered why they had not surfaced during our earlier discussions.

I was becoming concerned that the reason this ocean liner needed such a wide berth to turn was a culture of over analysis. I am all for minimizing our margin of error and the implications of any mistakes, but I also believe that delaying a decision due to protracted analysis is a mistake.

I dutifully spent the rest of the day making Emmett's revisions. When I left the office at quarter past six, I was confident all issues had been addressed, and I was ready for my meeting with Emmett the next morning. I noticed the lamp in Miss Adams' anteroom was already off. Apparently, I had now discovered her daily departure time as well.

As I walked past a newsie standing on the corner selling papers, I heard him declare, "Taft beats Teddy in New Hampshire primary! Read all about it!"

I couldn't believe my ears. Had President Taft actually bested the unbeatable Teddy Roosevelt in the New Hampshire Republican primary election for president? Everybody knew that whoever was chosen at the Republican Convention in Chicago in a few weeks was going to win the presidency. Were we really going to give Taft a second term? I handed the newsboy two cents so I could "read all about it."

Since it was a pleasant evening, I walked to the park along Southwest Park Avenue. I sat on an empty bench and began to read my paper.

About twenty minutes later, I noticed Miss Adams walking along the avenue on the other side of the street. My curiosity got the better of me when she turned a corner, so I got up and started following her. It was hard for me to imagine she had a life outside of OWR&N.

By the time I got to the corner, I spotted her about a block ahead of me. I quickened my pace to narrow the gap, but she suddenly halted and entered a building on her left. When I got closer, I read the sign out front:

Mount Zion Baptist Church
Rev. Tyrone Nelson
Sunday Worship 11 a.m. & 7 p.m.
Wednesday Service 7 p.m.
All are welcome!

So Miss Adams was a church lady! And she attended on Wednesday nights no less. That began to explain a lot of things. My mother had been a church lady. Even though I had attended for most of my life, I did not consider myself a church man. But I respected people who were—as long as they didn't try to impose their beliefs on me. I winced slightly as I recalled Rev. Cooper from the train.

But now I was even more curious about Miss Adams. What had drawn her to this church? I decided to go in and sit in the back out of view.

The congregation began to sing just as I stepped inside the doorway. As I opened the sanctuary door, a well-dressed man about thirty years my senior smiled at me and extended his hand in greeting.

"Welcome, mister," he said. "We're glad you're here. Can I help you find a seat?"

"No, I'll just sit right here, thank you," I said as I pointed to the back row.

"Suit yourself," he nodded.

I joined in the singing, making sure to keep my volume low so as not to attract any attention. I was familiar with both hymns from my days attending church.

When the singing concluded, a man who appeared to be the pastor came to the pulpit and said, "Please open your Bibles to Luke chapter fifteen, and let's read verses eleven through twenty-four:

Jesus said: "A certain man had two sons. And the younger of them said to his fa-
ther, 'Father, give me the portion of goods that falls to me.' So he divided his liveli-

hood. *And not many days after, the younger son took his portion, journeyed to a far country, and there wasted his possessions with prodigal living.*

But when he had spent all, there arose a severe famine in that land, and he began to be in want. Then he went and joined himself to a citizen of that country, and he sent him into his fields to feed swine. And he would gladly have filled his stomach with the pods that the swine ate, and no one gave him anything.

But when he came to himself, he said, 'How many of my father's hired servants have bread enough and to spare, and I perish with hunger! I will arise and go to my father, and will say to him, "Father, I have sinned against heaven and before you, and I am no longer worthy to be called your son. Make me like one of your hired servants."'

And he arose and came to his father. But when he was still a great way off, his father saw him and had compassion, and ran and fell on his neck and kissed him. And the son said to him, 'Father, I have sinned against heaven and in your sight, and am no longer worthy to be called your son.'

But the father said to his servants, 'Bring out the best robe and put it on him, and put a ring on his hand and sandals on his feet. And bring the fatted calf here and kill it, and let us eat and be merry; for this my son was dead and is alive again; he was lost and is found.' And they began to be merry."[1]

"In this parable of the lost son," the preacher continued, "we see two beautiful pictures: one of repentance, and the other of acceptance. The rebellious son comes to the end of himself—and realizes just how far he has fallen. He knows his selfish ways have led to failure and destruction. He has exhausted everything the world has to offer and has been left empty and broken—lying in a pigsty. He literally has hit bottom and knows there is only one choice. He can continue to remain in his filth, or he can seek his father's forgiveness.

"Having gone as far as he can on the path away from his father, the son makes a 180-degree turn back toward his father. That's the picture of repentance: coming face to face with the reality of our sin, lamenting over our sin and its effects on ourselves, on others, and on God. We must confess our sins and ask forgiveness from God and from those we have wronged. We admit we are powerless over our sin and make a 180-degree turn back to God.

"And God is there to meet us and accept us with outstretched arms, ready to forgive us and restore our relationship with Him. Picture the son's rags being exchanged for a fine robe, his once filthy feet now being cradled in his father's sandals, and the signet ring on his finger showing he has been restored.

"Then he is brought into a celebration banquet announcing to the world of his return. What a gift! Jesus extends that very same gift of forgiveness and restoration to 'notorious sinners' like me—and like you. There is no one too sinful to receive it, as long as we are not too hard-hearted or proud to accept it!"

I'd read that parable before. I'd even heard a sermon or two preached about it. But it was the preacher's last sentence that caught my attention: *"There is no one too sinful to receive it, as long as we are not too hard-hearted or proud to accept it!"*

I suddenly felt really uncomfortable. I quietly stood to my feet to slip out, but as I did, I noticed two people looking at me: the preacher . . . and Miss Adams.

---

1. Luke 15:11-24

23

THURSDAY, APRIL 25 – FRIDAY, APRIL 26

~

*S*uddenly, I felt more alone than I ever had. I looked around and discovered I was lying in a filthy sty surrounded by pigs. *What am I doing in this place?* The preacher was standing behind me saying, "Your selfish pursuit has led you here. Will you continue to lie here in this filth, or will you return to those you abandoned and embrace the dream God has designed for you?"

My father was standing before me looking helplessly across the distance calling out, "God, my son is lost! Help him find his way home!"

To my left, Miss Adams sat behind her typewriter pointing to a woman standing nearby. "You and she have been created for each other, Mr. Fearsithe. Nothing you do will ever be enough—without her by your side," she quietly whispered.

As I followed her gaze, I saw Sara, with her gentle smile and outstretched arms waiting to receive me.

No matter how much I struggled, I couldn't break free of that pigsty. I was sinking deeper and deeper into the filth. Finally I found the strength to sit up. As I did, I awakened to the reality I was in my bed, and the bedsheets were drenched in sweat. As my eyes adjusted to the darkness, I regained my senses.

What was that all about? I thought. *I'm not lying in a pigsty. I'm on the road to achieving more than I could have ever imagined. A week ago I had nothing, but now I am on the path to achieving everything I ever wanted!*

That preacher's sermon had played tricks with my mind, I decided. *That's what I get for walking into a church. I'll have to remember that the next time I'm curious.* Though it was only 5:30 a.m., I decided there was no sense trying to get any further sleep.

Instead, I got up and got ready for the day. I did not want to arrive at the office early because I knew Miss Adams had seen me leave her church—and I wanted to avoid an awkward conversation. I decided to enjoy an early morning walk through the streets of Portland. It would help clear my mind of that ridiculous dream.

On my way out of the rooming house, Reginald called me over to retrieve a message. He handed me a sealed envelope that contained a note:

Come by my home at 8:00 p.m. tonight.

When I walked into my office a while later, my mind was clear, hot coffee was in my carafe, and Miss Adams was busily working at her desk. I didn't really need any time to prepare for the morning's presentation. I knew the proposal and all of its nuances backward and forward. I gathered my papers and walked straight into Emmett's office.

Everything went smoothly, and I could tell Emmett was grasping at straws to find further revisions. But by the time we were done, even he had to admit that no more changes were necessary.

Before I left his office, Emmett said he wanted me to join him the following morning when he presented the proposal to the board.

"That way, if any questions arise for which I require your assistance, you'll be right there. Also, it will give me an opportunity to introduce you to the board members. Are you ready for that?"

"By all means," I replied. It was important that the board agree to proceed with the proposal tomorrow, so we could begin implementation next week. Otherwise, Archer would find himself overextended in his offers to the same cities, and his house of cards would come crashing down. "I look forward to it," I continued.

"And Gene, put the finishing touches on the tactical implementation plan today, so we can brief our full team tomorrow after we have board approval," Emmett added.

I spent the remainder of the day finalizing the plan. I chose to have minimal contact with Miss Adams, electing to keep our brief exchanges professional. To her credit, she made no reference to the prior evening and did not question whether I had been following her.

Promptly at six o'clock, I left the office to avoid the two of us leaving at the same time. I headed directly to the rooming house to get some dinner before my evening appointment. While I ate, I looked at the paper to catch up on the day's news and was surprised to read:

```
The RMS Olympic, sister ship of the White Star
ocean  liner  RMS  Titanic  was  barred  from
departing  Southampton,  England  for  New  York
```

City yesterday afternoon with its 1,400 passen-
gers because of a strike by ship workers over
insufficient lifeboats. The White Star Line has
now made arrangements to add sixteen "collapsi-
ble" boats which can quickly be deployed if
needed.

Whoever failed to make sure there were enough lifeboats—or worse, whoever decided against adding the number needed—most assuredly was now standing on the soup line. I wondered if the White Star line would be able to survive the negative publicity regarding passenger safety. I made a note to make sure OWR&N was in full compliance with all of our safety measures.

It was still light when I set out for Portland Heights, but the sun had set by the time I arrived. I presented myself at the tradesman's door as requested. Church appeared to be expecting me this time and immediately showed me to the library.

"Good evening, Gene," Archer said as he stood to greet me. "Thanks for joining me at this late hour, but I thought it best if we met after dark. Would you care for anything to drink? Coffee or tea, perhaps? Or something stronger?"

"Black coffee will suit just fine," I replied. Church immediately set out to get it for me.

"Gene, tell me about your week thus far," Archer requested.

"As I reported in my message on Monday," I began, "Emmett Hall embraced the proposal. Since then, we have been fine-tuning the presentation he will make to the board tomorrow morning."

"Oh yes," Archer chuckled, "I have heard about Union Pacific's infamous board meetings and their penchant for hammering their proposals to death. Their slowness in making decisions is one of their greatest weaknesses. Will you be with him when he makes the presentation?"

"Yes, I will. He asked me to join him in case a question arises that he and I have not yet discussed."

"Good," Archer responded. "I'm glad to hear it. Does he anticipate any resistance from the board?"

"The only one he has expressed concern about is William Moore, Esq. Apparently, Mr. Moore is on the boards of several railroad and shipping companies including OWR&N. He may have concerns over how our strategy affects those other companies, even though they do not compete in our region."

"Yes, I'm very familiar with William Moore," Archer said. "He will definitely ask the most questions. But when it comes down to it, he will not allow concerns regarding his other companies to affect what he believes is best for OWR&N. And I don't think he will suspect what I'm doing. So between his trust in Emmett, and the good impression you will make on the board, I think he will vote to approve the proposal. Where are you on the tactical implementation plan?"

"Assuming approval by the board, Emmett and I will brief the leadership team tomorrow afternoon," I replied. "My plan is for us to approach the Tacoma authority first at the beginning of next week. The director of the authority, Mr. Richard Anders, seems like he would be amenable to the proposal and the least resistant to grant OWR&N exclusive rights over the trade—both in and out of the port—as long as it benefits the port. Do you agree, Archer? Have I read him correctly?"

"Yes, you have, Gene," Archer confirmed. "I completely agree with your assessment. Actually, he is the first one I would approach as well. He also has influence over the other port directors. Once you have him on board, the others will more readily agree.

"Gene, I knew I had the right man for the job when I selected you! How quickly will you be able to approach the others?"

"Presuming Anders agrees, our plan is to complete our presentations to the initial seven ports in a two-week time frame," I replied.

"Excellent!" Archer declared. "And I assume you will be the one meeting with each of the port authority directors. That timetable is perfect. Well done! Let's plan to meet again next Saturday night at eight o'clock if you are back in town. If anything unexpected develops in the meantime, send me a message and we can talk sooner.

"By the way, Gene, I hear you are planning to take an apartment in the Marlborough Building. That is an excellent choice! I'm sure you will enjoy living there."

"Thank you, Archer. But how did you know about that?"

"Because I own the building through one of my landholding companies," Archer answered to my surprise. "The rental agent sent me your agreement to approve, which I have done and returned to him for you to sign on Saturday. I expect your weekly salary payment will help you settle your lease, will it not? And I included a $100 bonus for a job well done!" Archer added as he handed me an envelope containing $200. "By the way, you did a good job putting the agent in his place. I couldn't have done it better myself."

Archer rang for Church to come show me out, but not before he presented me with another one of those fine Cuban cigars! It made my walk back to the rooming house in the moonlight even more enjoyable. But I was also glad I had remembered to bring my billy club—just in case.

~

I arrived at the office the next morning dressed in my blue suit, tie, and shoes, as well as my newest shirt. I wanted to look my best for our presentation today. I had even stopped for a shave and haircut on my way home from Archer's.

I was grateful I hadn't had another restless night filled with unsettling dreams; I felt refreshed and prepared for my big day. Though I continued to avoid Miss Adams, as the day progressed, I had the sense she also wanted to avoid conversation.

Emmett stopped by my office on his way to the boardroom so we could walk together.

"Don't be nervous, Gene," he encouraged. "I know it's your first time to make a presentation to the board, but it's not my first time. Just follow my lead. I'll do all the talking unless I need your help on a detail. In that case, I'll make it clear that I'm asking you to speak. And if I do ask, it will be because I have every confidence you will do well."

We were the first to arrive in the room; the board members all began to arrive immediately after us. Emmett made a point to introduce me to each one as he entered. First was Mr. Henry Villard, the chairman. He is a distinguished gentleman who looks to be about sixty years of age. He served as the president of another one of Union Pacific's divisions until he was named chairman of OWR&N.

Next was Samuel Hill, also in his early sixties. He is a prominent businessman, philanthropist, and advocate for the development of a sound transportation infrastructure in the Northwest.

The third man I met was William Moore, whom I already felt I knew based
on the conversations I'd had with Emmett and Archer. He was younger
than I anticipated; I would guess in his early fifties.

The fourth was Julius Meier, who was by far the youngest member, probably in his late thirties. He is a Portland native, born of parents who had
emigrated from Germany. He is already a respected businessman and a
rising candidate in local politics.

The last member was Charles Ladd. In his mid-fifties, he is a prominent
banker and businessman.

Each of the men greeted me cordially and made me feel at ease. The group
appeared to have a good esprit de corps and clearly respected one another's abilities. They also conducted themselves, individually and as a
group, in a no-nonsense manner.

Henry Villard promptly called the meeting to order and invited Emmett to
make the presentation. Each member had a typewritten copy of the
proposal, which he had received the day before. Emmett did an excellent
job of presenting the proposal, and the members' initial questions indicated their favorable assessment.

As expected, William Moore raised the most challenging question.

"Mr. Hall," he began, "as you know there is much discussion taking place
in Washington, D.C., about restricting businesses from gaining exclusive
rights or control of services in order to eliminate competition. In many
respects, this proposal does just that. Though no laws have been enacted to

preclude an action like this, it is quite conceivable that one will be passed in the near future. How do you believe this action would stand up against such a law?"

"Mr. Fearsithe and I have discussed this at length, Mr. Moore," Emmett replied, "so with your permission, I would like him to address your concern."

"Please do, Mr. Fearsithe," he responded. "I look forward to hearing your opinion."

"Mr. Moore, as you know," I replied, "it is impossible to determine what such a law will look like when it finally makes its way out of Congress. So we do not know for certain what, if any, parts of our proposal would be restricted by such a law.

"However, Mr. Hall and I are not suggesting this proposal should be a long-term strategy. Rather, we anticipate it being two to five years. By then, we will have full control of the ports and the shipping lanes, plus be in a position to open up some opportunity for minimal competition. The timing and nature of those changes can be made as needed to ensure we are in full compliance with any new laws."

Emmett smiled and nodded at me indicating I had adequately addressed Mr. Moore's concern. And Mr. Moore's follow-up statement confirmed that no further details were needed.

A few minutes later, the board unanimously approved the proposal and recommended we move forward immediately. Since our part of the meeting had concluded, Emmett and I were dismissed with the board's compliments for a job well done!

I immediately telephoned Richard Anders in Tacoma and arranged to meet with him at ten o'clock Monday morning. I tasked Miss Adams with making arrangements for me to travel to Tacoma by train on Sunday afternoon.

Emmett and I briefed our leadership team and outlined the schedule. I would meet with each of the port authority directors over the next two weeks to gain their agreement, while the team made the necessary operational plans.

Around four o'clock, Emmett walked into my office and announced, "Gene, it has been a good day and an absolutely remarkable first week for you. Even I could never have anticipated what we could accomplish together in such a short period of time. But here we are—and I am so glad!

"Here is your first paycheck covering this week and last week. I don't believe there has ever been a first payroll check that was so well deserved. Why don't you get out of here a little early today since you'll be traveling Sunday?"

I appreciated Emmett's suggestion, particularly since I had not yet set up an account with a local bank. With the salary payments from both employers in my pocket, it was a matter of personal business I needed to attend to immediately.

∾

24

SATURDAY, APRIL 27 – SUNDAY, APRIL 28

◇

I t was half past eight when I woke up. I had decided to sleep in a little later than usual since none of the people I needed to see would be available before nine o'clock. I was moving out of the rooming house today, so I carried my packed suitcase with me down to reception.

As I approached Reginald, he said, "So today is the big day is it, Mr. Fearsithe?"

"Yes, it is," I replied, as I handed him the key to my room. "I believe I left everything in order, but if not, let me know when I come back later today and I will remedy it."

"Oh, I'm sure you did," Reginald responded. "What forwarding address should I use if I should receive any messages or inquiries?"

"The Marlborough Apartments on Morrison Avenue, apartment 1," I replied. "Speaking of which, I have several matters to attend to before I head over there this afternoon. Would it be too much trouble to ask you to watch my suitcase until I come back for it after lunch?"

"That will be no trouble whatsoever," he assured me.

My first stop was to see Jake at the *Journal* and give him my first weekly ten dollar payment. He inquired about my first week at my new job and reiterated his confidence that I would do well. I thanked him for his kindness and set out on my next errand.

I was just exiting the Goodnough Building when I ran into Miss Adams as she was entering.

"Well, Miss Adams, good morning to you," I said. "What a surprise to run into you!"

"Yes, we just seem to be running into each other all over town, don't we?" she replied. "But this is not per chance, I actually have come to see you."

"You have? What about?"

"I came to bring you your train ticket to Tacoma for tomorrow afternoon," she replied. "You left the office yesterday before the messenger delivered it, and I wanted to make certain it was in your hands."

"You are most kind, Miss Adams," I replied. "I had expected it would be waiting for me at the train station when I checked in tomorrow."

"I could have done that," she said. "However, I wanted to avoid any possibility that the ticket might be misplaced and your trip disrupted in some way."

"You truly are attentive to every detail, Miss Adams—going above and beyond, even on your day off!"

"I am a firm believer that if you are paid to do a job, you should perform that job to the absolute best of your ability," she remarked.

"And you do, Miss Adams," I replied. "You most definitely do."

I suddenly realized she was blushing at my compliment, so I changed the subject.

"What else do you have planned for this beautiful spring day?"

"I have not yet decided," she said. "But I see you are headed out. Where are you going?" She promptly blushed again. "Forgive me, Mr. Fearsithe. I did not mean to pry into your personal business."

"Think nothing of it," I said. "There is nothing secretive about my plans for the day. I am on my way to Lyman, Wolfe and Company to purchase a few pieces of furniture for my new apartment. But I dread going because my tastes are somewhat eclectic when it comes to furniture and furnishings. I fear my apartment will look like it was thrown together with whatever happened to be in the clearance bin."

Miss Adams laughed. "I doubt your taste is that bad. You seem to be very attentive to details in all that you do. I think you underestimate your own abilities, Mr. Fearsithe."

"Oh, I fear you are wrong, Miss Adams," I countered with a chuckle, "and if you are willing to take a short detour in your morning journey, I will prove it to you."

For a moment Miss Adams looked somewhat in a quandary as to what she should do.

"And if you would care to make any suggestions to save me from embarrassing myself, your recommendations would be greatly appreciated!" I added.

"I will join you, Mr. Fearsithe," she replied, "but only to convince you how capable you are in selecting your furnishings."

"You do me a great service, Miss Adams!" I exclaimed as we began our walk to the furniture store. "But I insist that if you are going to advise me on my home furnishings, you must call me Gene today. We'll return to being fellow employees on Monday morning."

Miss Adams hesitated for a moment. "Okay, Gene. But if that is the case, then you must call me Abigail."

"Abigail Adams? You mean just like John Adams' wife?"

"Yes, the very one!" Abigail responded, laughing. "My parents are both very passionate about U.S. history. That's why my older brother is named John, and my younger brother is named Quincy."

"I had no idea I was being assisted by such a celebrity," I said in jest. "I will make sure I show you the proper respect in the future."

"I will hold you to that," Abigail poked back.

"And I will trust you to use the same taste and skill you demonstrated when you furnished the White House!" I added, grinning.

As we walked along, Abigail confirmed that Lyman, Wolfe and Company was considered the finest purveyor of furniture and home furnishings in Portland.

"They most definitely are not the most inexpensive store in town, but they are known for their high quality," she elaborated.

When we arrived at the store, I was even more grateful that Abigail was with me. Once the salesclerk learned I was an executive at OWR&N, and I was taking an apartment in the Marlborough Building, he enthusiastically showed me a wide selection of styles. The more he showed me, the more confused I became. But Abigail came to my rescue.

The salesman initially thought Abigail and I were married—which proved to be a bit awkward. I explained we were friends, and that she had agreed to help me select furniture.

Abigail was able to discern from my comments that my taste leaned toward a blend of Art Nouveau and Colonial Revival. I was glad she knew what that meant! When she shared that with the clerk, he began showing me specific pieces of furniture that I really liked.

After almost two hours, I had all the furniture and furnishings I required to outfit my apartment. The salesman happily compiled a list of the items' cost, which exceeded $500. I never imagined making a purchase of such magnitude! The salesman was quick to point out that we had made the finest selections the store had to offer. "There is no question that Miss Adams has an eye for value," he said.

It was then I informed him I needed everything delivered that afternoon. My request obviously caught him by surprise. After some negotiating, he finally agreed to make delivery later that day. I, in turn, agreed to a price of $475. I wrote him a check, drawn on my new bank account, for ninety-five dollars, with the remaining balance payable in six monthly installments. My financial commitments were mounting, but given my income, I was not concerned.

It was almost noon when Abigail and I stepped outside from Lyman, Wolfe and Company.

"Abigail, I could not have done this without your assistance," I said. "I am forever in your debt. Will you permit me to take you to lunch as a small down payment on that debt?"

"Gene, you do not need to do that. It was my pleasure to help you. Besides, I have never had a hand in spending that much money in such a short period of time," she added with a smile.

"In that case, I can only imagine the appetite you have worked up," I laughed. "Do you like French food?"

"I don't believe I have ever tried any," Abigail answered thoughtfully.

"Then it's settled! You and I are going to enjoy a delicious French meal to appease our hunger and celebrate your prowess. It is the least I can do."

Abigail relented and we headed to the Lión Café. I had heard it was the premier French restaurant in Portland, known for its food, its service, and its atmosphere. And since it was also the only French restaurant I knew anything about, it was an easy choice.

As we walked, I continued to learn more about Abigail's family. They were still back in Iowa, working the family farm. Her parents had reluctantly bade her farewell when she chose to come out West. She had never lived in a city before Portland but loved it from the moment she arrived. She was hired by OWR&N on her third day here, thanks to the secretarial skills she had acquired in high school. She was fiercely loyal to OWR&N, and Emmett specifically, for giving her the opportunity.

Gradually she turned the conversation toward her faith.

"I surrendered my life to Jesus when I was ten years old," she said. "Since then He has been the most important person in my life. When I came to Portland, I knew I wasn't coming here alone. He had placed that desire in my heart. And I knew He was going before me to lead me every step of the way. So did my parents. That's why they sent me off with their blessing.

"The first few days I was in the city, I spotted Mount Zion Baptist Church and immediately knew I was supposed to attend there. I met Rev. Nelson the first Sunday, and our conversation confirmed it. I knew he had a heart to see Jesus known throughout the city. He wants the church to be a light-house in Portland, pointing people to Him—not only through words but also through our actions. I've never looked back.

"Gene, I must admit I was surprised to see you there the other night. I hadn't expected you to be a church-going man. What led you to the church this past Wednesday?"

I had considered what I might say if Abigail ever mentioned this subject, but I had never actually settled on a response. Given her honesty with me, I decided I had to be honest with her. I told her how I had spotted her on the street and followed to see where she was going. I admitted I probably would never have stepped inside the church if I hadn't been curious about where she was headed.

I could tell she was uncomfortable with what I divulged. But then she said, "We never know how God might use us in ways we would never expect. I never imagined He had used me to lead you to that service. What did you think of the pastor's message?"

I hadn't anticipated that question, and I knew I wasn't prepared to answer it honestly. But fortunately, we arrived at the restaurant and our conversation was interrupted.

The Lión lived up to its expectations! We both enjoyed our meal, and I was able to steer the conversation away from the pastor's message. I was thoroughly enjoying my time with Abigail, but I knew there was no prospect of our having a relationship outside of work. She was a sweet kid with a heart for Jesus—and my heart was pointed in any direction but that one.

I decided I needed to bring our time to an end.

"Well, I need to go to my apartment building and sign the lease so the deliverymen can bring the furniture in when they arrive. Can I walk you home?"

"Thank you for offering," Abigail replied. "That is very kind. But I, too, need to make a couple of stops on my way home. Thank you for such an unexpected adventure and for an exquisite meal. I have thoroughly enjoyed my time."

"So have I, Abigail. I am so glad we had this opportunity to get to know one another better. You are a remarkable young lady, and I am delighted we are working together."

"By the way, Gene, if you decide to visit our church for Sunday worship tomorrow, you are more than welcome."

"Thank you for the invitation," I replied. "I'll see what the morning brings in light of my trip tomorrow afternoon."

"Yes, of course," she said. "And I hope your trip and meetings go well, Mr. Fearsithe."

I picked up my suitcase from Reginald before making my way to the Marlborough Building. I gave him a two-dollar tip as an expression of my appreciation for all his help during my two-week stay. I don't think he expected it—and for a brief moment, a rare smile crossed his lips.

"All the best to you, Mr. Fearsithe," he said as I walked away.

"And to you as well, Reginald," I called back.

The rental agent was waiting for me at the apartment, as were the furniture deliverymen. I hurriedly reviewed the lease agreement, signed it, and gave the agent a check for the additional amount due. In exchange, he handed me the key to the apartment.

The deliverymen brought in the furniture and the other goods, and placed them where I instructed them. By the time they left, my apartment was well-appointed and befitting an up and coming executive of OWR&N. One month ago, I had nothing to my name other than a few dollars I had saved up for my journey. And now . . . I was becoming a swell. I liked the feeling!

～

When I looked at my watch the following morning, I remembered the church service at Mount Zion started at 11:00 a.m. I had never intended to go, but I wondered if Miss Adams was looking for me. I had gone out earlier to the café across the street and purchased a few sweet breads, a cup of coffee, and a newspaper so I could leisurely enjoy my first breakfast in my new apartment.

I was reminded the world was getting smaller as I read the headline stories of the day:

> *The shopping bazaar in Damascus, Syria, caught on fire Friday causing $10 million in damages and killing multiple people.*

> # # #

> *China canceled a $50 million munitions contract with a Belgian firm after protests from the United States, the United Kingdom, France, and Germany.*

> # # #

> *Civil war broke out in Paraguay with the former president, Albino Jara, commanding the rebel forces. Four Paraguayan warships bombarded the rebels, who returned fire with cannons and forced the troops to withdraw.*

> # # #

None of that seemed to have anything to do with Portland, Oregon, or my immediate plans. But I knew the world was changing. Seemingly unrelated events had implications that impacted the entire world as never before. The globe was no longer a collection of individual countries—we were becoming an international community. Today I was concerned about shipping lines within the Pacific Northwest, but I was certain my sights would eventually reach far beyond that.

At half past three I boarded my train for Tacoma. The four-hour train excursion gave me ample time to review the presentation I would be making to Richard Anders the following morning. The success of Archer's plan rested on the outcome of that meeting—and so did my future as a global shipping tycoon!

~

25

MONDAY, APRIL 29 – MONDAY, MAY 6

∽

T walked into the offices of the Tacoma Port Authority at five minutes before ten on Monday morning brimming with confidence. Between the information Archer had provided me and my own research, I felt like I knew Mr. Richard Anders almost as well as I know myself.

I had reviewed my notes about him once again earlier that morning:

Richard Anders was born in 1868 in a small coastal town in Massachusetts. In his early twenties, he ventured to the West Coast, lured by the promise of opportunity and adventure, just like the rest of us. He arrived in Tacoma in 1890 when the city was experiencing rapid growth due to its strategic location on Puget Sound. The bustling port, teeming with ships from all corners of the world, captivated Anders' imagination.

Eager to immerse himself in the maritime industry, Anders began working as a dock laborer, unloading cargo and assisting in the day-to-day operations at the Tacoma waterfront. His tireless work ethic, coupled with his keen intellect and natural leadership abilities, caught the attention of his superiors.

Recognizing his potential, Anders quickly climbed the ranks, assuming positions of increasing responsibility within the port. He displayed a remarkable aptitude for managing complex logistical challenges and demonstrated an uncanny ability to navigate the intricate web of shipping, trade, and government regulations.

In 1900, with his reputation for astute decision-making and his deep knowledge of port operations, Anders was appointed as the assistant director of the Tacoma Port Authority. Over the next seven years, he worked tirelessly to enhance the port's efficiency and promote its growth.

In 1907, he assumed his current role as director of the Tacoma Port Authority. Under his leadership, the port authority embarked on ambitious infrastructure projects, expanding wharves and dock facilities to accommodate larger vessels and increased trade. His innovative thinking extended beyond infrastructure improvements. He understood the importance of building strong relationships with shipping companies, local businesses, and the broader community. He fostered partnerships that encouraged trade and economic development, establishing Tacoma as a vital trade gateway to the Pacific.

Known for his integrity and dedication, Anders gained the trust of the Tacoma community as well as the other port authority directors throughout the Pacific Northwest. He tirelessly advocated for the port's interests, working closely with local and regional government officials and business leaders to foster the growth of the maritime shipping industry overall.

"Good morning, Mr. Anders," I said as I entered his office. "It is a pleasure to meet you."

"And you, as well, Mr. Fearsithe," he replied, shaking my hand with a firm grip. "You piqued my interest with your phone call on Friday, so I have been looking forward to this conversation. Please take a seat. Would you like coffee or tea?"

"Thank you for offering. I'll take coffee, black."

"Coming right up," he replied as he nodded at his secretary. "Did you travel here this morning on an early train?"

"No, I arrived yesterday afternoon," I answered. "I did not want to risk any delays that might prevent our meeting. Besides, it gave me an opportunity to discover a little of the natural beauty of your fair city this morning."

"Oh?" Anders commented. "What were you able to see?"

"I took a streetcar from my hotel to Point Defiance Park. The clerk at the hotel suggested the panoramic view from the park of Puget Sound with Mount Rainier in the distant background was breathtaking—and he was right! When I visit Tacoma again, I plan to allow more time to soak in that natural beauty.

"Then I surveyed your most impressive port facilities. I must say, if you will forgive the pun, you run a tight ship!"

"Thank you, Mr. Fearsithe, for your gracious compliment," Anders replied. "We do our best. I am glad to say it is a community effort that I believe will yield great benefits for Tacoma and the entire region in the years to come."

"Which brings us to the reason I have come to speak with you," I chimed in. "OWR&N shares your vision for the continued expansion of the maritime shipping trade, both regionally and globally. We desire to partner with you and the other port authorities here in the Pacific Northwest to make that a reality.

"Accordingly, we would like to propose a unique partnership never before seen between a steamship company and a port. We are aware the Pacific Steamship Company has offered you a flat fourteen percent of the freight revenue generated in and out of your port. And we know this overarching percentage exceeds your combined revenues from dockage, wharfage, pilotage, and tonnage fees. We also realize this very attractive offer will put you in a stronger financial position to continue future growth.

"Consequently, we are so fond of the proposal that we would like to offer you something similar. However, instead of paying you fourteen percent of our freight revenue generated through your port, we would like to increase that to sixteen percent—which will result in a significant increase in the port's operating revenue!"

I paused for him to respond, and I did not have to wait long.

"Mr. Fearsithe, I have questioned how PSC can offer fourteen percent and remain in business. How can OWR&N possibly pay us sixteen percent and stay in business?"

"Mr. Anders, that is a fair question, and I should quickly note that we would be asking for something in return. We want you to grant us exclusive rights for ten years. As the sole steamship company operating in and out of your port, we would benefit from increased production while reducing costs, thereby passing a portion of those savings on to you."

"Won't an arrangement like that be viewed as restrictive trade under the new anti-trust laws being considered by Congress?" Anders asked.

"We do not believe so," I replied. "Though it is impossible to state what the laws will look like after they make their way through committee, nothing in the current or proposed language precludes an arrangement like this. And we are confident that neither President Taft nor President Roosevelt—whoever wins this upcoming election—will take any action that would hamper this type of agreement. They are both seeking to grow our economic infrastructure, not restrict it."

"I would agree with that," Anders said. "But it was a surprise to see that Taft beat Teddy last week in New Hampshire. It's a reminder that nothing is sure in politics."

"True," I agreed, "but we're still a long way out from the convention in Chicago in June. I wouldn't count Teddy out too soon!"

"Yes, I agree with you on that as well," Anders replied. "But on a much closer note, will your board approve such a proposal?"

"They already have. Our board met Friday and gave the proposal their full endorsement. And they have sent me to make you this offer because of their great admiration for you and what you have done here in Tacoma.

"I must, however, add one more caveat. In order to make this work, we need at least six additional ports to agree to this arrangement. We have identified Kalama, Chehalis, Olympia, Victoria, Coupeville, and Port Townsend as the other six."

"Have you spoken with any of them?"

"No," I replied, "we wanted to come to you first. If you approve this offer, we ask that you help us broach the idea with the others. We know you have been a champion of the ports working together, so as the saying goes, 'A rising tide lifts all boats.'"

"Well, you have given me a lot to think about," Anders responded. "When do you need an answer?"

"Because of the nature of our proposal, we do not have the luxury of waiting long. If this news reaches the other port authorities before we present them our offer, it will weaken our ability to build consensus. We know you need to discuss this proposal with your board, but once you do, the risk of news getting out increases exponentially. That said, we will need your answer by the end of the day tomorrow. We're trusting that gives you enough time to assemble your board and look at this from all angles."

I waited for him to reply. What he said next would indicate whether or not he was in favor of our offer.

"I can let you know by the end of day tomorrow," he said.

"Then I will be waiting for your answer. I am staying at the Tacoma Hotel, room 201, if you have any questions. Otherwise, I look forward to hearing from you by . . . shall we say 6:00 p.m.?"

"Six o'clock it is," he agreed. "Until then I hope you have an enjoyable night exploring Tacoma!"

I arrived back at my hotel around noon. As we previously arranged, I telephoned Emmett to update him on the meeting. Abigail, of course, answered the call.

"Hello, this is Mr. Emmett Hall's office. How can I assist you today?"

"Good afternoon, Miss Adams, I trust your week is off to a good start."

"Yes, it is, Mr. Fearsithe. And Mr. Hall is looking forward to hearing from you. Let me put you straight through."

"Gene, is that you?"

"Good afternoon, Emmett," I replied. "I have a good report for you. Anders seems favorable to our proposal. We have set a deadline of 6:00 p.m. tomorrow for him to get back to me with their answer."

"Excellent news!" Emmett exclaimed. "Did he raise any questions we did not anticipate?"

"No, not at all. Everything unfolded exactly as planned. However, we don't want to put the cart before the horse. Let's wait to celebrate until we receive their definitive answer."

"Well done, Gene," Emmett said. "Keep me apprised. What's on your to-do list for the remainder of the day?"

"I plan to book my steamship passage to Port Townsend, Coupeville, and Victoria immediately after we have an answer."

"Well, be sure to take a few minutes to enjoy the city," Emmett added. "It has a lot to offer. And be sure to call me as soon as you have an answer."

"I will."

By late afternoon I had worked up quite an appetite, so I asked the front desk clerk for a dining recommendation. He pointed me to the Elks Club Dining Room just two blocks from the hotel. It did not disappoint!

I decided to remain at the hotel Tuesday in the event Anders tried to contact me. I didn't want anything to hinder him from meeting our deadline. Since the majority of my day was spent waiting, the hours passed slowly.

At five minutes before six, my telephone rang.

"Hello, this is Gene Fearsithe."

"Mr. Fearsithe, this is Richard Anders. Would you care to join me for dinner this evening?"

"Yes, I would enjoy that," I replied. "When and where?"

"Well, I am downstairs in your hotel," he said unexpectedly. "How about we eat at the restaurant here in the hotel. Does now suit you?"

"I'll be right there!" I answered, as I put on my coat and dashed out the door.

The dining room was elegant with a refined atmosphere. The number of empty tables suggested they were used to serving a later crowd. But that worked to our advantage; there were no prying eyes and ears close by.

Once we were seated, Anders began.

"Mr. Fearsithe, I am pleased to inform you our board has decided to accept your proposal—with one minimal revision."

"What's that?"

"Since our acceptance of this arrangement will likely influence the other port authorities to do likewise," he continued, "we think it is only fair that Tacoma receive an additional quarter of one percent over the life of the agreement. We consider that to be a collaboration fee for our assistance in gaining the support of the other ports. By structuring it in this way, we can assure the other ports we are all receiving the same percentage for dockage, wharfage, pilotage, and tonnage."

I pretended to consider his request. Unbeknownst to Anders, our board had already agreed to pay Tacoma an additional amount not to exceed half of one percent.

"I will need to get our board's approval of your request," I lied, "but I am certain Mr. Hall and I will be able to convince them of the value of that additional amount. I am confident I can go out on a limb and tell you that we have a deal!"

After we shook hands, I told him I would bring him the agreement by ten o'clock the next morning. Fortunately, I had asked Miss Adams to type up two copies that included an additional quarter of one percent, even though I had never expected to use them.

We celebrated our alliance over a delicious meal of Dungeness crab, a prized delicacy found in Puget Sound. Though the meal was delightful, my mind kept wandering to the next appointments I needed to arrange.

~

I woke early Wednesday morning and set up my next three appointments, then noted them in my calendar.

Wednesday, May 1, 2:00 p.m. - Philip Easterly - Port Townsend Port Authority

Thursday, May 2, 11:00 a.m. - Robert Simpson - Coupeville Port Authority
Friday, May 3, 10:00 a.m. - Jeffrey Jackson - Victoria Port Authority

After meeting with Richard Anders at 10 a.m. to sign our agreement, I set out on my journey to meet with the other port authority directors. Each meeting went off without a hitch. Not surprisingly, once I told them we had already signed an agreement with the Tacoma Port Authority, any reservations they had evaporated.

I gave each of the men twenty-four hours to gain the approval of their respective boards and arranged to retrieve the signed contracts on Monday of the following week. That meant I would spend the weekend in Victoria, British Columbia, before traveling back south.

That Friday, I made three important phone calls. The first was to Emmett to report that Port Townsend and Coupeville had both agreed to the proposal, and all indications were that Victoria would do the same. I would be back in the office next Tuesday with all four signed agreements.

My second call was to Church. "Please let Mr. Winslow know I will be back in Portland on Tuesday and can meet at eight in the evening if that is convenient for him," I said.

My third call was to Jake to let him know I would pay him his ten dollars on Tuesday.

I spent the weekend in Victoria's Empress Hotel, which had been completed just four years earlier. I was impressed by the ornate decor, including its lavish chandeliers, intricate woodwork, and fine furnishings. My room was spacious and adorned with elegant furnishings. The hotel boasts of its modern amenities, such as electric lighting, telephones, and hot and cold running water in every room. Located on the waterfront, its most breathtaking feature is the view of the Inner Harbor.

It was a comfortable and luxurious weekend retreat, courtesy of OWR&N. My only regret was that I didn't have someone with whom to share it.

26

TUESDAY, MAY 7 – FRIDAY, MAY 10

◞

$\mathcal{I}$t was good to be back in my own bed, although I woke before the sun rose. It looked like it was going to hide behind rain clouds all day. Even though it was just drizzling, I've never been particularly fond of rainy days—so I was glad Portland was headed into its dry season.

I made a dash to the bakery across the street for an assortment of fresh pastries and to fill my carafe with fresh coffee. I made a mental note to stop by Lyman, Wolfe & Company to purchase a coffee pot so I could make my own. Nonetheless, I was starting to wonder just how much time I would actually spend in my apartment.

I settled in for a quiet breakfast, reading a copy of *the Oregon Journal* I'd picked up the night before. One particular article caught my eye:

```
On April 25, a deputation of seamen on the RMS
Olympic witnessed a test of four collapsible
lifeboats that had been placed on board. One
boat proved to be unseaworthy, and the crew
```

```
threatened to strike if the boat was not
replaced. Fifty-four sailors left the ship,
which canceled the Olympic's launch. All of the
sailors were arrested and charged with mutiny
when they went ashore. On May 4, Portsmouth
magistrates found the charges against the muti-
neers    valid, but discharged them without
imprisonment or fine due to the special circum-
stances of the case. Fearing public opinion
would be on the side of the strikers, the White
Star Line allowed the sailors to return to
work.
```

And this one struck me as a uniquely Western news event:

```
John Graham, a 63-year-old bear trapper, was
killed over the weekend by a bear on Crevice
Mountain near Yellowstone National Park.
According to some accounts, the bear lost three
toes on one paw due to one of Graham's traps.
The bear was now being called "Old Two Toes."
```

I arrived at the office at half past seven, allowing me ample time to prepare for my eight o'clock meeting with Emmett. Miss Adams made a point of stopping by my office to congratulate me on my successful week.

"Several board members stopped by to see Mr. Hall to get a report on your progress," she said. "They were all quite impressed with what you accomplished—particularly once they realized it was only your second week on the job. Each one congratulated Mr. Hall for recognizing your talent. It appears you are on your way to achieving that dream you left Pennsylvania to pursue, Mr. Fearsithe!"

"You are most kind, Miss Adams, but I am fully aware that those congratulations belong to everyone involved, including you. So, congratulations to you! And I look forward to sharing more successes with you in the days ahead."

Just then, Emmett stuck his head out of his office to see if we could begin our meeting a few minutes early. I presented him with the four signed agreements and gave him a detailed report on each conversation.

"When will they be notifying the Pacific Steamship Company of their decision to give us exclusive rights to their ports?" he asked.

"We all agreed to wait until next Monday to give me time to make our presentation to the Kalama, Chehalis, and Olympia port authorities. They also agreed that once we had signed agreements with all seven ports, we should not have any difficulty convincing the others. In fact, Richard Anders has agreed to personally contact his counterparts in Portland, Seattle, and Vancouver to bring them on board when the time is right.

"Our control of the Pacific Northwest shipping lanes is within sight, Emmett!" I declared.

"When do you meet with the other three?" he asked.

"I will be contacting them once you and I are finished here. Barring any unexpected reluctance, I plan to meet with Kalama tomorrow, Chehalis on Thursday, and Olympia on Friday."

"In that case, I will not hold you up any longer," Emmett replied. "I will work with our operations team the remainder of this week to finalize preparations for taking over the shipping business in the seven initial ports."

We stood and shook hands. As I left his office, Emmett said, "Let me know if you need anything, Gene!"

I contacted the three remaining port authority directors and arranged to meet with them. I had a suspicion they already knew what I wanted to talk about. The private networking between directors was most certainly working in our favor. Once the appointments were confirmed, I noted them in my calendar:

Wednesday, May 8, 2:00 p.m. - Douglas Andrews - Kalama Port Authority
Thursday, May 9, 11:00 a.m. - Peter Bentley - Chehalis Port Authority
Friday, May 10, 10:00 a.m. - John Lemoine - Olympia Port Authority

I then tasked Miss Adams with making my steamship reservations before leaving the office to pay Jake a visit.

"Look who's here," Jake called out sarcastically as I walked into his office. "You're rising so quickly in Portland society, I expected you might send your butler with an envelope for me."

"Well, I was going to send him," I retorted, "but I needed him to attend to other important matters!"

Then I added with a laugh, "How've you been Jake?"

"I'm doing well, even though my best debt collector abandoned me," he said with a slight grin. "But I would venture I'm not doing half as well as you are. I hear you moved out of the rooming house and have your own apartment in the Marlborough Building with the rest of the swells."

"Where did you hear that?"

"From Constable Burton," Jake replied. "He apparently went to your old rooming house looking for you and found that you had moved."

"When did you talk to him?"

"He came by to see me yesterday," Jake answered. "He told me they'd had a development in your case. Seems they got a match on the fingerprints they took off your wallet. When he found out you had moved, he came here thinking you were still working for me."

Then Jake wisecracked, "I told him nobody who works in my department can afford to live in the Marlborough Apartments!

"I did pass along that I expected to see you today," Jake continued, "so he asked me to give you the message to come see him."

"I never expected to hear anything more about the robbery," I replied. "I will go by and see him when I leave here.

"Speaking of the theft, here's a check for twenty dollars, which should cover last week and this week. I'm headed back out of town tomorrow and won't return until the weekend, so I figured I'd give you this week's payment ahead of schedule."

"Like I told you before, I'm not worried," Jake assured me. "You have more than proven that you're good for it. So, I see you're writing checks now instead of paying in cash?"

"Yes, that keeps me from having to carry around my billy club," I said, only half joking.

"Well, I do hope the coppers catch whoever robbed you so you can get your money back."

"Even if they are able to catch the guy, I'm certain the money is long gone," I said. "I'm not holding my breath about seeing any of the cash."

"Well, I hope for your sake, they do," Jake reiterated.

""Thanks, Jake. I need to get back to my office. It was good seeing you."

"Say hello to the other swells for me," Jake said with a smile, "and don't forget to stop by and see the constable."

When I arrived at the police station, Constable Burton told me everything Jake had already relayed. But then he added, "I want to show you a photograph of the guy whose prints match those on your wallet.

"We arrested him a few years ago for petty theft. He spent a year in jail, but no one has seen him since then. We've run down his former associates and his last known address, but they all say they haven't heard from him and don't know where he is. They seemed to think he has left town."

The constable pulled a photograph out of a file and showed it to me.

"Does he look familiar?"

The guy had dark hair and appeared to be about my size and age. But that description would probably match hundreds of guys in the city.

"There is something familiar about this guy," I responded after studying the photograph. "But I can't place where I've seen him. What's his name?

"Thomas Buckholt," the constable replied. "Does it sound familiar?"

"No, I can't say that it does," I answered. "But if anything comes to mind, I'll let you know."

I returned to the office for the rest of the afternoon and gathered all the information I could about the three port directors I would be meeting. I reviewed the proposals and the steamship tickets Miss Adams had gotten for me. When six o'clock had come and gone, I finally decided everything was in order, and I was as prepared as I would ever be.

As I walked past Miss Adams on my way out, I wished her a good night.

"Good night, Mr. Fearsithe," she replied. "I pray all goes well with your meetings. I'm sure it will. And don't forget—the invitation still stands for you to join us at Mount Zion this Sunday."

I was hungry for a dinner of fish and chips, and Clyde had mentioned a place on the riverfront called the White House Restaurant. He said it wasn't anything fancy, just good food. Though it was in the opposite direction from Archer's home in Portland Heights, I decided I had plenty of time to dine there and still make my eight o'clock appointment.

Clyde's recommendation was right on the mark. Since the meal took slightly longer than I planned, I decided to catch a streetcar. It traveled along one of the most scenic views in Portland and dropped me off at Council Crest Park. From there, it was just a few minutes' walk to Archer's home. Dusk had begun to settle in when I knocked on the tradesman's door.

"Good evening, Gene," Archer greeted me as I entered the library. "Church has already poured you a cup of black coffee. I hope that's correct?"

"Oh, yes, that will do just fine."

"Wonderful! Well, go ahead and update me on your time since we last met. I understand through my network that your meetings have been successful."

"Yes, indeed they have," I replied. "OWR&N now has signed agreements with Tacoma, Port Townsend, Coupeville, and Victoria. And I expect to have them with Kalama, Chehalis, and Olympia before the week is out."

"Well done, Gene," Archer said. "By the end of the week, you will have put everything in place to tie up the shipping lanes for PSC—and you will have accomplished it in only three weeks' time. Between my ability to plan and yours to execute, we are a pretty effective team, Mr. Fearsithe."

"So, what happens next, Archer?" I asked. "I mean, with these agreements in hand, it appears that OWR&N now owns the shipping lanes. What happens to change that?"

"This coming Tuesday, the dock workers are going out on strike," Archer said smugly. "And I'm going to be the only one who can settle the strike."

"How are you going to do that?"

"I can't disclose all my secrets, Gene," Archer chuckled, "even to my vice president for special assignments. Just keep doing what you are doing, and everything will end just the way it needs to end.

"That reminds me, here is your salary for both last week and this week," he added. He took an envelope off the table and handed it to me. "You'll find I have also included another reward for a job well done!"

Inside the envelope were six, crisp fifty dollar bills.

"Thank you, Archer," I said, "for that added recognition. It means a lot!"

"Well, like I said, Gene, I reward initiative and you continue to show it. Let's plan on meeting again next Tuesday night at the same time. And if everything goes according to plan, there should be no reason for us to continue meeting in secret after that. The whole world will soon know about your important role in all of this!

"How does that sound?" Archer asked as he opened his box of cigars and offered me one.

"That sounds great!" I acknowledged as I held the cigar under my nostrils to take in its aroma. But at the same time I was beginning to question just how great it was going to be. Everything was starting to feel very wrong.

"I'm going to have to get you your own box of Cuban cigars, Gene," Archer chortled. "I think you enjoy them even more than I do!

"Church will show you out, and I look forward to seeing you again next Tuesday night."

As if on cue, Church appeared at the library door. I was beginning to sense that everything about Archer Winslow was carefully orchestrated, and no detail was ever left unplanned.

As Church walked me through the house, I spotted the same man I had seen on my first visit. He was slouched in the sitting room, folding the newspaper he had just finished reading. As I passed by, he nodded and gave me a slight smile.

It was at that moment I recognized him, but I did not let on.

When we arrived at the tradesman's door, I turned to Church and innocently asked, "Is that man one of the servants here?"

"No," Church replied, "I would never allow him to serve in this house. He's another one of Mr. Winslow's employees—just like you."

"What's his name?" I asked nonchalantly.

"Thomas," Church answered. "His name is Thomas Buckholt. Good night, Mr. Fearsithe."

Over the next three days, I successfully executed agreements with all three port directors. When I called Emmett to report my results, he was extremely pleased and conveyed his appreciation for a job well done.

I knew Archer, too, would have commended me for securing the contracts. I had done exactly what he had hired me to do.

I continued to try and unravel Archer's next move. I knew he was always several steps ahead of me. Thomas Buckholt was proof of that. But what were those next steps? Did I need to confront Archer? Should I disclose to

Constable Burton the whereabouts of Thomas Buckholt? And should I warn Emmett that something untoward was in play?

All those questions swirled in my mind as I arrived back at my apartment Friday night.

27

SATURDAY, MAY 11 – MONDAY, MAY 13

∾

$\mathcal{I}$ woke up Saturday morning with those same questions still churning in my head. But one thing I had no concerns about—the trajectory of my career. I doubted I would be working for OWR&N much longer. And though I would lose my second salary, I would be officially stepping into my role at PSC with an expected increase in pay. Archer Winslow knew I was an invaluable resource capable of getting the job done. And he had shown that he rewarded such initiative.

So I settled in for an enjoyable weekend. I relaxed with a great tasting cup of coffee, made in my own coffee pot, on my own stove, in my own apartment. The cherry on top was smoking the Cuban cigar Archer had given me.

I decided to do three things to celebrate my achievements. First, I stopped by my old rooming house to see Clyde. Reginald said he had already gone out, so I left him a message:

Pick you up at six o'clock for a celebratory dinner - my treat!

Next, I set off to see Albert Frank. He was busy with another customer, but when he saw me, he called out, "Your suit isn't quite finished, Mr. Fearsithe. But I should have it done by next Saturday as promised."

"Thank you, Mr. Frank, but I didn't come to inquire about my suit. Rather, I came to order two more. But I will wait until you are done with this gentleman."

"I should be about ten minutes," he replied. And just like the last time, he was true to his word.

"So, Mr. Fearsithe, what can I interest you in today?"

"I need to expand my wardrobe, Mr. Frank," I replied. "A successful businessman cannot continue to function with just three suits. I need at least two more to complete the work week. What do you suggest?"

"I would recommend the same style as the one I am currently making for you. But how about one in dark brown and another in black, so you have one you can also use on more formal occasions?"

"Those are excellent suggestions," I affirmed.

"I won't need to take any measurements today since I already have them," Mr. Frank continued. After looking at his calendar, he added, "And I should have these two finished by June 8."

"Excellent! And I will also need two dress shirts."

"I can have those ready for you at the same time. The total cost will be $125, and I will throw in two neckties."

We shook hands, and I paid him a fifty percent deposit before leaving the shop to seek out my next purchase. I had actually seen it the other night on my way to the White House Restaurant. It had called out to me from behind a massive plate glass window.

There weren't a lot of automobiles on the streets of Portland yet, but I knew the number was increasing daily. I also was aware the drivers of those automobiles were young, successful businessmen like me. When I saw that red Gentleman's Roadster, I knew it was the car for me.

When I arrived at the Packard Motor Car Company showroom, I was pleased to see the roadster was still there.

"Good morning, sir," a salesman greeted me. "What brings you in today? Are you in the market for an automobile?"

"Yes, I am, as a matter-of-fact," I replied. "Fearsithe is the name, and I have my eye on this beauty right here. What can you tell me about it?"

"Well first, I must tell you, Mr. Fearsithe, that you have excellent taste! This gentleman's roadster is a 1910 Packard Model 30. It clearly communicates that its driver is a man who knows what he wants, and he reaches out and grabs it. It's a high-end luxury car equipped with all the comforts.

"A customer traded it in when he purchased the 1912 model. But as you can see, it looks brand new—both inside and outside. It has been well maintained, and I will tell you this is the finest value we have had available for some time. Frankly, I have two other gentlemen who have their eyes on this beauty; both told me they plan to come back today to buy it. But as I told them, it's available to the first person who writes us a check.

"I do not say that to pressure you into making a decision. I just want you to know this is such a good buy I do not think it will be here by the end of the day. What questions do you have for me, Mr. Fearsithe?"

"What's the price?"

"It is priced at $4,000," the salesman replied, "but my boss told me I could go as low as $3,950."

"Well, that's very generous of him, but I was thinking more along the lines of $3,800," I countered.

"I fear that given all the interest in this particular automobile, my boss will not be receptive to an offer that low," he replied.

We continued to haggle back and forth. Once he learned I was an executive at OWR&N and lived in the Marlborough Apartments, he became more earnest in his negotiation. We finally agreed on a price of $3,850. I wrote him a check for $350 and signed an agreement, promising to pay the remaining balance over the next thirty-six months.

After the salesman maneuvered the car out onto the street, I said, "Now I only need you to do one more thing—show me how to drive it!" I was glad it wasn't too complicated, and after a thirty-minute lesson, I felt confident enough to drive it on my own.

It was a beautiful spring day, so I spent the remainder of it driving around the city. I made my way over to Front Street and drove along the west bank of the river. I caught glimpses of several sailboats gracefully navigating the river, their sails billowing in the gentle breeze.

I crossed the river and turned north on East Water Street. I hadn't yet been in this part of East Portland. It was a bustling thoroughfare lined with warehouses and mills. However, I decided I wanted a more scenic route, so I made my way back across the river.

As I drove through the western edge of the city, I was able to pick up speed. The breeze blowing through my hair was thrilling. However, I had to slow down whenever I encountered a horse-drawn carriage. They are not quite ready to share the road with an automobile, and they can act a little skittish! Still, it was a wonderful way to spend an afternoon.

I arrived back at the rooming house promptly at 6:00 p.m. Clyde was outside waiting for me. I could have knocked him over with a feather when he saw me pull up in my new roadster!

"Okay," he declared, "so I see they have now made you president of the company!"

We both had a good laugh as I took him on a drive around town. We ended up back at the White House Restaurant for a dinner of fish and chips. The most astounding news Clyde shared during our meal was he had asked Elenore to marry him—and she had accepted! I couldn't have been happier for them both.

But at the same time, I couldn't help but be reminded of the emptiness in my own life. I was finding that I was missing Sara more and more. I missed her smile and her laugh. I missed our time together listening to music and dancing.

Still, all in all, it had been an enjoyable day and night. For the most part, I felt like I was on the top of the world. And it felt pretty good!

I decided not to go for a drive Sunday since it was raining. At 11:00 a.m. I thought of Miss Adams and Mount Zion Baptist Church, but I immediately put them out of mind. I stayed in my apartment all day, except to run across the street for a sandwich in the middle of the afternoon. Otherwise, I planned for what I knew would be a busy week, full of new developments. I just didn't have any idea what *kind* of developments.

∾

Monday started as a day of celebration at OWR&N. I was congratulated by everyone who passed me in the halls, most of whom I did not yet know. Each one of the board members stopped by to congratulate and praise Emmett and me.

All seven ports announced their new agreements with OWR&N. They lauded the new era of trade now made possible through our innovative partnership. Businesses currently shipping through their ports were encouraged to discover the expanded opportunities. The port directors also challenged those who had not yet begun to ship their goods along the northwest shipping lanes to reconsider the many benefits.

Our operational team—deployed throughout the seven cities in full force —was giddy as members entered into those conversations. The team reported agreements being executed with new customers at an unprecedented rate.

The *Oregon Journal* got wind of the story and sent a reporter to interview Emmett. He was asked if the Portland Port Authority had been approached about a partnership.

"We look forward to entering into agreement with the Portland Authority, and the other ports along the shipping lane, as soon as they are prepared to do so," he replied.

Meanwhile, I was busy making arrangements with those port directors to do just that. Portland was at the top of my list, followed by Astoria, Seattle, and Vancouver, British Columbia. And since they now knew why I was contacting them, they were eager to meet with me. Richard Anders was doing a remarkable job of spreading the excitement.

I requested a meeting with James Porter, director of the port here in Portland, for that afternoon at two o'clock. He immediately accepted the appointment. I had a feeling that any previous engagements on his calendar were now being rescheduled.

As soon as I got off that call, Miss Adams told me Emmett wanted to see me in his office.

"How did your interview go with the reporter from the *Journal*?" I asked as I approached his desk.

"It went well," he replied. "He appeared to have already captured the excitement among the port authorities regarding the boon this could usher in for the shipping trade. But he did catch me by surprise with one question."

"Oh, really! What was that?"

"He told me when he reached out to Archer Winslow for a comment from PSC, he gave the reporter this response:

> *"'I applaud OWR&N for their creativity. I only hope they, as well as the port authorities, have taken into consideration the concerns being expressed by the waterfront workers. As the leading shipping company serving these ports until now, we have been in protracted negotiations for several weeks to stave off a workers' strike.*

"'Since we no longer will be the leading shipping company, we hope OWR&N is successful in stepping into our role in those negotiations. Otherwise, I fear all the excitement will dissipate under the weight of a lengthy workers' strike.

"'We do, however, want the port authorities, OWR&N, and all the businesses that rely on the shipping lanes to remain open, to know that we stand by to assist in any way we can.'

"He asked me to respond to the comment."

"What did you say?" I asked.

"I told him we were not aware of any concerns nor any negotiations being undertaken with the union by PSC. But we would be reaching out to the leaders of the International Longshoremen's Association (ILA) to ensure that any and all concerns are being adequately and fairly addressed."

"How did he respond to your answer?"

"It seemed to satisfy him for now," Emmett replied. "But we need to find out immediately what Winslow was talking about. I'm going to reach out to Richard Morgan over at ILA to see if I can make sense of this."

"Would you like me to join you?"

"No, you continue to meet with the port authority directors to get these agreements signed and I'll take care of ILA," Emmett stated. "Hopefully, it is merely a matter of Winslow creating a tempest in a teapot to detract from the success we just achieved. Besides, we know he was planning a similar approach with the ports. We just beat him to it, as a result of your brilliance and loyalty to OWR&N."

Those last words pained me, but I tried not to show it. I knew it wasn't any brilliance or loyalty on my part; it had all been part of Winslow's plan. And now everything was about to unravel.

I returned to my office and successfully scheduled meetings with the port authority directors in Astoria, Seattle, and Vancouver beginning Wednesday afternoon. They all cleared their calendars and assured me their boards had already expressed interest in our proposal.

As I was preparing to go to the Portland Port Authority office later that afternoon, Miss Adams informed me Richard Anders was on the phone. She said he indicated that we must speak right away. I knew I needed to take the call.

"Gene, this is Richard Anders," he began. "Have you heard what's happening at ILA? They are saying that OWR&N has refused to meet with them, and they are threatening to strike."

"Richard, that's not true. We only learned a short while ago that they have been negotiating with PSC. Neither we nor any of the other shipping companies were aware of any such negotiation. My boss, Emmett Hall, is reaching out to them now to request a meeting so we can address their concerns.

"Please be assured that no one here has refused to meet with them," I continued, "and we are earnestly attempting to do so. Please tell whoever provided you with that incorrect information that we are doing everything we can to bring any issues to an expedient conclusion."

"I will, Gene," Richard said. "But you need to know there are a lot of concerns up here about this. I hope OWR&N can diffuse this situation quickly before it blows up. I'm being bombarded by calls from customers who are criticizing us for entering into an exclusive agreement with your company. Not to mention some of our board members are jumping on that bandwagon. The clock's ticking, and it's got a short fuse!"

~

I was immediately ushered into James Porter's office at the Portland Port Authority when I arrived a few minutes late.

"Mr. Porter, I apologize for my tardiness," I said. "Regretfully, I was unavoidably detained by another matter. Thank you for agreeing to meet with me at such short notice."

"Mr. Fearsithe, unfortunately your late arrival causes our meeting to get started on the wrong foot," Porter replied. "But I trust you will set that straight and impress me with the details of this new business arrangement we have been hearing so much about."

Mr. Porter's coolness showed signs of dissipating as I explained our proposal. I was able to answer all of his questions to his satisfaction—until he asked about the statement just issued by Richard Morgan at the ILA.

"I regret that I am unaware of his statement," I replied. "Can you share it with me?"

"He indicated the ILA was not aware of any exclusive agreement between the ports and OWR&N until this morning, just like the rest of us. He went on to say OWR&N has not been at the table addressing any of the concerns the ILA put forth. Actually, he said, 'only PSC has been working with us to address the inequities their workers are experiencing. And now at this late hour,' he added, 'OWR&N rushes in and supplants PSC at the table, negating all the good faith progress that has been made.'

"Mr. Morgan also implied that given the late hour of this development, a strike may be unavoidable. He acknowledged that Emmett Hall, from your company, has reached out to enter into dialogue, but he added, 'I fear it may be too little too late!'

"Mr. Fearsithe, until this matter is resolved, the Portland Port Authority has no interest in discussing your proposal. However, we will be more than happy to reconsider when this dispute with the ILA is settled."

28

TUESDAY, MAY 14

~

*R*ichard Morgan, a longshoreman himself, had emerged as a key leader over the years within the International Longshoremen's Association (ILA) Local 8, which represents the dockworkers in Portland. His leadership and ability to mobilize had proven to be instrumental in rallying support for the workers' cause.

Under his guidance, the longshoremen had fought for better wages, shorter working hours, and improved working conditions. He had successfully united the workers and maintained their solidarity. He had been so successful, in fact, that his influence had spread to the other locals up and down the northwest shipping lane. His voice seemingly represented all the locals.

Emmett had successfully arranged a meeting with Morgan that lasted long into Monday night.

"Mr. Morgan, rest assured that neither OWR&N nor any of the other shipping companies were aware of your discussions with PSC," Emmett began. "Our absence from those discussions was not from lack of concern.

"I can guarantee my company would have been present if we had known. And further, we would have informed you of our intent to negotiate an exclusive shipping agreement with the ports."

Emmett told me later that Morgan didn't seem to believe a word he had said; their conversation remained combative the entire evening. Morgan was leaving no room for negotiation, and the concessions he was seeking for the workers would increase our shipping costs by about eight percent.

OWR&N would be unable to absorb those costs, together with the increases that had been promised to the ports in our agreements—even with the increased revenue we anticipated from the eight percent rate increase and our expanded customer base. It was a no-win proposition for OWR&N, and according to Morgan, the ILA was unwilling to make any concessions since Archer Winslow and PSC had already agreed to these terms.

Emmett and I sat in his office Tuesday morning hashing over the company's dilemma.

"I cannot believe Archer Winslow would agree to any such thing," Emmett avowed. "The numbers don't even work with the fourteen percent he was proposing to the ports. It's as if he were intentionally creating deals to put PSC into bankruptcy. Gene, can you explain it?"

I could—but I most definitely didn't want to. Archer never had any intention of keeping those agreements with the ports or with ILA. He was simply setting up an expectation that OWR&N would be forced to live up to or abandon. And the only way OWR&N could abandon the agreements would be to walk away from the shipping business. That would leave PSC free to walk back in as the hero. I had to admit it was a brilliant plan.

"No, Emmett, I can't explain it," I lied. "Archer Winslow never uttered a word to me about his negotiations with ILA. It makes absolutely no sense!"

Over the course of the day, our entire management team and board struggled to come up with solutions. Emmett returned to the table with Morgan twice with counter proposals designed to avert a strike. Both offers were rejected and, to our surprise, Morgan never offered his own counter proposal. He was not going to budge at all. I had a hunch that Archer was calling the shots.

At four o'clock that afternoon, Morgan publicly announced the waterfront workers were going on strike effective immediately in the seven ports working exclusively with OWR&N. However, because of the agreement struck between PSC and ILA, work would continue at the ports being served by PSC—but with them only. That meant PSC now had exclusive shipping rights in the ports where they were operating.

Immediately following that announcement, the seven port directors—with whom I had just secured agreements—advised me that unless we immediately settled with ILA, they were severing our contract based on the "failure to perform" clause. And, as Richard Anders told me during our conversation, "Because of your failure to perform, we will no longer permit OWR&N to have any access to our port whatsoever."

In one day, OWR&N had gone from the rising star of the shipping business to a persona non grata. Short of agreeing to ILA's demands, we could not salvage this. And there was no way we could financially agree to those demands.

Emmett and I were still in his office attempting to find a solution when Miss Adams interrupted us.

"The board is requesting the two of you come upstairs and meet with them." Though they may have used the word "requesting," Emmett and I both knew it wasn't a request.

As we entered the meeting room, our reception was completely different from the day before. The smiles and backslaps had been replaced by the somberness of a funeral.

Henry Villard, as chairman, was the first to speak.

"Gentlemen, we have just received a directive from our parent company, Union Pacific, to shut down the steamship division of OWR&N. They have determined that any continuing effort would do nothing more than further erode their reputation. They advised us they reserve the right to return to the steamship business at some future point through one of their other subsidiaries. All OWR&N employees in that division are to be terminated unless there is a suitable position in another division. All assets of the steamship division are to be liquidated.

"Statements to that effect are now being publicly disseminated. The agreements with the seven ports are being declared null and void. The steamship shipping industry in the Northwest is returning to what it was three weeks ago—with the exception that OWR&N is no longer a party to it.

"We will leave it to the two of you to decide whether you would like to resign your positions effective immediately or be terminated."

Silence filled the room as everyone awaited our response. No discussion was needed. No attempts to justify decisions would be required. It was simply resign or be fired.

I couldn't look at Emmett. He had invested twenty years with Union Pacific, and he had planned to retire from here—perhaps retaining a seat on the OWR&N board. But now he was being shuttled out the back door in disgrace. And it was entirely my fault.

"You will have my resignation within the hour," Emmett said as he rose from his chair to leave.

"And mine as well," I stated as I followed him out.

We did not speak as we returned to our offices. Other company representatives were already breaking the news to the remaining employees in the division. The mood in the office was heartbreaking. I looked at Miss Adams and thought about how loyal she had been to this company and to Emmett. I could scarcely breathe as I felt the weight of the pain I was causing her, Emmett, and so many others.

Archer Winslow had just issued his own public statement, which was circulating around the docks, our office, and throughout the city. Miss Adams had typed it up and placed it on my desk, and presumably, Emmett's:

> *"To the good men and women who enable the free flow of goods and passengers up and down our northwest shipping lane, whether you work on the docks, in the offices, on the steamships, or for the companies that entrust us all with your goods:*

> *"We at Pacific Steamship Company are distressed by what has occurred in our industry and in your lives over the past few days. We promise to assist you in getting past this turmoil so we may all return to the free flow of our shipping lanes and the way of life we have enjoyed prior to these unfortunate incidents.*

"Please know that your welfare is our priority and our commitment.

"Archer Winslow, President"

I quickly prepared my resignation:

I hereby resign my position with Oregon-Washington Railway and Navigation Company effective immediately this 14th day of May 1912.

R. Eugene Fearsithe

I slipped it in an envelope and left it on top of my desk before walking out and closing the door. I couldn't face Abigail or Emmett. I didn't have any words, so I simply left.

Mrs. Brown was sitting at the reception desk, efficiently attending to every detail. I'm not sure whether she was unaware of what had occurred, or just didn't want to add to the pain.

"Good night, Mr. Fearsithe. Have yourself a pleasant evening."

I now felt conspicuous as I climbed into my red roadster. At what price had this extravagance come? Unquestionably, this car had been my way of saying, "Hey, look at me! I am important and I am successful!"

But now I didn't want people to look at me. I was embarrassed by the man I'd become and what I had done.

I drove back to my apartment and isolated myself until it was time to go to Archer's. I didn't feel much like driving the roadster, so I took the street-car. I arrived promptly at 8:00 p.m.

As Church showed me into the library, I could hear Archer humming. His celebratory mood was the direct opposite of how I was feeling.

"How are you on this fine day, Gene?" Archer greeted me. "Don't you just love it when a plan works out? Please take a seat and help yourself to a cigar. You deserve it!"

I looked around for a cup of coffee, but clearly Archer had not told Church to prepare one. Undoubtedly, this was going to be a short meeting.

"So what happens now?" I asked, probably more to myself than to Archer.

"What happens now?" he replied in disbelief. "We celebrate! I now control the northwest shipping lanes, and I achieved it in such a way that I look like a savior. I've saved the ports, the waterfront workers, and the compa-nies that ship their goods."

"Yes, but what about the good people who lost their jobs today?"

"They'll find other jobs, Gene. As a matter-of-fact, tell them to come work for me. I'm going to need more people to help handle all the new business coming my way. That's how it works. Businesses come and go. Jobs come and go. But the survivors move with them and seize the next opportunity!

"Just like you, Gene! You're a survivor. A month ago, you didn't have two nickels to rub together. But now you're living the good life. How do you refer to it? 'Living among the swells'? You're wearing fancy suits, living in a posh apartment, driving a fancy car, and smoking a swell cigar! Think about it Gene—after only a month's time.

"It's almost as if somebody were watching out for you, isn't it?"

"Yes, you were watching me, weren't you, Archer?"

"What do you mean, Gene?"

"You had Thomas follow me that night after I came to collect the money you owed the *Journal*. You told him to rob me, didn't you?" I accused.

"Why would I do that, Gene? I mean, look around. Does it look like I needed whatever money was in your pocket?"

"No," I replied. "I figure you were angry the *Journal* had the audacity to send someone here to collect a mere twenty dollars as if you were a nobody. So you decided you wouldn't give them, or me, the satisfaction. You sent Thomas to knock me out and bring back whatever money I had. After all, any good businessman wants a return on his investment!"

"So you think I am that petty, Gene, to care about a measly twenty dollars?"

"No, it wasn't the twenty bucks; it was the principle. For some reason, you had Thomas keep an eye on me. Maybe it was to see if I would trace the theft back to you. But then you saw me get right back up on the horse—this time carrying a billy club. Perhaps you liked my spunk and determination."

"Actually, I did, Gene. But I liked you for another reason."

"What was that?" I asked.

"Thomas had actually seen you before that night," Archer began explaining. "He spotted you on the train when Emmett Hall told you he had a job for you. Thomas was on that train to keep an eye on Emmett for me. And the night he knocked you out, he recognized you and told me. That's when your part in the play began to come together. I figured if you were out collecting five-dollar debts, Mr. Hall must not have come through with that job—and you would have an axe to grind with him.

"And yes, you impressed me with your grit. So I decided to invite you over and see if you'd bite. And you bit, Gene. You bit hard! And I really do want to thank you, because you played a starring role."

"And just so we're clear about the $135 Thomas borrowed from you that night in the alley. I have more than paid you back with bonuses you received over and above your agreed salary. There was even enough to cover your hospital bill. So you can consider that debt paid in full."

"I presume my position as vice president of special assignments has been dissolved?"

"Yes, you did such a good job that the special assignment has been completed," Archer replied. "Besides, Gene, I can't have someone working for me who was one of the key executives involved in the disastrous demise of OWR&N's steamship division. I mean, how would that look?

"My one regret is that we will no longer have these enjoyable chats. I like you, Gene. I like your spunk. And I am confident you are a survivor. But I do need to warn you. If you tell anyone about any of this, you'll end up in more trouble than I will. Because you knowingly convinced Emmett Hall and OWR&N to enter into a scheme I had orchestrated to defeat them. I'm afraid you wouldn't come out clean on that.

"Also, you're going to have to deal with a few other problems. You see, the Marlborough Apartments just informed me that you were forced to resign from OWR&N for questionable reasons. In fact, a whole division was forced to shut down because of whatever you did. And the Marlborough has some pretty strict standards about who they allow to reside there. I should know, I actually wrote them! So tomorrow, you will be served with an eviction notice, including a demand for payment of your remaining lease commitment. I do believe, however, they might settle for $1,000 if you're lucky.

"And Packard Motor Company is going to be looking for your roadster back since you are unemployed and have no way to make your installment payments. And sadly, Lyman, Wolfe and Company will be repossessing all that fine furniture for which you still owe them.

"Yes, I'm afraid you're going to have a really busy day tomorrow, Gene. And I regret, nowhere to sleep tomorrow night!

"But do have one more cigar for the road."

29

WEDNESDAY MORNING, MAY 15

*H*arold Wolfe was the first to knock on my door early Wednesday morning. He presented his business card to show me he was one of the owners of Lyman, Wolfe and Company.

Accompanying him were the two able-bodied movers who had delivered my furniture a little more than two weeks earlier.

"Mr. Fearsithe, I am afraid we have come regarding a quite serious matter," Mr. Wolfe began. "We have learned that you are about to be evicted from this apartment and you no longer have the means to satisfy your debt to our company. Although we accept installment payments, we do so with the realistic expectation the customer has the resources to honor his obligation. Since that is no longer the case, we have come to take possession of the goods you purchased from our company.

"Should you, however, be able to present me with full payment of the $380 you owe us, we will not trouble you any further. Otherwise, I regret that my men here will be forced to load your furnishings into our wagon."

"Considering I just became unemployed yesterday, doesn't your company allow a customer a reasonable period of time to get back on his feet?" I asked, already knowing his response.

"Ordinarily that would be true, Mr. Fearsithe," Mr. Wolfe replied. "But given the nature of your dismissal, our sources indicate it is highly unlikely you will find another position with a comparable salary to maintain your standard of living. It is in your best interest, as well as ours, that the furnishings be returned to us today so we may recoup our money."

"And what if I refuse?" I questioned, looking at the two hefty associates standing on either side of him.

"Mr. Fearsithe, you could always choose to refuse—but it would not be wise," Mr. Wolfe said sternly. "As I said, if we repossess the furnishings today, your indebtedness to us will be canceled, and you will have no further obligation. However, if you force us to take time to get a writ from the judge, your furnishings' value will further decline and you will not only need to surrender it, but you will still owe us some portion of the balance. I truly believe returning your furniture today is your best option."

"Well, Mr. Wolfe, considering your persuasive argument, your solution is probably the best. Please have your men proceed. However, do leave the coffee pot—I paid *cash* for it!"

No sooner had Mr. Wolfe and the movers departed, than a second visitor arrived at my door. It was the man from Packard Motor Car Company who had sold me the roadster. He, too, was flanked by two burly men, though the actual reason for them being with him remained vague throughout our conversation.

Our exchange was similar to the one I had with Mr. Wolfe and resulted in the same outcome. I handed the key to the gentleman, and he and his associates drove away in that beautiful red roadster—which had been in my possession for less than five days.

My final visitor that morning was a solicitor named Mr. Henry Robertson, Esq. He represented the company that owned the Marlborough Building. Surprisingly, he did not have two brawny men with him!

"Please come in, Mr. Robertson," I said. "If you had arrived earlier, I could have offered you a chair. What can I do for you?"

"Mr. Fearsithe, it has been brought to the attention of my client that you are in violation of paragraph seven of your lease agreement. That clause pertains to the standing of the Marlborough's tenants in the community. As you know, the Marlborough has the reputation for leasing only to people with character that is above reproach and who exemplify the utmost propriety. The company maintains a strict watch over each tenant's compliance to ensure the property's reputation is maintained.

"Regrettably, it has come to the attention of the company that recent events in your life now call the state of your character into question."

"To what events do you refer, Mr. Robertson?"

"Your dismissal from OWR&N," he replied.

"I wasn't dismissed from the company, Mr. Robertson. I resigned."

"Yes, technically that may be true, Mr. Fearsithe. But it is well known your employment would have been immediately terminated for what some describe as reckless performance of your duties, and others consider extremely questionable business practices. At the very least, you are regarded as one of the key employees of OWR&N who, together with a

Mr. Emmett Hall, almost brought the steamship shipping trade in the Pacific Northwest to an abrupt halt. As you know, that particular industry is a leading source of employment and revenue in our city. Therefore, your failures—or perhaps more aptly, your indiscretions—have already gained great notoriety, calling your character into question."

"So, I am tried and proven guilty without a judge or jury present to weigh my guilt?"

"The issue of moral turpitude, as it relates to your lease, is not so much about what is proven as much as it is about perception. And in this instance, Mr. Fearsithe, I am afraid the court of popular opinion has already cast its verdict and found you lacking. Accordingly, my client is demanding you vacate these premises forthwith."

"So your client expects me to leave today without any arrangements as to where I will sleep this evening?"

"Unfortunately, Mr. Fearsithe, that is not my client's concern. And judging from your empty apartment, it appears you only require one or two suitcases to transport your earthly possessions as you leave today. So, yes, you will return your key to me, and we will both leave these premises together.

"I must also point out that paragraph twelve in your lease agreement says if the lease is terminated early, due to breach of contract on your part—such as your failure to maintain the character described in paragraph seven—the Marlborough has the right to demand full payment for the term of your lease agreement. As you know, the full amount due for the year is $1,200 which, after subtracting the amount you have already paid, leaves a remaining balance of $1,050."

"Let me make sure I understand this. I am to leave today, yet pay for the remainder of the year, even though I have only resided here for less than three weeks?" I asked in disbelief.

"Yes," he replied, "that is what's stated in the agreement you signed. Incidentally, if you will permit me to say so, might I suggest in the future you engage the services of your own solicitor before entering into such a weighty agreement.

"I regret there is also one last item," Mr. Robertson said with a sigh. "Another clause you agreed to in your lease, specifically paragraph twenty-two, grants my client the right to draft your bank accounts in order to recover the amount to which they are entitled. Accordingly, a draft to First National Bank of Portland was presented this morning for the full amount of your indebtedness.

"To my client's surprise, they were advised you only had $52.50 in your account. My client was paid those funds, leaving your bank account with a zero balance, as well as leaving a remaining balance that you owe my client of $997.50. I must ask, and you are obligated to tell me, if you have any other bank accounts or assets upon which my client can rely for payment."

I had not expected anyone to drain my bank account of its small balance, but at this point it was the least of my worries.

"No, I have no other assets—unless your client would like a slightly used coffee pot," I retorted sarcastically.

"No, Mr. Fearsithe," he replied smugly, "I think you can keep that with my client's good wishes. I must advise you, however, that we will be filing a writ with the court demanding full payment of the amount still due us. That means we will be able to garnish any future wages you earn and seize any future assets you possess until your indebtedness is paid in full.

"Unless you have any further questions, I believe that concludes our business. If you would now quickly pack your bags, we can vacate the premises together."

There was no point arguing. Archer had played this out masterfully, and I knew there was nothing I could do. It took only a few minutes to pack my bags. When we exited the building, the solicitor climbed into his automobile—a red 1912 Packard Model 30 Gentleman's Roadster—and drove way. No doubt he was headed to Archer's to provide a complete report.

I decided to walk across the street to the café. I had twenty dollars and a few coins left to my name. I splurged on a pastry and a cup of coffee and sat at one of their outdoor tables as I contemplated what to do next. I looked around as passersby continued going about their daily lives just as they always had. Well, at least most people. I knew there were others— former employees of OWR&N—whose lives had changed abruptly. The burden of what I had done was weighing heavily upon me . . . but I didn't know what to do about it.

I knew I couldn't carry my bags around town, so I decided then and there where I needed to go first.

"Mr. Fearsithe, what are you doing here? And why are you toting your suitcases?" Reginald asked in surprise.

"Well, I need a place to stay. Do you have any rooms available?"

"Certainly," he answered, "but nothing that can compare to the Marlborough."

"That's just fine, Reginald," I said, "because I've decided that's not really my kind of place."

"I'm sorry to hear that, Mr. Fearsithe. I know you're down on your luck right now. I read in the newspaper about what happened at OWR&N and how you and Mr. Emmett Hall were being blamed for everything. But I decided a long time ago there are always two sides to every story, and I'm certain your side has yet to be told. I have always found you to be a gentleman, Mr. Fearsithe, so there will be a room for you here as long as I'm at this desk."

"You are most kind, Reginald, at a time when I really need kindness but don't deserve it."

"Don't say that! Everyone deserves kindness—maybe some more than others. That's why I keep a snarl on my face. That way I can decide which ones need it more. And right now, Mr. Fearsithe, you fit into that category. Do you have the twelve dollars?"

"I do," I said. "Here you go, but don't tell anyone I'm staying here, or they might try to collect the twelve dollars from you," I added, only half joking.

"Should I tell Mr. Sheets that you've returned?" Reginald asked.

"No, I'll tell him myself later on."

After I set my bags down in my room, I set out for my next appointment. I heard that familiar voice call out as I walked through the door.

"I'll be right with you!" When Mr. Frank turned and saw me, he added, "Mr. Fearsithe, I didn't expect you today. Your suit is still not ready."

"I know it's not, Mr. Frank. That's not why I came. I'm hoping you haven't started on the suits and shirts I ordered this past Saturday, because I need to cancel the order."

"No, you're in luck! I haven't started on them yet."

"Please go ahead and apply the deposit I gave you for those to pay the balance for the suit you are working on," I said.

"Why don't I just refund your deposit for the two suits, and you pay me the balance for the one suit when you pick it up?" he offered.

"Because I want to make sure you get paid."

"Well, if that's what you want, that's what I'll do," he replied. "Let me see; you paid me a deposit of $62.50 for your new order, and you owe thirty dollars for the first suit. So, I owe you $32.50."

After he refunded my money, Mr. Frank admitted he had read about what happened in the newspaper. By this point, I was fairly confident everyone had. But what he said next surprised me.

"I know both you and Mr. Hall are fine gentlemen. Your coming to my shop today to make sure I got paid for my work is further proof to me. So please know I don't believe everything I read."

"Thank you, Mr. Frank," I replied as I shook his hand. "I'll be back Saturday to pick up the suit."

As I was walking out the door, another customer was coming in. We startled one another before I realized it was Emmett Hall.

"Gene!" he exclaimed. "I wasn't expecting to run into you."

"Nor I you, Emmett," I replied. "I was just here canceling an order with Mr. Frank."

"Yes, I'm here to do the same," he said. "Why don't you wait until I have finished here, then the two of us can go somewhere and talk. We didn't get to do that yesterday. Everything happened so abruptly."

I didn't know what to say. Emmett was the one person I was most ashamed to meet face to face. What would I tell him? But I knew we needed to talk, so I replied, "Certainly! I'll wait right here."

In a few minutes, Emmett came back outside.

"Gene let's walk to the El Rey Café. It's just three blocks down. We should be able to find a table there where we can talk without people gawking at us."

"Yes, since you are so well-known in the city, I'm sure that's happening to you a lot," I sympathized.

"Yes, I've always thought it was a good thing to have your name in the paper—until now," Emmett said with a rueful smile. "Gene, I am so sorry I got you into this. You are a talented go-getter who has a bright future ahead of you. And I caused you to trip and fall right out of the gate because I failed to look at all the possibilities."

"Emmett, I think you got that backward," I said. "I'm the one who came to you with this proposal. You never would have pursued it if I hadn't persuaded you. I'm the one who owes *you* an apology."

"Yes, but I was the senior manager; you were the new kid on the block. It was my job to make certain we explored all the possibilities and thought through all the contingencies. And I totally missed the union piece. I never anticipated that being an issue. And now a whole division of people are unemployed due to my negligence."

"But Emmett, you weren't negligent," I said, "you were set up!"

We had just arrived in front of the café, and Emmett stopped, turned to me, and asked, "What do you mean, I was set up?"

30

WEDNESDAY AFTERNOON AND EVENING, MAY 15

∼

*W*e stepped inside the café, and Emmett requested a table that afforded us some privacy. I waited until we were seated, and the waitress had brought us both a cup of coffee, before answering his question.

"We were all pawns in a game designed by Archer Winslow," I explained.

"How do you know that, Gene? I mean, I know you had information he divulged to you during your job interview. But that doesn't mean he knew you were going to bring it to us or come up with a strategy to beat him at his own game."

"Yes, it does, Emmett," I responded guiltily, "because that was all part of his plan." I paused, knowing if I continued there was no turning back.

"Because he hired me to come work for you!" I exclaimed.

"He what?!" Emmett asked in shock.

"He hired me, then told me everything to say in order for you to hire me," I admitted in shame. "But what I didn't know until last night was he had someone following you on the train who heard you promise me a job. He had orchestrated every piece of this for weeks prior to your hiring me. He planned it so he would end up controlling the shipping business and look like a hero for rescuing everyone."

"Wait a minute!" Emmett said emphatically. "There are a lot of steps between he had someone spying on me and he swept in 'like a hero.' Fill in the gaps—and don't leave anything out!"

Over the next hour, I walked Emmett through every detail—from my resentment toward him when he didn't offer me a job, to the theft in the alley, to the way Archer lured me in and hired me, and the way he coached me in what to say and when to say it.

In some respects, I felt like I was unloading a burden by telling Emmett the truth. But in other ways, I was overcome with guilt as I heard the words coming out of my mouth.

When I had finished, I told him, "But I had no idea what Archer had planned regarding ILA. He never divulged that to me. I knew he master-minded events so he would come out on top, but I did not know any details. I believe he somehow manipulated the ILA; otherwise, how would PSC be the only one at the negotiating table? But I was completely left in the dark about those particulars."

When I finished, an awkward silence hung in the air.

Finally, Emmett said, "You may have been left in the dark about those details, but you left me in the dark about all of it. I trusted you, Gene—

probably more than I have ever trusted a coworker. But you betrayed my trust. And now a lot of innocent people are suffering because of it. Good people, Gene, who did not deserve to lose their jobs! Some of them have worked for OWR&N for a long time. They have families . . . and mortgages . . . and hopes for the future that have been dashed.

"And why? So you could come out here to Portland and pursue your dream? What about their dreams, Gene? Did you ever think of anyone besides yourself? I'm not sure there is anything criminally wrong with what you did, but I do know it was morally wrong. And it will weigh on your conscience for the rest of your life.

"I thank you for having the courage to tell me now. I expect you'll be leaving Portland, because I can assure you no one in this part of the country will hire you now. Actually, they won't be interested in hiring either one of us! But you don't really have any roots here like the rest of us do. So you can travel back to Pennsylvania, and live out your life with no one being the wiser.

"I don't plan to tell anyone what you've done—that would just make me look even more incompetent. You see, I bypassed every employment practice in our company to hire you, Gene. I had a hunch . . . unfortunately, it didn't pay off."

Emmett slowly rose from his seat, put a dollar on the table, and said, "The coffee's on me."

As he walked away dejectedly, Emmett looked like he had aged a decade in the past twenty-four hours—and the majority of it was in the past hour.

He was correct; I would be heading back to Pennsylvania. But I couldn't leave Portland without somehow making things right. And I had no idea how to do that. I spent the afternoon walking the streets trying to discover the answer to that question. But it wouldn't come.

Suddenly I realized I was walking on Salmon Street and a familiar sign came into view:

Mount Zion Baptist Church
Rev. Tyrone Nelson
Sunday Worship 11 a.m. & 7 p.m.
Wednesday Service 7 p.m.
All are welcome!

I looked at my watch; it was seven o'clock on the dot. I looked up at the sky and said, "Okay, I'll go in."

The same gentleman who had greeted me when I was last there, pointed me to the same seat in the back row. The congregation seemed particularly energized as they sang and clapped their hands in time to the music. But I didn't feel much like singing, so I just listened to the familiar songs.

When the singing was over, the preacher stepped up to the pulpit and said, "Beloved, turn in your Bibles to the Gospel according to Matthew chapter eleven, and let's read verses twenty-eight to thirty:

> *"Come to Me, all you who are weary and burdened, and I will give you rest. Take My yoke upon you and learn from Me, for I am gentle and humble in heart, and you will find rest for your souls. For My yoke is easy and My burden is light."*[1]

I don't recall much of what the preacher said after that. Those words continued to revolve over and over in my head. "Come to Me, all you who are weary and burdened!" I felt like I was back in that pigsty from my dream, lying in that filth. My burden of shame and guilt was pressing me down further and further.

Before I realized what was happening, I had bowed my head and tears were flowing freely down my cheeks. After several minutes, I looked up to see if anyone was watching. There, beside me, was Abigail. She was quietly praying as she knelt by my side.

The fresh realization of all the pain and hurt I had caused her and so many others made me weep even more. After a few moments, she reached out and took my hand between hers.

"Let Him take your burden, Gene, and allow Him to give you the rest you need," she whispered.

When the preacher finished his message and concluded the service, I became self-conscious about someone seeing me in this state.

"We need to go," I anxiously told Abigail.

"No, Gene," she said tenderly, "you're right where you're supposed to be. And none of these people will bother you. Allow the Lord to exchange your burden for His rest."

The tears started to flow again. I hadn't shed a tear since the day my mother died. I'd been holding them back for a long time, and now I couldn't make them stop.

After most everyone else exited the church, the preacher came over to us. I didn't know what to say. Fortunately, Abigail did.

"Pastor Nelson, this is my friend, Gene Fearsithe, and he needs to talk to you—even though he doesn't quite know what to say. He's been through a lot these past few days, and I believe God led him here tonight to speak with you. I'll step away so the two of you can talk."

I took a firm grip of her hand and said, "Abigail, please stay. There is nothing I need to say you can't hear. And I believe there isn't anything he's going to tell me that you don't already know."

I slid over so she could sit beside me. The preacher entered the pew from the other end.

"Gene, what do you believe God has been saying to you tonight?" he gently asked.

"I don't know, preacher. I don't even know if it was God. But I've been carrying a weight for a long time. And I don't want to carry it anymore."

"Tell me about that weight, Gene," he said. "When did you first notice it?"

I told him how it had all started with the death of my mother, and how I had come to resent my father. I told him about leaving my father just to spite him, even though he needed me. I explained how I had left my life behind—including my girl—because I was going to prove something to my father. And I admitted I felt like that son he had preached about three weeks earlier.

Then I told him about all I had done since I arrived in Portland. I felt Abigail tense up as my story unfolded, but to her credit she continued to hold my hand. I told the pastor about the shame I felt over the pain and loss I had caused so many people. I told him I would never be able to make right all the damage I had done. I would never be able to obtain the forgiveness I now desired.

At that point, Pastor Nelson stopped me and said, "You're wrong about that, Gene. You *can* experience that forgiveness. Just like He said in those verses we read tonight, 'Come to Me, all you who are weary and burdened, and I will give you rest.'

"Gene, you sound pretty weary and burdened to me—and Jesus promised to give you rest."

"But I don't deserve it, preacher!"

"No, you don't," the preacher conceded, "because none of us do. There's no denying you're a sinner, Gene; but so am I, so is Abigail, and so are all of us. None of us deserve His grace. But He freely gives it to us, though it wasn't free to Him. He paid for it with His shed blood by dying on a cross 1,900 years ago.

"The apostle John writes, 'If we confess our sins, He is faithful and just to forgive us our sins and to cleanse us from all unrighteousness.'[2] All unrighteousness, Gene! There isn't anything He can't cleanse, and there isn't anything He can't forgive."

"Yes, but I have hurt so many people," I said between sobs.

"And He will be faithful and just to forgive you, son," the preacher replied, "because that's what He promised."

"But what about the people? How can they possibly forgive me?"

"Some of them may not be able to, Gene," Pastor Nelson said, "that's not your choice to make. But it *is* your choice to confess what you've done and seek their forgiveness—after you first seek the forgiveness of Jesus. And the good news is once you do, He'll lighten that burden and go before you as you seek forgiveness from those you've hurt—both here in Portland and back home in Pennsylvania."

"I hear you, preacher, and I believe you. I just don't know how anyone could forgive me."

"I forgive you, Gene," Abigail said as she squeezed my hand.

Those simple words triggered a floodgate of fresh tears. Abigail had done nothing to deserve losing her job—and yet she had. And now she was willing to forgive the man who was responsible!

"I think you'll find there are others who will forgive you as well, Gene," the preacher consoled me. "But, first, are you ready to seek forgiveness from the One you have sinned against the most . . . and the One who loves you the most?"

"Yes, I am."

The preacher led me in a prayer, and as I prayed, it was like a weight was lifted off of me. The tears kept coming, but now they were tears of joy. After a few minutes, we all stood. I embraced the pastor and then Abigail. I thanked them both for being there for me that night—and for pointing me to the truth.

The preacher explained that I now needed to be baptized as a public testimony of my faith in Jesus. I assured him I'd be back Sunday, and he could baptize me then. He asked me if I had a Bible.

"Not since I was a kid."

"Well, pick one up at a store," the preacher said, "and start reading all the promises Jesus has given you as you walk with Him. You can start by reading the book of First John and learn just how much Jesus loves you."

I promised to do just that as the three of us walked out of the church together. After I wished him a good night, I turned to Abigail and said, "This time you have to allow me to walk you home—if you're not afraid to be seen with me."

She laughed as we began walking toward her building. On the way, I learned she had not been let go. She had been transferred to another secretarial position within the company.

"So you need not be concerned about my welfare, Gene," she said. "I am doing just fine. Honestly, the majority of employees in our division were transferred to other positions. Only a handful, in addition to you and Mr. Hall, are no longer employed by OWR&N. So, if that has been bothering you, please know you don't have to worry over it anymore.

"But I understand your desire to make things right. And if you come up with a way to do so, and I can be of any assistance, count me in."

We arrived at her boardinghouse, and I told her good night. My steps were much lighter on my way back to the Goodnough Building.

---

1. Matthew 11:28-30
2. 1 John 1:9

31

THURSDAY, MAY 16 – FRIDAY AFTERNOON, MAY 17

∼

I had the best night's rest I had enjoyed in a long time. I truly felt rejuvenated. But I was also determined. I now knew I would be returning to Pennsylvania—not because I wouldn't be able to get another job in Portland—but rather, because I now knew that's where I was supposed to be. Portland is a wonderful place, with a lot of great people, and now some very dear friends. But Williamsport was where my dream was. It had been there all along. I had just needed to travel to Portland to discover it.

I sat down and wrote two letters: one to my father and one to Sara. I told them both I loved them. I also told them I was headed back home, though I didn't yet know when. I told them I hoped they would forgive me and take me back—but assured them I understood if they couldn't. I closed both notes by explaining I had a task to finish here before I could return, but I would see them soon.

Reginald provided me the envelopes and stamps in exchange for four pennies, and I deposited my letters into the box for the postman. My rumbling stomach reminded me I hadn't eaten breakfast, so I proceeded to the dining room. I spied Clyde eating alone, and he looked surprised to see me.

"How are you doing, Gene?" he asked sincerely. "I've been reading in the newspaper about the unfortunate affair at OWR&N. I hope you are surviving all of this mess."

"I am, my friend," I replied, "and thank you for asking. There is much we need to discuss, but I know you need to begin your workday. Let's meet back here for dinner this evening at six o'clock. Does that work for you?"

"Absolutely," Clyde answered. "Am I to presume you are now living back here?"

"Yes, at least for now. I look forward to catching up this evening."

After a quick bite of toast with jam and my morning cup of coffee, I returned to the reception area. Before I went up to my room last night, Reginald had handed me a message:

I have thought more about our conversation. We need to talk. I'll meet you at half past seven in the morning here at reception.
Emmett

"Punctual as usual," Emmett said, as he reached out and shook my hand. "Let's head over to Southwest Park, and we can talk as we walk through the gardens."

He told me he had thought a great deal about how we might make things right for those who lost their jobs at OWR&N. He also wanted to repair the company's name and reputation.

"Do you genuinely desire to help make things right? Or were you simply saying that to assuage your conscience?" Emmett asked pointedly.

"It is the only reason I am remaining in Portland. And I have no plans of leaving until I try to right my wrongs," I replied.

"Good! Well, let's put what happened between us behind us and work together to come up with a plan," he declared. "Though Archer Winslow was the author of much of what we planned together, I still think we made a pretty good team.

"Is there anyone who witnessed the conversations you had with Archer Winslow?" Emmett continued.

"The only two who witnessed us meeting together were his butler, Church, and his nefarious employee, Thomas Buckholt," I replied. "And I doubt either of them will say anything against his employer. There is, however, one piece we might be able to use. I'm just not sure how yet.

"Part of Archer's game to recruit me was to have Thomas Buckholt knock me out and steal all my money my first week here. The police found Buckholt's fingerprints on my wallet, and they are searching for him for questioning. There is a clear trail to him for assault and robbery, but other than Archer's admission to me, there is nothing directly connecting him to Buckholt as it relates to the assault.

"Perhaps," Emmett replied thoughtfully, "but let's not discount it entirely. What else do we have?"

"Well, there is the question regarding the union negotiations supposedly taking place between Archer and Morgan. That all sounds pretty sketchy. And why was Morgan so unwilling to negotiate with you? Why should he care which of our companies was paying the workers? Furthermore, do we know for a fact the workers are being paid what Morgan demanded of us? Like you said, there is no way to make those arrangements financially viable even with the lower amount being paid to the port."

"And for that matter, do we truly know what Winslow is paying the ports?" Emmett added.

"How can we get answers to those questions without it getting back to Winslow?" I asked. "I doubt any of the port directors will even take my call, let alone be that forthright with me. And Morgan will most certainly not tell you anything."

"That's true. But I learned a long time ago, if you really want to know what is happening inside an organization, don't ask the bosses. Ask the ones who truly make it happen—the secretaries."

"I completely agree," I said, "but I don't imagine any of the secretaries will talk to us."

"Without question," Emmett responded. "But what if another secretary were to ask them in a less direct way? Perhaps someone we can trust, such as Miss Adams?"

"Who, incidentally, I found out last evening was not terminated but is working in another division of OWR&N," I conveyed with a sigh of relief.

"Well, good for her," Emmett replied. "That may also prove helpful for us. Since you continue to stay in touch, perhaps you could ask if she would help us put all of this right."

"That's already done," I said. "She told me as much last evening!"

Emmett and I spent the next couple of hours putting together a list of questions for the ports and the union. I agreed to contact Abigail and solicit her assistance.

When I called her, Abigail enthusiastically agreed to help gather information. We met at the general store near OWR&N during her lunch break so I could give her the list of questions. She was confident she could get answers by that afternoon. We planned for her to meet Emmett and me at the park across the street from her boardinghouse at half past seven that evening.

After I left Abigail, I decided to stop by and see Jake. He, of course, had read all about what transpired at OWR&N. He asked how I was doing in the midst of everything.

"Believe it or not, Jake, I am doing remarkably well," I said. "I might even say, better than I ever have been. I have a peace I have never known and a sense of purpose I have always struggled to find."

"How can that be," he asked, "in light of the fact you were sacked?"

"Well, technically I wasn't sacked," I said. "But that's not an important distinction. I now have peace and purpose because I have come to know Jesus. I realized I've been running from Him for most of my life. But last night I stopped running. And Jake, I can tell you that it's made all the difference."

"I'm happy for you, Gene" he said. "I always say, 'Whatever works!' And it appears that's working for you."

"Thanks, Jake, and if you'd ever like to know more about Him and what He can do for you, I'll be happy to tell you what little I know. In the meantime, I'm in need of employment to pay the rent."

"I doubt I can pay you enough for your rent at the Marlborough Building!" Jake exclaimed.

"In that case, it's a good thing I no longer live there," I laughed. "I'm back at the rooming house here in the building. So what do you say, do you have any debts you need collected?"

"We've always got people who owe us," he said. "You're hired. Same deal as before. When can you start?"

"How about tomorrow?" I asked. "And by the way, no one needs to know I'm working for you. Otherwise, there's an attorney in town who will garnish whatever I make."

"Your secret's safe with me, Gene," Jake replied. "I've got to protect my best collector! See you tomorrow."

I went back to my room and finished unpacking. It actually was good to be back at the rooming house. Life seemed so much simpler here. At a few minutes before six I went down to the dining room to meet Clyde. It was meatloaf night, and that was fine with me!

Clyde asked a slew of questions about what had taken place, and I tried to answer him as best I could. I also told him about the decision I had made at Mount Zion Baptist Church; his reaction was similar to Jake's. But I still offered to tell him more if he was interested.

Then our conversation turned to his work and what was happening there.

"You know, I met this fellow, Richard Morgan," Clyde said.

"You have?" I replied. "Where?"

"Well interestingly enough, he came in last week and ordered a custom dining room set," Clyde answered. "It's the kind of set you ordinarily see in only the finest homes. We don't usually sell furniture like that to men who work on the docks, even the head honchos. But he had the cash, so we're building him a custom ensemble. He said it was something his wife had always wanted.

"Anyway, I was surprised to see he was somehow mixed in with what happened to you. It's a small world, isn't it?"

"Yes, it is!"

It was time for me to go meet Emmett and Abigail, so as I excused myself, Clyde added, "Tomorrow night is the next to last performance of *The Merry Widow* and Elenore has gotten me two tickets. I don't suppose you'd like to go and see it with me?"

"Yes, I would. I'd very much like to see Elenore and Maggie perform. Thanks for the invitation. What time?"

"Let's plan to leave here at half past seven," he answered.

∾

Emmett and I both arrived at the park at the same time, and Abigail joined us five minutes later. After we exchanged pleasantries, Abigail briefed us on what she had discovered.

"First," she began, "I had to pretend to be a payment clerk in the bookkeeping office of PSC in order to obtain the answers. But I've already confessed my sin to God, and He has forgiven me!"

Emmett looked at me and shrugged, and I looked at Abigail and smiled.

"Second," she continued, "I confirmed that PSC is paying the ports the agreed upon amount of fourteen percent of their freight charges. However, I contacted a few of the accounts we served until recently, those with whom I had a close relationship, and I found out PSC increased the freight rate they are paying by five percent."

"Well, that's reasonable," I said. "We were going to raise their rate by eight percent, so they're actually doing better than they would have with us."

"Yes, that's true," Abigail replied, "but PSC has not reflected that rate increase on what they are paying the ports—which means the ports are being cheated out of that portion."

Abigail now had our full attention!

"Third," she went on, "I learned from a friend at ILA that the rate increase received by the waterfront workers amounted to five percent, not the ten percent Mr. Morgan was demanding OWR&N pay. And apparently, the five percent increase was what the rank and file voted to approve the beginning of last week.

"Though Morgan presumably discussed it with Archer Winslow two weeks ago, he had been directed by the workers to enter into discussion with *all* the shipping companies. His failure to do so was never reported. Apparently when the question was raised on Tuesday at ILA, the presumed stonewalling being attributed to OWR&N kept that issue from ever being pursued any further.

"So the bottom line, gentlemen, is the waterfront workers were unknowingly used by their leader as a ploy in our negotiations. And Mr. Archer is obviously defrauding the ports of funds they are otherwise due."

"And," I added, "Mr. Richard Morgan appears to have recently come into a windfall of cash. Makes you wonder where that might have come from, doesn't it?"

Emmett spoke up for the first time.

"Though all of this is incriminating information, I doubt seriously it would result in any criminal charges against Winslow or Morgan."

"I agree, Emmett," I responded, "but we don't need criminal charges to turn the tables. We only need to alert the ports and waterfront workers how they are being used—and allow them to deal with Winslow and Morgan. I suspect if OWR&N put their original agreement back on the table, adjusted downward to the fourteen percent the ports were willing to accept from PSC, OWR&N could be back in the steamship shipping business. And, PSC would need to put their boats into dry dock.

"What's more, I imagine the ILA will soon be looking to elect a new leader, and I fear Mrs. Morgan will not be getting her new dining room set!

～

The next morning, Emmett contacted Henry Villard and requested to meet with the OWR&N board to advise them of pertinent information he and I had just received. Out of respect for Emmett, they agreed to do so.

As Emmett and I presented what we had learned, the board members became incensed by the spurious business practices of Archer Winslow and the unethical actions of Richard Morgan. They unanimously made the following recommendations:

First, Chairman Villard will contact the executive leadership team at Union Pacific and advise them of these new developments, requesting that the shipping division of OWR&N be reinstated, and all employees returned to their positions with no loss of income, an added week's pay, and our sincere apology for the disruption of their lives.

Second, a formal and public apology be issued to Mr. Emmett Hall and Mr. R. Eugene Fearsithe for statements made or inferred that have maligned their professional ability and personal character, as a result of an orchestrated fraud being perpetrated by one of our more disreputable competitors.

Third, that the leadership of the shipping division immediately advise the port authorities of the fraud currently being perpetrated against them.

Fourth, that the rank and file of ILA be advised of the fraudulent manner in which their interests have been represented by their current leadership.

Fifth, that OWR&N stands ready to be the leader of the steamship shipping industry in the Pacific Northwest.

Once the formal part of our meeting concluded, backslaps and praises were again being generously directed toward Emmett and me.

"Gene, we look forward to having you back on board," Henry Villard said. "You are unquestionably one of the most talented young men to have joined this company in a long while. You will go far here, and we look forward to seeing it happen."

"Mr. Villard, I thank you for your kind comments and good wishes," I replied, "but over the past several days, I have discovered exactly where I need to be. And it's not here in Portland. It's in Williamsport, Pennsylvania, beside my father and my girl—if she will have me as her husband. Because there is where my dream is, and they are the ones I want to share it with."

∾

EPILOGUE: FRIDAY EVENING, MAY 17 – FRIDAY, MAY 31

∽

I immediately jumped to my feet Friday night as the curtain came down. The play had been remarkable, and Maggie and Elenore had taken my breath away. They both will enjoy long and successful careers on the stage, if that is what they choose.

Clyde and Elenore were planning their wedding for the end of June. Clyde asked me to be his best man, an honor I regretfully declined since I would no longer be in Portland.

Maggie and Samuel Jacobs, the director of the play, were apparently now an item. I was happy for them both. They shared the love of the stage. He would provide wisdom and stability to their relationship, and she would provide the fun and excitement to their lives.

I wished Maggie a fond farewell that evening, because I knew it would be the last time I saw her.

"You have discovered your dream, Gene," she said sincerely, "and you now recognize that Sara is your one true love." As she gave me a kiss on the cheek, she added, "And I am very happy for you. *Au revoir, mon chéri!*"

On Saturday, I picked up my new suit from Mr. Frank. I truly believe it is the finest suit I will ever own. Not only because of the quality of the fabric and his excellent workmanship, but also because I believe Mr. Frank puts a little bit of himself into every suit he makes. I will always be a grateful recipient of that gift! I plan to wear it for the first time on the day I next see Sara.

On Sunday, Rev. Nelson baptized me at Mount Zion Baptist Church. Clyde and Elenore attended the service at my request. I told them I needed some fellow Pennsylvanians there to share in the joy with me. They were gracious, though I'm not sure they understood why it was so important to me. My prayer is that someday they will.

I told the preacher I had bought a Bible, like he had suggested, and I was reading it each day.

"You've probably finished First John," he said. "Try turning to the Gospel of John and reading that book. It will help you get to know Jesus even better."

"Oh, I've already done that, preacher," I said. "In fact, I've read all four of the Gospel books. I'm getting ready to start reading the book of Acts." The preacher just smiled.

Of course, the one face in the congregation that radiated the brightest that day was Abigail's. God had brought her into my life just when I needed her most. She had been a steady, positive influence with a firm hold that had helped me get to the other side. I hope and pray there is someone who will be that for her. I noticed a young man in the congregation who appears to be quite taken with her—so I believe that prayer may already be answered.

On Monday, OWR&N informed the ports and the workers of the ILA about what had been committed against them. The ports immediately declared their contracts with PSC null and void. They then issued public apologies to OWR&N, which now enjoys exclusive rights in and out of all ports on the northwest shipping lanes.

Pacific Steamship Company closed its doors and laid off all its employees. Archer Winslow refuses to make any comments to the *Oregon Journal* and has sequestered himself inside his home in Portland Heights. I sympathize with the innocent employees of PSC; I am well aware of how they must feel. Hopefully, most of them will find their way to the many new job openings OWR&N has recently posted in its shipping division.

Thomas Buckholt was arrested for assault. Constable Burton is investigating possible charges against Archer Winslow for his role in the assault.

The ILA immediately fired Richard Morgan and attempted to have criminal charges filed against him. As of my departure, no charges have been filed, but I also understand he has gone missing. No one seems to have any idea as to his whereabouts.

Jake kept providing me with accounts to collect each day until I finally earned enough to pay off my debts to the newspaper and the hospital, plus purchase my train ticket home. Yesterday, I returned the billy club he had loaned me and presented him with a gift—one I knew he needed—my coffee pot. He did something totally unexpected. He came out from behind his desk and gave me a hug—though he made me promise not to tell anyone!

Emmett Hall actually came to see me off at the train station. He handed me an envelope just before I boarded.

"It's a parting gift from all of us at OWR&N," he said. "It's our investment in your dream. Invest it wisely!"

In the envelope was $500 in cash. Since it was not earned compensation, it was not subject to garnishment by the Marlborough Apartments—a distinction that brought a smile to my lips.

As I waved goodbye to him and all of Portland, I was struck by the good memories I would take with me from this place. Somehow the challenges I had faced were already fading. The city had lived up to everything I had imagined it would be. It had kept its part of the bargain. I had come to Portland looking for my dream—and I had found it. Now all I needed to do was travel 3,000 miles back to Williamsport to seize it.

I had sent a telegram just before I left the train station. It read:

> Your prodigal son is on his way back home! See
> you this Friday!

~

PLEASE HELP ME BY LEAVING A REVIEW!

i would be very grateful if you would leave a review of this book. Your feedback will be helpful to me in my future writing endeavors and will also assist others as they consider picking up a copy of the book.

To leave a review:

Go to: amazon.com/dp/B0CK3XLKD4

Or scan this QR code using your camera on your smartphone:

Thanks for your help!

THE NEXT BOOK IN "THE PARABLES" SERIES

A Belated Discovery (Book 2)

(*releasing Spring 2024*)

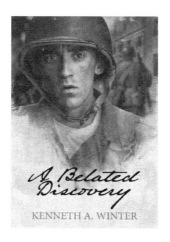

R. Eugene Fearsithe's nineteen year old son, Bobby, enlisted in the army on the fifteenth day of December 1941 to fight for his family, his friends, and his neighbors. Along the way, Bobby discovered just who his neighbor truly was.

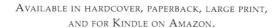

AVAILABLE IN HARDCOVER, PAPERBACK, LARGE PRINT, AND FOR KINDLE ON AMAZON.

Scan this QR code using your camera on your smartphone to see the entire series.

For more information, go to *kenwinter.org* or *wildernesslessons.com*

"THE CALLED" SERIES

Stories of these ordinary men and women called by God to be used in extraordinary ways.

AVAILABLE IN PAPERBACK, LARGE PRINT, AUDIO, AND FOR KINDLE ON AMAZON.

Scan this QR code using your camera on your smartphone to see the entire series.

ALSO BY KENNETH A. WINTER

THROUGH THE EYES

(a series of biblical fiction novels)

Through the Eyes of a Shepherd (Shimon, a Bethlehem shepherd)

Through the Eyes of a Spy (Caleb, the Israelite spy)

Through the Eyes of a Prisoner (Paul, the apostle)

THE EYEWITNESSES

(a series of biblical fiction short story collections)

For Christmas/Advent

Little Did We Know – the advent of Jesus — for adults

Not Too Little To Know – the advent – ages 8 thru adult

For Easter/Lent

The One Who Stood Before Us – the ministry and passion of Jesus — for adults

The Little Ones Who Came – the ministry and passion – ages 8 thru adult

LESSONS LEARNED IN THE WILDERNESS SERIES

(a non-fiction series of biblical devotional studies)

The Journey Begins (Exodus) – Book 1

The Wandering Years (Numbers and Deuteronomy) – Book 2

Possessing The Promise (Joshua and Judges) – Book 3

Walking With The Master (The Gospels leading up to Palm Sunday) – Book 4

Taking Up The Cross (The Gospels – the passion through ascension) – Book 5

Until He Returns (The Book of Acts) – Book 6

ALSO AVAILABLE AS AUDIOBOOKS

THE CALLED

(the complete series)

A Carpenter Called Joseph

A Prophet Called Isaiah

A Teacher Called Nicodemus

A Judge Called Deborah

A Merchant Called Lydia

A Friend Called Enoch

A Fisherman Called Simon

A Heroine Called Rahab

A Witness Called Mary

A Cupbearer Called Nehemiah

∼

Through the Eyes of a Shepherd

∼

Little Did We Know

Not Too Little to Know

∼

ACKNOWLEDGMENTS

I do not cease to give thanks for you ….
Ephesians 1:16 (ESV)

… my partner and best friend, LaVonne,
for choosing to trust God as we walk together with Him in this faith
adventure;

… my family,
for your continuing love, support and encouragement;

… Sheryl,
for your partnership in the work;

… Scott,
for using the gifts God has given you;

… a precious group of advance readers,
who encourage and challenge me in the journey;

… and most importantly,
the One who goes before me in all things
– my Lord and Savior Jesus Christ!

∽

ABOUT THE AUTHOR

Ken Winter is a follower of Jesus, an extremely blessed husband, and a proud father and grandfather – all by the grace of God. His journey with Jesus has led him to serve on the pastoral staffs of two local churches – one in West Palm Beach, Florida and the other in Richmond, Virginia – and as the vice president of mobilization of an international missions organization. Today, Ken continues in that journey as a full-time author, teacher and speaker. You can read his weekly blog posts at kenwinter.blog and listen to his weekly podcast at kenwinter.org/podcast.

And we proclaim Him, admonishing every man and teaching every man with all wisdom, that we may present every man complete in Christ. And for this purpose also I labor, striving according to His power, which mightily works within me.
(Colossians 1:28-29 NASB)

PLEASE JOIN MY READERS' GROUP

Please join my Readers' Group in order to receive updates and information about future releases, etc.

Also, i will send you a free copy of *The Journey Begins* e-book — the first book in the *Lessons Learned In The Wilderness* series. It is yours to keep or share with a friend or family member that you think might benefit from it.

It's completely free to sign up. i value your privacy and will not spam you. Also, you can unsubscribe at any time.

Go to kenwinter.org to subscribe.

Or scan this QR code using your camera on your smartphone:

Made in the USA
Monee, IL
07 October 2023

44148238R00185